WOLF'S BETRAYAL

USA TODAY BESTSELLING AUTHOR

EVE L. MITCHELL

WOLF'S BETRAYAL

Foreword

This is a continuation of The Blackridge Peak Series. This is Book 2 in a three-book paranormal romance series. This book cannot be read as a standalone.

Book Description

Sent back to the human world by my brother and the shaman, I found refuge among humans, reconnecting with an old friend who urged me to embrace the life I left behind. Yet, my shelter was short-lived when the alpha, Cannon, captured me once more.

In his pack, I witnessed the stark differences between the pack I came from and the Blackridge Peak Pack. I longed to belong to a community as free as this—all the while resisting the magnetic pull towards the alpha.

Meanwhile, someone who was once close to me could hold the key to unlocking the mysteries of humans hunting shifters. While some truths remained hidden, I feared the answers lay within the heart of my old pack.

As external pressures intensified, threatening to shatter the delicate trust building between Cannon and me, I came to realize that it's not our bond we should have been resisting.

It's betrayal.

Content information: Wolf's Betrayal is a paranormal romance, and is the second book in The Blackridge Peak series. Recommended reading age is 18+ due to sexual content, mature language, violence, and some mature themes. This is Book 2 in a continuing series and ends on a cliffhanger.

CHAPTER 1
Kezia

"Zia! I need more trays."

The bartender's voice was so high-pitched and sudden that I banged my head off the top of the dishwasher that I was currently half in as I tried to unsnag the broken tray from the slider along the bottom of the machine.

"Ow," I protested, finally wrenching the tray free and almost staggering backward. When I looked up, Nicola was watching me, her gaze darting between me and the tray. "It broke before I took it out," I defended myself instantly.

She looked around the small glasswashing area with a disdainful sniff before pointing at the stacks of clean glasses. "Them, now."

The door swung shut behind her, blocking anyone from seeing me flick her the finger. "Oh, no, your ladyship," I grumbled. "Please, don't try to help. You couldn't possibly lift a tray by yourself. Luna forbid you try, you lazy shit."

The trays were high-sided wire baskets for glasses. They got stacked and went into the glasswashing machines in rows of two. They could be stacked when they came out to cool. The bar was busy tonight—Thursday Night Football always drew a crowd—and the crews from the logging plant halfway up the mountain were down with their end-of-the-month paychecks. They all drank draught and were keeping me and the machine busy.

The glasswashing area was separate from the bar and the kitchen, tucked in a tight space with room for only one person, two machines, and a low counter that ran the length of the wall to allow the trays to be stacked. There was an open hatch in the wall that allowed me to put the dirty glasses through after I'd collected them, and the clean ones could rest there so I didn't need to fight the door to the main bar area while carrying glasses.

I slid two trays onto the hatch area and then hurried through the door to grab them. Working the machines was hot and steamy work on busy nights, and tonight was no exception. My T-shirt was sticking to me, my jeans felt like they were glued on, and my hair felt heavy despite being piled high onto my head in a bun. The apron I wore to "protect" my clothes was heavy and thick, and I was sure the only thing it did was increase my body temperature.

It had been five months since I was on the Peak. Kris had given me enough money to *blend* as he called it. I'd moved around furtively to begin with, and then when I realized no one was coming for me, I'd stopped being so frantic.

It was a hard fact to swallow. Again. The Anterrio Pack wasn't interested, not even my so-called "mate" Landon.

I'd come here over a month ago and found a one-bed apartment easily. Due to the logging station further up the mountain, the locals were used to a high turnover of people coming into their town. I was just another pair of feet traveling through, looking for work before I moved on. The whole town was so used to it that I didn't need to blend, as no one ever asked me any questions.

Carrying the trays, I navigated my way through the crowd to the bar. I slid them onto the counter and got no acknowledgment from Nicola. I was used to her attitude. I'd been here for three weeks now, the longest I had stayed in one place since coming off the mountain, and she'd taken an instant dislike to me when I got the position of glasswasher.

I wasn't a hypocrite—I didn't like her either. She smelled weird. Not in a she-has-bad-taste-in-perfume way or even the odd scent that Mal had; she was just *off*.

Making my way back to my steamy refuge, grabbing some empty glasses along the way, I thought of the scent that Mal had, the doc from the Blackridge Peak Pack. *His* pack. I tried very hard not to think of the alpha of the Blackridge Peak Pack. I told myself I didn't miss him and I hated everything about him. Pressing my lips together, I tried not to scowl at the hollow-sounding lie.

As well as not being a hypocrite, I also wasn't a liar. Well, not about the things that mattered.

Not that *he* mattered. *He* meant nothing to me. As I obviously meant little to him since he hadn't followed me off the Peak either. I didn't *want* to be followed, but if I *was* his mate, wouldn't he be curious about where I was? Had he really not bothered to check on me since that night in the shaman's house?

"Mate, my ass," I grouched as I routinely emptied dregs from glasses and shoved them into the trays to be washed. I felt my wolf stir, and I ignored her as well. She'd been quiet since we came off the mountain, only letting me know she was pissed with me a few times a month.

I let her run free whenever we could, and if she ran, hunted, and had fresh meat for dinner, so far, she'd been content to keep her judgment to long stares and a general rumble of discontentment.

I'd learned in my time off the mountain to count the small things as blessings, and so far, the fact my wolf was keeping her general displeasure to herself, I was taking it as a blessing.

"Zia!"

I jumped again and turned to glare at Nicola through the hatch. "What?" I barked with as much attitude as she gave me.

"Where's the glasses?"

"On the bar," I snapped, turning fully, my hands on my hips to stop me from reaching through the hatch and dragging her skinny ass in with me where I was sure I could cram her into the machine and put her on a cycle to clean up her attitude.

"Two trays?" Her voice was at near-piercing levels, and I felt my wolf stir. "I need more than *two* trays!"

Despite what Nicola thought, she wasn't the boss. Despite *that*, she was still the one who *slept* with the boss, and therefore she had the slight advantage over me that, if I did smash her head off the counter, by accident, then he'd probably take her side.

Maybe. He was a bit of a wild card.

Instead of throttling her, I smiled wide and fake in her face. "Well, *honey*, all you had to do was say."

I bit back my laughter as I watched her flounce away. My temper may get me in trouble one day, but my sass was going to get me fired sooner or later, I knew it.

I took two more trays of clean glasses and placed them on the hatch, ready to carry them out to the bar. The night pretty much went through the same rinse-and-repeat cycle: I slowly dehydrated in the glasswashing area, Nicola grated on my very last nerve, and by the end of the night, I was eagerly waiting for the pickup truck behind the small apartment block I'd been staying in since I came to town.

I saw the familiar shape of the truck, and before it was fully at a stop beside me, I was climbing into the cab.

"You're late."

"Am I?" Vance asked with a smirk, pulling away from the sidewalk. "Why do you look pissed off and..." He glanced at me. "Damp?"

"Because glasswashing is humid and tiring. And that witch is just begging me to punch her in the face."

Vance threw his head back as he laughed. His hair was shorter than when I last saw him, his muscles were more pronounced, and he had a golden tan that was definitely working in his favor.

"You look good," I told him with narrowed eyes. I sniffed. "And you're wearing cologne." Turning in my seat, I gawked at him. "Were you on a *date*?" I asked him incredulously.

"It hurts me that you think I'm incapable of such a thing, Zee."

"I told you I hate *Zee*."

"Which is exactly why I use it," he told me with a grin. He laughed again when I punched him in the ribs, but his complete dickishness caused me to smile.

It had been two towns before this one, where I ran into him again. I hadn't even been looking for a fight. I walked into a café for a takeaway coffee, and he was in the line. We'd both stared at each other in shock for a good few minutes before Vance grabbed me and practically carried me to his truck and locked me in, demanding to know everything.

I hadn't told him everything, but when I told him why I was no longer wanted for murder, he no more believed the "it was mistaken identity" storyline than I believed pigs could fly.

However, he knew when to stop, and eventually, reluctantly, he dropped it.

My hair was still my natural blonde-white color—I had no reason to dye it—and it amused me that Vance thought the white-blonde was hair dye and not my natural coloring.

We'd gone back to the café, he bought me coffee and a bacon sandwich, and then he told me how he'd left the old town. He had too much attention on him, so he packed up, left town, and moved state. He hadn't settled down in one place, he followed the fights as they moved, and a few times now, he'd called me to suggest he pick me up. I'm not sure Kris would appreciate I had given out the number on the phone he gave me, but hey, a girl had to get by somehow.

We never arrived at the fights together; Vance dropped me off and I made my way there. He would tell me the details I needed, he would tell me the odds, and then he'd place the bet for both of us.

He wasn't completely unknown. He had his fighters who moved around with him, but after what happened with Bullet, he made sure no one connected us.

I liked these fights more. They were open to anyone. It wasn't a case of who won stayed in the ring, it was one or two fights only, and if you got the second fight, your odds were better. I had two lined up tonight, which was unusual for me. We both knew not to push me too much. I was recognizable. No matter that the fights were more open, I was still a girl with white-blonde hair and an unbeaten track record—a point of surliness for my companion.

Vance wanted me to throw the first fight tonight. He said it would better the odds for the second fight if I hit the mat and stayed down. I disagreed about the odds. I also refused to throw the fight.

I saw him looking at me out of the corner of his eye, and I rolled my eyes. "I can *hear* you thinking," I grumbled, looking out at the empty road as we traveled.

"Is that right?" I could hear his amusement. "How do you *hear* someone thinking?"

"Your skull's empty, so that one loose thought is just rattling around like a penny in a tin can."

Vance barked out a laugh, turning the truck onto an old dirt road. "That's quite the insult," he said as he glanced at me.

"I liked it." Putting on a black hoodie, I got ready to get out of the truck. "Directions."

"We're a few miles up this track first," he told me. "This is a bigger fight—" He held up his hand to stop me from interrupting. "I know I told you that already, but you have two fights tonight. You're going to draw attention as it is, and even more with two. The first one is against a woman, Rita. She's good, fast." Vance looked me over. "She has more bulk than you."

"Muscle means shit," I reminded him. "Speed is what wins."

"Yeah, well, she's also fast. I got you an energy drink." He jerked his head to the back seat. "Forgot to give it to you," he added.

An energy drink would burn through my metabolism quicker than alcohol. I said nothing though, instead turning in the seat to fish around the back seat before realizing it was on the floor, in a grocery bag. Inside were two energy drinks, a deli sandwich, and a candy bar.

"All for me?"

"The candy's mine."

I shook my head, dropping it in his lap. "You have such a sweet tooth."

Was it weird I knew this? Ever since we were back in each

other's lives—and even that made me blanche—we knew more about each other. I knew he would take three sugars in his coffee, and he knew if he didn't put caramel creamer in mine, I would moan about it until he did. I knew if he smiled when a fighter was talking to him, it meant he wasn't taking the fighter on as one of his. He knew that if I smiled when a fighter was talking to me, I was more than likely going to be savage in the ring.

I knew that if he was thinking about what to say next, I wouldn't like what he was about to suggest.

"Spit it out," I told him, unwrapping the sandwich and taking a bite. Turkey, meh, it was worse than chicken. "I hate hearing that penny rattling."

"If you take the fall against Rita, it could work in your favor."

I took another bite and chewed slowly. "If I take a fall, which I won't, I lose my undefeated status. You want me to lose *that* against a girl?"

"You're a girl."

I took another bite. "I don't see the point."

"We can play it as she took you unawares."

"No one takes me unawares," I reminded him. Except for Bullet the night he ambushed me. Or the night the alpha stepped out of the shadows and caught me. "No one in the ring takes me unawares," I amended. Balling up the wrapper, I tossed it in the grocery bag. I popped the ring pull of the energy drink and took a large swallow, instantly grimacing at the taste. "This is vile."

"You're welcome."

I grinned at his dry humor. "Who's fight two?"

"Some big bruiser. He's also undefeated, so your odds against him will be shit." Vance met my gaze. "Do not lose."

"If my odds are shit, then winning against...what was her name?"

"Rita."

"Then winning against Rita won't make a difference."

"You miss the point," Vance said with a sigh.

I studied him as he drove us through the darkness. What was I missing? And then I realized. "You're all dressed up," I said with a delighted smile. "You have on a shirt. A nice one. And smelly stuff. You cut your hair. Vance?" I leaned towards him in my seat. "Do you have a crush on Rita?"

"I'm twenty-seven years old, Zee. I don't get crushes."

I was practically bouncing in my seat. "Oh man, you like her!" I exclaimed in glee. "You want me to throw a fight so you can have sex?"

"Shut up," he muttered, but I think his face was reddening. "This is where you get out." He pointed to the faint light from over the hill. "Head over there, keep to the plan, keep your head down. You speak to no one except the fight organizer. I'll see you on the other side."

I put my hand on the door handle to leave. "I won't throw it. Live with the fact you need to charm her with your personality."

He was already shaking his head. "Get out of my truck."

Jumping out, I zipped up my hoodie. "See you on the other side," I called out.

Yeah, it was strange how our relationship had changed since we first met, but I didn't think I hated it as much as I thought I would.

Weird.

CHAPTER 2

Kezia

CRESTING THE HILL, I LOOKED DOWN AT THE CROWD OF cars and the amount of people milling around outside a large barn. Barn was an insult. It looked like an industrial warehouse, similar to the one I woke up behind the night Bullet got me.

Unease pooled in my belly as I remembered how easily he had caught me. I'd been distracted. Comfortable. Dare I say, happy? Making my way down the hill, I used my shifter sight to pick the easiest route. Keeping my eyes and ears alert, I felt my wolf come forward, alert as ever.

She hadn't liked being shot three times with silver any more than I had. I felt her familiar presence and took comfort. She may be pissed at me for taking her away from *him*, but she was still always ready to protect me. It made no sense to me that she wanted to be where he was. Did she believe we were mates? I was still in denial, but the shaman had thought it too...and that worried me. However, he had said distance would help, and that was what I did. Put distance between us.

I didn't know what it was helping with. Despite everything I did, I still thought about the alpha asshole every day. There was a longing inside me, sometimes it almost felt like a tug, pulling at me. Was it him? Or was it indigestion?

Although I knew little about the mate bond, I was sure if it *was* a gift from Luna, then would it matter how many miles there were between us? Mates were mates. Right? Or was it so simple to put us in different states and wait for whatever it was that bonded us together to fade? I snorted a laugh as I jumped clear of the incline onto the flat ground.

In black jeans and my black hoodie, I was merely another shadow of the night as I moved closer to the venue. Weaving amongst the crowd, I made my way inside. If I'd thought there were a lot of people outside the barn, it was nothing to the crowd inside.

Working my way through the tightly packed bodies as they mingled and jostled for a position closer to the ring, I made my way to the corner of the room, where the organizer was. I couldn't remember his name, but Vance had taken me to him once before and seemed to like him. A fact which was solidified when I spotted Vance beside him. Two of Vance's regular fighters were nearby, and as always, it amused me that they doubled as his muscle *and* fighters. Not that Vance needed muscle. I knew he always carried a gun and at least two knives on him.

Vance saw me approach first and nudged the organizer, who immediately stopped talking as he watched me come closer. I didn't like the way he looked me over, nor the fact he smiled widely when I stopped in front of him.

"Thought you wouldn't make it," he told me.

I kept my gaze on him, even though I noted that Vance was paying more attention than he was supposed to. "Why wouldn't I make it?" I asked him casually, keeping my voice low but still loud enough to be heard over the noise.

"You're late."

I shrugged. "I'm here now."

His loud burst of laughter caused several people to look at us. "Your first fight is next." He pointed to a door behind him. "Stash your shit, be back here in five minutes."

"My odds?"

His eyes narrowed as he watched me. "Get worse the longer you stay in front of me."

I did look at Vance then, briefly, and saw him frowning. So did the guy.

"Fine," I bit out, taking two steps away from him. "But when I beat her ass in under five minutes, you better pick up the odds for the second fight."

He laughed again and I imagined throat-punching him. The thought made me smirk, and I shouldered past his hired help on my way to the door at the side of the room.

The back room was what I assumed to be the staff break-out area. There were lockers on one side, a few tables and chairs, and located at the very back was a door, which probably led to the restrooms.

A handful of the fighters were there, some bloodier than others, and it would be a safe bet that they'd already fought. My attention drifted to the only other female in the room.

She was white, had bright red hair, and was at least a foot taller than me. Her shoulders were broad and strong. She wore a sports bra and a pair of shorts like the wrestlers did in the made-up wrestling matches on TV. The boots on her feet were as solid as the rest of her, and without her being aware I was in the room, I watched her for a few moments as I unzipped my hoodie.

Someone nudged her, pointing to me, and I chose not to pretend I hadn't been openly assessing her. She looked me over casually and then gave me her back. My head dipped as I hid my smile at her obvious dismissal.

It seemed Rita didn't think I was a threat. That worked for me.

The door opened again and as I pushed my hoodie and phone into a locker, handily supplied with a key, I watched as Vance entered the room. He didn't look at me, making his way straight to my opponent. This time, I tried not to stare as he laughed at something she said, and... Was he *flirting*? He was smiling at her. Widely. That was the second time he reached out and touched her arm.

Oh my Luna, was I jealous?

The thought came out of nowhere, and I turned my back abruptly on the room so no one could see me freaking out over the fact that I was reacting to Vance in the company of another woman.

He was Vance.

Vance.

The guy who made a living off other people fighting and bleeding in a ring.

I heard his laughter and a throaty female laugh along with him and winced as my nails dug into the palms of my hand. What the hell was going on with me? This was insanity. I knew insanity, had tasted it more than I should, and I absolutely could not, *would* not accept that I was reacting to Vance with another woman.

Another woman? As in not me. What was I thinking?

Scrambling, I looked to my wolf, who was watching me, her head resting on her paws.

Vance?

She sniffed.

Vance!

Lazily she lifted her head, tilting it to the side.

I tried to decipher her look, she simply put her head back on her paws. Frowning, I wondered if I was near my heat. I looked down at the top of my jeans, which sat just below my navel. I didn't feel the familiar itch like I had before when my heat was threatening. Rubbing my tummy, I smoothed my hands over my lower abs. I didn't feel *off*. I pressed my hands into my belly, trying to flatten out the potential need I may start to crave soon.

I thought you liked Cannon? I asked my wolf, blurting his name out with a wince.

Her ears perked up and she looked at me with approval, as her tail flicked.

Vance is here. I felt her grumble of disapproval. *Is my heat coming? Am I overreacting to Vance's flirting?* A rumble of agreement.

Okay. Not the green light to bump uglies with Vance. Got it.

I felt her become less present and risked a glance over my shoulder at the man who stood with my opponent. To my surprise, Vance was watching, and he met my look with his usual blankness. Until he saw whatever was on my face, because I saw his head tilt to the side, and I saw the small curl of his upper lip as he held my stare.

He really *did* look good tonight. His hair wasn't slicked back like it usually was, it was more tousled and soft-looking. His black shirt pulled nicely along his shoulders, and the dark shade complemented his skin tone, making his blue eyes more striking. I swallowed as I looked him over. When I met his gaze again, his playful smirk was gone and his eyes had narrowed slightly, a look in them that was familiar, but *not* a look I was familiar with from Vance.

I bit the corner of my lip as I watched him watch me and saw his eyes darken. That tug in my lower abdomen tightened.

Holy Goddess, was *I* flirting with Vance?

The thought made me turn away and once more give the room my back as I scrambled to control myself. Shit shit shit. Vance? This was bad.

"Next fighters in the ring!"

The loud shout brought me crashing back to reality, and I slammed the locker shut, twisting the key to lock it, and tucking the key in my bra, under my boob to keep it safe. When I turned around, I was face-to-face with Vance. I gulped as he looked down at me, a question in his eyes.

"Yeah?" I forced out, looking past him to the door where it had closed behind Rita. "You need something?"

"Gimme the key," he said quietly. "I'll keep it safe."

Looking around, I saw most of the fighters had left, and of the ones who were left, no one was paying attention to us. Under his watchful eyes, I dipped my hand into my shirt and pulled out the key. Vance held his hand out and I pressed the key into it. His fingers caught around mine, holding them for longer than necessary. And I *let* him. I looked up as he looked down, watching me.

"Yeah?" he asked gruffly.

Shit shit shit. I didn't know what to do. I pulled my hand free, not looking at him, and stepped back. Brushing past him, rushing for the door, I fled. I needed to escape, and the ring was calling.

The ring was safe, and I didn't trust myself right now with Vance. He was giving off signals that were confusing me. Or, more likely, I was giving him signals that were confusing both of us.

Ignoring the people around me, I made my way to it. It was a bona fide boxing ring, elevated for better viewing. The ropes were drawn taut, and I rolled under the lowest one, blocking out the usual shouts from the crowd as I bounced to my feet and took the corner opposite Rita. She was still laughing and talking. I knew why she was doing it. It looked to the observer that she wasn't worried about me, and why would she be? I was half her weight and shorter than her.

Tugging at the waistline of my jeans, I swept a glance over the crowd. Vance stayed at the back as was usual for him, and without thinking, I pulled my white tank top over my head, dropping it carelessly at my feet as I watched him drink me in greedily. Had he always looked at me like this? Maybe he had, and I'd been blind to it.

Seeing his interest now, it was my turn to smirk as I gave him my back amidst the loud cheering of appreciation from the crowd.

Stupid really. Rita and I both wore tight-fitting sports bras. As the emcee ran through the rules, I quickly braided my hair. I should have done this in the locker room, but I had been too busy freaking out over my sudden attraction to the most unlikely male.

Who was I kidding? I was *still* freaking out.

"Oh my Luna, will you focus, Kezia?" I growled at myself as Rita stood in the center of the ring. "Time to fight, freak out on your own time."

Standing across from Rita, I heard the bell and immediately stepped to the side when she flung out a quick jab my way. Her follow-up was wild and too loose, and I realized something very quickly about Rita as she danced backward. She looked the part, but she couldn't fight for shit. Not against me, anyway.

A well-executed roundhouse kick, a swift uppercut, and one final full punch to the side of her face, and Rita was out cold on the canvas.

Standing back, I looked down at her before I looked up at the emcee as he declared me the winner. At the ropes, I grabbed my tank top and rolled out of the ring. I made my way to the back corner where the fight organizer was, pulling my shirt on.

"I should have said sixty seconds," I told him as he watched me. "Five minutes was generous."

"You're mouthy, I don't like mouthy."

"My odds for the next one?" I asked him, ignoring his dislikes. They didn't interest me.

I saw the gleam in his eye. "You beat the next one, baby, I'll give you an all-star bonus."

I was under no illusion as to what he meant by bonus. *Asshole.*

With a snort, I turned on my heel, hearing him yell out that I had twenty minutes until the next fight. Blowing out a breath, I slipped outside, seeing Rita get helped from the ring. It was quiet around the back of the warehouse, and I let the night air cool my overheated skin. I'd barely broken a sweat against Rita. She hadn't landed one punch on me.

"You good?" Vance asked, and I felt irrationally angry as I heard him approach.

"Why the fuck would I throw the fight to *her*?" I demanded as I whirled to face Vance. "Are you out of your mind? Your redheaded crush can't even punch properly!"

Vance pushed me back as I got in his face. "Because losing to *her* means your odds would have been worse for the next fight, and we would make more money when you *won*." He looked down at me.

I scoffed as I looked away, crossing my arms across my chest. "Yeah, well, dickhead in there is giving me shit odds anyway."

I heard him chuckle and looked his way. "Yeah, well," he mimicked me, "I forgot that your natural ability to piss most people off would work in my favor."

Ducking my head, I hid my grin. "Sorry about Rita."

Vance laughed louder. "No, you're not."

I was already nodding. Resting against the wall, I turned my head to look at him. "True." I grimaced as he pulled out a cigarette. "Smoker's breath, really?" Turning away from him, I looked up at the moon. "Thought you'd have more game."

"Meaning?" I felt him move closer as he leaned against the warehouse, one leg raised as he tilted his head to look up too.

"For Rita, she might not want to kiss you if you're all nicotine and stuff."

"Why am I kissing Rita?" he asked, and I felt his hand brush the back of mine, and I didn't move away.

"Your date?" I cleared my throat. "Right?"

"I'm not going on a date with Rita," he said, but out of the corner of my eye, I saw him put his pack of cigarettes away.

"You got dressed up," I pointed out, reaching over and tugging the hem of his shirt.

"I got *dressed*. Like I do every other day."

Our eyes locked and held. "Right."

Vance's eyes searched my face, and I saw him lean forward before he pulled himself back. He took a step away from me. "You're giving me some strange signals, Zee."

I felt my eyes widen. Pushing off the wall, I turned to face him. "Me? You're all date-mode and cologney!"

"Cologney? I wear cologne every fucking day."

"Well, I smell it more tonight."

"So? What difference does that make?" Vance shoved his hand in his pocket, the other scratched his jaw. "Is there something you want from me, Zee?"

Was there? I didn't know. I didn't think there would be, but the tug in my abdomen was confusing me. I broke eye contact and huffed out a breath. "Maybe?"

CHAPTER 3

Kezia

"Maybe?" He was watching me intently. "Zee, what are you saying?" Vance asked.

A soft touch, his thumb running lightly over my jaw, caused me to look back at him. His hand cupped my cheek, and his fingers slid into my hair.

"I don't like *Zee*," I protested weakly, meeting his gaze. Vance's lips twitched. When he took a step closer, bringing our bodies flush against each other, I couldn't deny the thrill I got when I felt him pressed against me. "What are you doing?" I asked him, feeling his fingers tighten in my hair, his hand cupping the back of my head.

"I don't know," he answered honestly. "On one hand, I'm thinking that you're, what...eighteen?"

"Nineteen," I corrected. In human terms, I was nineteen. In shifter terms, I was an adult now that I had gone through my first heat. No one would bother counting years anymore, as shifters lived much longer lives than humans. An adult was an adult. Age was a number a shifter cared little for.

"Okay, on one hand, I'm thinking you're nineteen." Vance

leaned down slightly, bringing our mouths dangerously close to each other.

"And the other?" I whispered, watching him closely.

"On the other hand, I don't care."

His lips covered mine. His tongue swept in, dancing with my own. This wasn't like when Landon had kissed me. That had been weird. Landon's tongue in my mouth was as alien to my body as the idea of Landon being my mate was to my soul.

When Cannon kissed me, I was overcome with need, want, and hormones. *Him* I wanted in a way I never thought I would crave anyone.

When Vance kissed me, I was very aware of what it felt like, and I took the time to explore the sensation. He knew what he was doing, I'd give him that. He took charge of the kiss, his mouth hard and soft at the same time. His right hand was fisting my hair, and his left was running down my back, resting on the curve of my hip.

Slowly my hands slid over his chest and around the back of his neck, my fingers twisting into the hair at the nape of his neck. His hair was shorter than Cannon's. I could feel the product he used for his hair, giving it a strange texture, and it left an unpleasant coating on my fingers.

Vance was also shorter than Cannon, so there wasn't as much stretch to kiss him. He also wasn't as broad-shouldered; I hadn't met anyone who was as wide as my alpha. I felt his hand slip from my hip as he ran it over the curve of my ass, and I remembered vividly what happened the last time the alpha learned someone had touched my ass.

In fact, all I could think about was *him.*

Cannon.

I broke the kiss abruptly, taking a step backward. "Um..."

"Yeah," Vance agreed with a short laugh. He watched me, his look assessing. "I...we're good?"

I nodded. "Yeah, of course." Smoothing my hands over my thighs, I tried to keep the awkwardness out of my voice. "I need to fight."

Vance stood back, his hand rubbing the back of his neck. "Yes. Absolutely. You go ahead." He pulled out his cigarettes. "I'll need a minute," he told me with a rueful laugh, resuming his pose against the wall, his foot flat against the wall with his leg raised to hide his arousal.

"And that's my cue," I told him as my face flamed after all. "See you in there." Hurrying around the side of the warehouse, I couldn't believe I'd just made out with Vance. "It better be my heat," I growled, tugging my braid free and shaking out my hair. Goddess knew what it looked like after Vance had his hands in it.

I rejoined the main crowd and grabbed a bottle of water from one of the buckets. When I first started fighting, Vance had warned me against drinking from these and told me to always check the seal. Human drugs didn't affect shifters. Much like alcohol, it burned out of our systems very quickly. However, until Bullet, I wouldn't have been wary of a gun, and now that I knew some bullets could hurt me, I checked the caps of bottles.

I drank the bottle in three gulps, seeing the last fight had ended, and looking around, I saw the organizer watching me. He gestured to the ring, and I gave a curt nod to show him that I understood. Jumping onto the skirt of the ring, I rolled under the ropes, and getting to my feet, I saw I was the first one in.

The emcee gave me a nod of acknowledgment but went back to talking to someone at the ropes. Once again, I braided my hair, tighter this time. I didn't know who I was fighting, and if they were a hair puller, I would rather have a sharp tug on a braid than lose a handful of hair.

I watched the door more than I should, and when Vance entered a few minutes later, giving me his usual look, I felt the tension between my shoulder blades ease. Looking at my tank, I opted to keep it on. I'd made enough rash decisions tonight.

Bouncing lightly on my feet, I was surprised when the emcee approached me, pointing at my boots.

"Lose the boots."

"Why?" I asked him, coming to a standstill. I looked at the canvas. "Have you seen this canvas? There's blood all over it. I'm keeping the boots."

"You keep the boots, you forfeit." He looked bored as he spoke to me. Sure, the germs and stuff on the canvas weren't bothering me, but had I not protested, it would have brought more attention than I needed.

"Says who?" I demanded.

"Boss says." He shrugged. "Lose them or get out."

Turning, I looked to the back and saw the organizer watching me. He grinned and I searched the crowd for Vance. I spotted him talking to someone, and it looked like he was arguing. His head snapped up and he looked to the ring and saw me watching. He looked worried and I watched him make his way to the back of the warehouse.

"You losing the boots?"

"Ugh, fuck it." I kicked my boots off and placed them in my corner.

"Socks too."

"You better tell your boss to be ready to pay my medical bills," I grouched, pulling off my black socks. The canvas was cold under my feet, which surprised me, considering how hot it was in here.

The ring was also wet, and I knew they'd hosed it down, but still... ick.

Stuffing my socks in my boots, I looked around the empty ring. Where was my opponent?

"Zee!"

Turning in surprise, I looked at Vance. We were supposed to be strangers to each other, why was he blowing it all to hell? "What are you doing?"

"They changed your opponent," he told me, getting closer to the ring. "I don't know who it is."

Looking up, I met the knowing smirk of the organizer. "You just let him know you know me," I growled. "How bad could it be?" I asked him as I turned my attention back to him, crouching down to speak to him without shouting.

"It could be very fucking bad, babe," he said with exasperation. "Drop the fight. We'll get another somewhere else."

No. I needed that money in case I had to run again. Shaking my head, I stooped closer to Vance, speaking in his ear. "It'll be fine. If he's a monster, I'll take the dive you asked of me."

Vance jerked his head back to look at me, the question clear in his eyes. "Don't be a hero," he warned me.

"Me?" I teased him and was rewarded with the familiar eye roll.

Vance looked around and then back at me. "Well, they'll all know now you're one of mine," he said. Reaching up, he tugged my head down and planted a kiss firmly on my lips. "Make it fast or get out quick," he whispered as he pulled away.

Resting back on my heels, I ignored the nearby catcalls. Pushing myself onto my feet, I jumped lightly on the spot, shaking my arms loose. The warehouse was packed, the atmosphere electric. The noise levels were loud, so many different smells as people crowded close to each other. I'd learned early on to breathe through my mouth only. There were too many scents for my nose that it caused me a headache.

Rolling my head on my shoulders, I turned to ask the emcee what the holdup was when I saw the crowd part to make way for someone.

I tracked his every move as he walked with confidence to the ring, head and shoulders above most here. My heart was hammering against my rib cage, my breathing felt labored. We made eye contact, and I took a step back at the animosity that was blasted my way. His hair was slightly longer than fashionable, and his face looked harsh in the light, all sharp angles and hard planes, emphasizing the almost severe jawline, the high cheekbones, and the perfectly straight nose.

Effortlessly he jumped onto the skirt of the ring, grabbed the top rope, and in a move of athleticism and incredibility, swung himself into a handstand, balancing on the top rope before his body flipped into the ring. The crowd went wild.

I was sweating as he landed squarely on his feet and looked me up and down. His feet, like mine, were bare. His jeans were loose but molded in all the right places. The dark gray T-shirt was sculpted to his chest and accentuated his biceps.

Watching me, he reached behind him, and in one slow move, he pulled the shirt over his head and tossed it aside. His golden bronzed skin was perfect and flawless under the harsh unforgiving lights.

My mouth was dry, sweat beaded along my top lip, and my clothes felt sticky and heavy.

The lazy smirk as he looked me over made my body heat ratchet up a few degrees. The pull in my belly constricted, my core tightened, and heat erupted all over my skin.

His nostrils flared, his head tilted slightly, and I watched as hooded eyes narrowed further.

The emcee was speaking, and I saw him gesture to us as the crowd screamed. Habit made me walk to the center of the ring, and I watched as he mimicked me until there was only one measly human who stood between us.

"Cannon."

Cannon ran his eyes over me. I saw him inhale slightly before his lips twisted in an ugly sneer. "You smell of filth."

My body wasn't ready for him. My head wasn't ready for him. But more importantly, my heart wasn't ready for this confrontation.

"How are you here?" I whispered, ignoring the emcee and everything he was saying.

"Your lucky night?" Cannon answered mockingly. "Or did you already get *lucky* tonight, *Zee?*"

It was getting harder to breathe. His scent surrounded me, making me feel foggy and disoriented. Shaking my head to clear it, I looked up at him, seeing his green eyes hard like granite as he watched me. "Stop it," I whispered, hating the desperation in my voice.

The emcee had finally realized we weren't listening to him and had stopped talking.

Cannon ignored my plea. "Forfeit, walk outside right now."

"Who waits for me outside?" I asked him bitterly.

Cannon flashed his teeth at me. No humor. No mirth. "Or you stay in here, and I get to kick your ass like you deserve."

My wolf stirred and I pushed her back. "When I kick *your* ass, I'll leave. Will you let me leave?"

"No."

Frustrated, I sucked my teeth. "So, you win, you take me back.

You lose, you take me back."

This time, there was maliciousness when he smiled.

"Fuck you." I turned away from him.

His hand caught my braid, jerking me back into his body, tugging my head back to look up at him. Cannon glared down at me, ignoring the fact I was struggling or that my fingers dug into his forearm as his hand tightened in my hair. I could only imagine what we looked like in the middle of the ring. The fight hadn't even started, and he had me locked in his grip.

"Fuck me?" he growled, his hand tightening even more. "Fuck *me*?" I looked up into the barely controlled anger. "You smell of *him*, you *reek* of him. Walk outside *now*."

Anyone else would be running at the fury in his eyes. Anyone else would be on their knees in front of the alpha, bowed in submission.

"Emcee!" I shouted over the noise of the crowd. "Start the fight." I stared back at Cannon, furious at the situation I was in. "Get your fucking hands off me."

He let me go abruptly, pushing me away from him forcefully, causing me to stumble. The crowd cheered. I got back to my corner and once more loosened my hair as I watched Cannon in his corner, recognizing Royce with another shifter I didn't know at the edge of the ring. Both were watching me.

I dare not look for Vance. Cannon was already furious, and I didn't need to make it worse for my friend.

Twisting my hair, I tied it back in a tight bun, and as the alpha watched me, I knew I'd need an advantage because my alpha was fucking huge. I remembered his words to Kris that night in the kitchen of my cottage. The *alpha* in him didn't like anyone looking at me unless I was covered. I pulled my tank up and tossed it behind me, relishing his rage as his eyes narrowed to slits.

With a wicked smirk, I reached for the top button of my jeans, and the alpha charged forward. Dimly I heard the bell ding for the commencement of the fight, but my attention was on the male in front of me.

I expected him to punch, but he didn't. I expected him to dodge *my* punch, but he didn't. My fist connected in his gut, and he didn't even grunt. Instead, Cannon picked me up and tossed me clear over his shoulder. I landed flat on my back, the wind knocked out of me.

With a cough, I rolled, but I saw his large hand circling my ankle, and the alpha asshole picked me up with one hand by the ankle and dangled me in front of him like I was a worm on a hook.

The crowd was cheering maniacally, and as I twisted to break free, a hard smack landed on my ass, causing me to yell out in surprise rather than pain. I punched out and connected with his dick. Cannon dropped me, and I sprang away from him while he folded over in pain.

As he crouched, I scissor-kicked, my right foot connecting with his chin, knocking his head back, my left foot landing squarely on his chest, kicking him backward.

Cannon took a step back, and I ran to the ropes. Throwing myself against them, I used their momentum and flung myself, launching myself at his unprotected back, intent on wrapping my arm around his throat. I knew I wouldn't beat him physically, but I sure as hell could choke the fucker.

Cannon spun, catching me in midair, and used my power against me to throw me clear across the ring. I landed face down on the canvas, and I heard a hiss of sympathy as I landed with an oomph. Looking up, I met Royce's stare.

"Hey," I groaned, rolling over onto my back. I saw the alpha coming for me and quickly did a backflip to regain my feet.

Cannon stood still as he watched me. The crowd was going wild, but all I could feel was the sense of violence that lurked beneath his skin. He'd tossed me across the ring, dangled me upside down, and smacked my ass like I was a naughty puppy, but he hadn't hit me.

A desperate plan began to form. Desperate because I wasn't sure I could hold my own against this male. But still, I wanted him to fight me, *really* fight me, not play with me.

Cannon's eyes flared briefly as he watched me move. Feinting right, I spun to kick him at the last moment, but he grabbed my leg, hauling me to him. I tried to fight the wave of heat that rolled over me as Cannon gripped my thigh over his hip, his fingers digging into my ass.

"You won't beat me," he goaded, dragging his hand down the curve of my spine as he arched my back.

"I don't want to beat you," I told him with a snarl. "I just want to see you bleed." My punch didn't have the normal weight behind it, but I hit him right above his eye, a soft area that was prone to bursting open like a dropped watermelon, and I hummed in satisfaction as that exact thing happened when I struck him.

Cannon twisted my body, and somehow, I got his knee in my gut and was once again winded and on the canvas. Sensing him near me, I rolled, my legs kicking out with sharp precise movements, connecting with his shin and upper thigh. He didn't budge, but his arrogance also meant he didn't move, and I aimed a forceful kick to the back of his knee, causing him to stumble. I rolled away, knowing how quickly Cannon would recover, and springing to my feet, I jumped again as I threw myself at him, my punches and kicks wild and unrestrained.

I knew I got him a few times, because I could hear the crowd shrieking. But more often than not, he blocked me. With every kick, sidekick, punch, and jab I attacked him with, he let a few past his defenses, but mostly he blocked. Cannon's fist knocked into my belly; it was nothing more than a tap, but it knocked me flat on my ass because I hadn't been expecting it. He reached down for me, dragging me up by the strap of my sports bra, and turning me in his grip, he kicked my ass, literally kicked my ass, sending me lurching across the ring as I tried to steady myself.

"Bastard," I muttered as I regained my footing. Turning, I met his cold hard stare. "Fight me."

Cannon snorted in answer.

I knew he'd been holding back. I knew he hadn't hit me once, not really. I think I threw myself into his fist more than the other way around. I'd fought and trained with my brother. I knew fighting. I *could* fight. Cannon was insulting me by refusing to fight. I knew the crowd was seeing something more violent, but they didn't know how hardy shifters were.

How hardy I was. He *would* fight me. Licking my lower lip, I looked him up and down.

"Do you hate the fact he touched me?" I asked softly, knowing only a shifter would hear me over the din of the crowd. "Do you hate that his mouth was on mine?" I circled him as I watched his hands curl into fists. "He knows how to kiss. I can still taste him," I added with what I hoped was a contented sigh.

The alpha pounced. But not towards *me* like I'd planned.

No.

Cannon jumped the ropes in one move and landed in the middle of the crowd.

CHAPTER 4

Kezia

"Cannon!" I raced to the ropes as I watched him push past people. "*No!*" I knew exactly where he was headed, and I knew I wasn't going to get to him before he got to Vance. "Shit."

Climbing through the ropes, I jumped onto the ground, ignoring the roughness of the concrete floor as I ran after the alpha. I saw Royce and the stranger battling through the crowd too and then lost sight of them as bodies crowded around me.

Fighting my way through the crowd, I pushed and shoved until I was clear, but by then, Cannon already had his hand wrapped around Vance's throat and had him pinned against the wall, his feet off the ground. Running at Cannon's back, I came to a sudden stop when he reached behind him and grabbed me, halting my advance.

His strength and speed were scary, and I staggered as he pulled me roughly into his side. Cannon kept his attention on Vance as his fingers dug into my hip, his hold tight.

"Cannon—"

"Shut your mouth," he snarled. "You've said more than

enough." He glanced down at me, and I bit back my retort when I saw his normally green eyes were almost turquoise as he fought to hold back his wolf. Knowing what was at stake, I pressed my lips tightly together.

Looking up at Vance, I winced when I saw his lips turning blue and couldn't hold my silence. "Cannon, you're hurting him," I pleaded quietly. "I didn't mean any of it," I told him honestly, trying to fight against his hold on me. "Let him go. I'll come with you, I won't even fight it."

Cannon pushed Vance higher up the wall, but he turned his head to look down at me. "You let him touch what's mine," he growled.

What's his? I wasn't *his.* But right now was *not* the time to be pedantic.

"And I will let you kick my ass," I assured him quickly, my hands in fists at my side as I tried my best to reason with a crazy person. "Just, let him go." I swallowed my pride. "Please, Alpha, let him go."

Cannon's nostrils flared and he scoffed. "You're a shit liar. You're covered in his scent."

"Then cover me in *yours!*" Twisting out of his hold, I pressed myself between the two of them.

Cannon snarled in disgust when Vance's limp body touched mine. Cannon released Vance, letting him drop to the ground as he jerked me forward, away from him. I was in his arms, not how I imagined our reunion, I admit, his arms wrapped around me like a vise.

"Cannon," I whispered. "Everyone's watching."

"You think I care?" His eyes were turning back to their normal forest green. Vance groaned behind me, and I tried to turn, but the alpha caught my head, forcing me to look at him. "Eyes on me," he warned softly.

"Cannon," Royce spoke lowly behind us. "We need to move."

"I know," he answered, watching me. Only me.

I felt some of the tension leave his body but not enough to relax me. I was still pinned in his arms, my friend regaining consciousness at my feet.

"You stink of him," he told me again. "Tell me why he should live." Cannon's eyes narrowed slightly.

"Because you're overreacting," I hissed at him. "Like the colossal asshole you are." I felt his arms loosen slightly as the alpha stared down at me.

"You kissed him."

"For the first time, tonight!" I said in exasperation. "Everyone's staring at us while you have your jealous fit of rage. Can you just get your shit together? Things are bad enough without you being a possessive dick!"

Vance moved and I tried to look, but the alpha's grip stayed firm. "No."

I saw the shift of his eyes, and I moved closer. "Let's leave," I urged him. "We can talk, fight, or whatever you want."

"Fuck?"

I swallowed hard, but I was already nodding. "Whatever you want," I told him as I pressed closer, hoping he didn't call my bluff. "We need to *go*."

"To the pack?"

I nodded again, slower this time. "Of course."

"Say it."

My wolf was alert and wary, but she remained silent. "Say what?" I asked, unsure, unable to look away from his hard stare.

"Tell your *alpha* what you *want*." The blue eyes of his wolf mingled with the green, and I knew how close he was to losing control, even though I wanted to smack him with something hard and heavy off the side of his head.

"I want to go back to the pack," I spoke softly but clearly. "With you, Alpha."

I didn't expect the cold, almost cruel smile as Cannon released me and stepped back. His eyes were clear of any wolf presence, but they stayed on mine as he spoke to Royce. "You heard her, she wants to go back to the pack, with *me*. Let's go." Royce stepped forward, his hand reaching for me. "Leave her," Cannon barked. "Kezia, now."

Jumping at the command in his voice, I hurried to his side, resenting his tone but prepared to run as soon as we got outside.

"And him?" Royce asked from behind.

Cannon smirked at me as he spoke. "Bring him."

"You can't take Vance!" I hissed at the alpha furiously.

"Watch me." He turned away from me, and for the first time, I noticed the sheer number of shifters who had surrounded us, keeping the humans back. "Move out."

I had no choice but to follow as they cleaved their way through the confused but excitable crowd. Looking over my shoulder once, I saw Royce half carrying a still stunned Vance. The beta looked at me, and I saw his warning look before the low growl from in front jerked my head around so I was once more staring at the broad back of the alpha.

Outside, the cool air brought little clarity as a shifter, who I didn't know, spoke quietly to the fight organizer, and I saw him hand over a large wad of cash. There were several Jeeps, some full cars, some open tops, and I realized the shifters were getting into them. My time to flee was running out, but when I saw Royce place Vance in the back seat of one of the covered Jeeps, I knew I couldn't leave him.

As I turned to look for Cannon, my breath caught when I met his gaze, anger still riding his emotions. Cannon jerked his head to the back of the warehouse, and I hesitated as I understood his intent. He raised an eyebrow in challenge, and I felt my wolf grumble in retaliation.

"Just go," Royce mumbled beside me, almost inaudible amongst the noise of the shifters revving engines and getting ready to leave. "He needs to calm down," he added. "The Jeeps will hide you."

"My stuff?"

"We got it." Royce looked over my shoulder and I took the hint.

I slipped between the cars, making it look like I was getting in one of the few with tinted glass, so anyone looking at security footage later didn't see me run to the back of the warehouse. I hurried to the back of the building, hoping that I was quick enough to shift and run. They wouldn't hold Vance, I was sure of it. I could shift and run and come back and get him.

My plan was ruined when I saw Cannon already waiting for me. His alpha speed was far faster than I could ever be, I realized.

"Planning on running?" he mocked me as he stood still under the moonlight.

"No," I lied and saw his lip curl upward in a sneer. "Fine, I thought about it."

"What else have you *thought* about tonight?" Cannon folded his arms across his chest. He was still shirtless, and I was having a hard time not looking at his body.

"My fights," I struggled to answer without losing the fake confidence I was clinging to.

"Your *friend*?" he sneered.

"Jealousy is a poor fit for you," I snarked back. The speed with which he moved forward made my knees shake.

"Strip."

"Fuck you."

Cannon's head tilted slightly. "You said whatever I want," he reminded me. "You said to cover your body with *my* scent."

I couldn't swallow, my throat was too dry. I was too far out of my depth. "Here?" My question was a whisper, but he heard me.

"Here." Cannon's voice was harsh and cold. "Take off your clothes, or I'll rip them off."

I was in jeans and a sports bra. He'd seen me naked before. Shifters were used to nudity—we were werewolves after all—but this felt...different. My sports bra had a front zip, and with shaky hands, I tugged at the zipper, freeing my breasts to the cool night air, tossing it to the side once it was off. Keeping my head lowered, I unsnapped my jeans, pushing the denim down my hips, kicking them off and stepping to the side.

"Underwear."

My jaw clenched as I followed his command.

"Shift."

Surprised, I looked up at Cannon to see his cold hard glare as he watched me. "Wh-what?"

"I said *shift*," he told me. "When we get back to my pack, I want his stench off you as much as possible."

The nausea in my belly settled. "We're running back?" I said in understanding. "You don't want..." My head dipped again, and I saw the bare feet of the alpha as he stepped into my space.

"Want *you*?" he asked me gruffly. "Want a female who's so

terrified her scent is making my stomach turn?" he added harshly. "You think so little of me?"

I couldn't look up at him, my relief warring with my lingering anxiety. "You implied..."

"I'm not a monster," he growled at me. "You're my mate, remember?" I heard the sneer even though I wasn't looking at him. "While you may want to fuck a human, the bond still exists between us," he told me bitterly.

"I didn't," I whispered, feeling tears burning my throat. "My heat is near, I...I was thinking of you—"

"As you stuck your tongue down another's throat? Gee, I'm thrilled." Cannon let out a bitter laugh. "Shift."

I had nothing else to say. Nothing I *could* say. I knew how it sounded. Goddess, I knew how it looked. I had no excuse, so instead, I let my wolf forward and turned my head as Cannon took off his jeans. I felt the heat of flames, and she turned her head as he set fire to our clothes in the exact spot I had stood when Vance kissed me. I'd unpack that later when I was calmer and he was in more control of his temper.

Run.

His voice in my head was warm and comforting, a contrast to who he was in his human form. We ran to the woods to start the journey north to the mountains that housed the Blackridge Peak Pack. I was under no illusion he was taking me home.

WE RAN FOR DAYS. He kept quiet for most of it. We hunted together, our wolves sharing our kills, but the alpha maintained his silence. Still, it was impossible not to enjoy the journey. His wolf was huge, a large black wolf with no hint of any other color, and bright electric blue eyes watched me and the terrain, seeing far too much of both, I suspected.

My wolf was content beside him. I knew she wanted to sidle up to him, but I kept her back from him. When she caught two rabbits, dropping them at the alpha's feet rather than eating her fill first, I pretended not to notice how easily she submitted to the more dominant wolf.

All too soon, the familiar peak rose above us, and with reluctance that our time was nearing the end, I followed the alpha as he ascended the mountain.

We were near his pack lands when he turned to look back at my wolf.

Shift.

She did so willingly. I had a lot more questions, and as I rose from the crouching position, pulling my hair over my shoulder, I heard Cannon sniff.

"Better," he grunted. "Not good, but better."

My snappy retort was lost when I heard the command.

Sleep.

I heard the distant snort of amusement as I whispered "asshole" as sleep covered me like a warm welcome blanket.

The fact I woke in the same cell that I'd escaped all those months ago didn't surprise me. What did surprise me was seeing Cannon stretched out in a chair in front of my cell, eating a chicken leg and reading a document. He looked as I sat up, and pointed wordlessly to the corner of my cell with his half-eaten chicken leg.

Turning my head, I saw the plate of covered food, and with hunger gnawing at my belly, I crossed the cell and brought my tray of food back to my bed. Uncovering it, I ate the first two chicken legs without looking at him.

"How long was I out this time?" I asked him, opening my bottle of water.

"A day."

"And Vance?" I asked, picking up the third leg and taking a bite.

"You no longer have his stench."

My gaze flicked up from my plate to his, and I watched him lick his fingers clean. "That's not what I meant." I was dressed in gray sweatpants and a white tank.

"Don't care," Cannon said with a shrug, his attention going back to his document. "Do you know that your heat surfaces every time I'm near?"

They'd mentioned it last time, and I hadn't been sure, but as soon as he said it, and knowing how I reacted to him, I realized that it made sense. I wasn't in control of my body any time I was in the same space as him.

Hormones.

A shifter's cycle was a cruel joke of the Goddess's.

"And do you know, when your heat spikes, you make really, *really* bad choices?" he added, turning the page of his report without looking at me. "First with that limp dick Landon and then, I actually don't know if it's worse, some horny human."

"Been naked or next to naked with you a few times too," I added with more bite than I intended. I pretended to think about it. "You're right, I make really, *really* bad choices."

"My mate," Cannon drawled sarcastically. "The tramp."

I was on my feet, the tray at my feet as I surged towards the bars. "I hate you," I hissed at him. "If you despise me so much, *Alpha*, let me be free, *away* from you."

Cannon stood, slowly uncurling from his relaxed pose. In one step, he was in front of me, glaring down at me. "You are not free," he reminded me. "Your crimes are as yet unanswered. Your brother and your shaman have not aided you by letting you run."

"I was in seclusion," I defended Kris immediately. "I ran. He doesn't know."

"You are as poor a liar as you are a judge of character."

"Says tons about you, *mate*."

Cannon smiled as he watched me. "I am the only thing that's keeping you alive right now, pup."

"By locking me up? Again?"

"Would you rather stand in front of the Pack Council and tell them how you cannot control your wolf? Tell them that you are feral and rogue, or how about you tell them you fight illegally in human fight rings, using your supernatural strength to beat men for money?"

"I fight as a human!" I shouted angrily.

"No. You don't," he said, grabbing the bars. "Because you are *not* human, and you never will be." Cannon's hard glare cut into me. "Until you control your wolf and accept you are a shifter who has superior strength to a human, you will stay in this cell."

I stepped back in confusion. "Until when?"

"Until I am convinced you are not a danger."

"I'm not dangerous," I protested weakly.

"Which is exactly why you remain here, pup. You are the most dangerous thing I've ever met."

The heavy silence hung between us until the alpha turned, scooped up his stuff, and left me in the cell.

It had been months. Months of freedom. Why then was I back in this cell, having the same conversation with a male who refused to hear me? Tiredly, I sank onto the bed and closed my eyes.

A rhythmic knocking brought me out of my wallowing.

Turning my head, I looked at the wall to the side of the room I was locked in. There was someone else here. Snapping my eyes open, I sat up in bed. I wasn't alone here, there *was* someone else here, and they were here because of *me*.

Because of my stupidity.

"Vance!"

CHAPTER 5

Kezia

CANNON HADN'T COME BACK. IF I DIDN'T KNOW better, I would say he was avoiding me. Which couldn't possibly be true, because that would mean he was pissed off with me still—wait, who was I kidding? Of course he was still pissed off. The man was grumpier than Cass without coffee.

I was lying on my cot, staring at the ceiling, when I heard the door open. I recognized Royce's scent and, turning my head, I also recognized the delicious smell of lamb stew.

"Dinner!" I called out with a happy clap, earning a chuckle from Royce as I swung my legs over the cot.

"You had lunch four hours ago," he reminded me. "You're not starved."

"Not like last time," I conceded, watching Royce slide my tray through the cell door opening. When he had stood back, I crossed the short distance to the tray, retreating with it to my cot. "Why is that? Why am I suddenly on three meals a day?"

Royce looked away from me as he shrugged. "You'll have to ask Cannon."

Lifting the plate covering, I snorted. "Yeah, because he comes to visit me so frequently." Lamb stew, mashed potatoes, carrots, and broccoli. My wolf eyed the veg with distaste, but my human form was delighted to see my favorite vegetable on the plate.

"I'm sure it's not intentional," Royce said gruffly as he took the seat that Cannon had left days ago.

"Mm-hmm." The stew was delicious. Better than mine, it was seasoned perfectly. "This is so good." I scooped up some mashed potatoes. "He *is* avoiding me," I said determinedly. "It's been a week." I frowned as I thought about it. "Hasn't it?"

"Give or take," Royce confirmed, shifting in his chair uncomfortably.

"Has he taken Vance back?"

"You know I won't talk about this with you, Kezia." Royce's look was firm but gentle. "You ask me every day."

I kept my head bowed as I ate. I'd stupidly mentioned I could hear the banging when Cannon had returned the next morning after my first night. He'd glared at me, refused to speak, and then left with such fury that I was surprised he hadn't internally combusted.

The banging stopped. Royce had, eventually, confirmed that Vance was still alive, but he said nothing else.

I hadn't seen *Alpha Asshole* since that morning.

"You don't tell me anything, he's too chicken shit to come in here and face me, and all you leave me with is my thoughts and imagination." I looked up when Royce snorted, failing to hide his laughter. My eyes narrowed. "You think it's funny?"

"You have quite the flair for the dramatic," he said with a grin. "And *thoughts*? Plural?"

I threw a head of broccoli at him, which he caught easily and, to my dismay, ate happily. "This is why you're his beta: you're also a dick," I grumbled as I resumed eating.

"Cannon is busy," Royce told me, quickly looking over his shoulder towards the closed door. "He is an alpha, and alphas are needed by their pack." He glanced once more at the door. "You were gone for months, Kezia."

I chewed the meat thoughtfully as I considered the male before me. "What's that got to do with anything? I was in seclusion."

Royce rolled his eyes as he got to his feet. "You don't have a bread roll," he said, pointing to my tray. "I'll be back."

Looking between the tray and the beta, I frowned. "I'll be finished by the time you come back." My smile was wide and innocent. "Unless...you want to bring me back more stew too?"

Shaking his head, the beta left to go fetch me a bread roll and, hopefully, more dinner. Despite being held in a cell, it was easier this time. Whether it was because I knew what to expect or because I was getting more regular meals, I wasn't sure. Maybe it was both. It helped that Royce was friendlier and more open. He was loyal to his alpha and spoke little of the pack life itself, but we had plenty of other things to talk about.

At first, I thought he was trying to trick information from me, but then I realized the beta wasn't keen on uncomfortable silences either.

Royce had also brought Mal with him twice, which was nice. I liked the doctor, and when he came the first night to make sure I was healed, fit, and healthy, he had also been more open than he had been before.

I wanted to believe it was because they knew I wasn't a threat. I feared it was because Cannon used the term "mate" too loosely and they were worried their alpha's future wife may resent the fact they locked her up in a cell for weeks, if not months, at a time.

Wife.

The idea made me laugh. Like I would ever be his wife.

"What amuses you tonight?"

My head jerked up as I watched Cannon cross the floor. I hadn't heard the cell door open or even sensed him. I didn't know of any other alpha that could hide their presence as well as he could.

I finished my dinner while I tried to control the impulse to throw the plate at his head.

He watched me as I finished my bottle of water, ignoring his question and him. He stood in his usual pose, legs spread, arms folded across his chest, back straight, and his head held high.

He dripped of authority, confidence, and overall arrogance. What had Luna been thinking? How the heck had I been bonded to him? I was none of those things, and I found none of the qualities attractive.

I ignored my wolf's huff of amusement.

Quiet.

"Where've you been?" I placed the empty bottle of water on the tray.

"Did you miss me?" Cannon taunted, his eyes roaming over me. "Where did you get the clothes?"

"I squeezed between the bars, shimmied up the wall, found a loose shingle, forced myself through, crept into one of your pack's homes, raided their wardrobe, and then when I took their clothes, I came back here to this cell so I could have fresh clothes every day and look pretty for you."

"So, Royce then?"

"Or that." I shrugged as I looked away from him. "My version has more flair."

"Your version is a lie."

"Isn't everything?" I met his look once more. "Isn't that what you expect from me? A lie."

Cannon frowned but he cleared his expression quickly. "You're unbelievable."

"Thank you."

"Kezia..." he warned with a sigh as he sat down. "Or is it Zia?" His look was mocking. "Or *Zee*?"

I wasn't rising to his bullshit. Not today. I had delicious lamb stew in my belly and the promise of more coming on Royce's return. If he returned. "Royce is coming back, right?"

Cannon gave me a flat stare. "All you think about is food."

"Well, you shouldn't have starved me the first time," I snapped back.

"You know why I did it," he grumbled irritably.

"Yes, I remember. You needed me to *want* you." I pinned him with a glare. "And *apparently* the only way to do that is by starving me until I'm desperate."

Instead of being insulted, Cannon threw his head back and laughed. I hated that his laugh was infectious. I hated that he was genuinely amused. I hated the way he looked at me when he let his guard down.

I hated that I didn't hate it as much as I should.

Cannon wiped the corner of his eye as he relaxed in his chair. "I spoke to your brother," he told me with no preamble. "I told him you were here."

I knew I was gaping at him, because I felt my jaw unhinge as it dropped to the floor. "Wh-what? You? *What*?" I was on my feet, excitement coursing through me. "When is he coming?"

Cannon had lost his humor and was watching me, his face blank of any expression. "He isn't."

I blinked. Shaking my head, my teeth gnawing at the corner of my lip, I took a step back from the bars. "No, he wouldn't leave me here. When is he coming?"

"He isn't." He continued to watch me, and I felt my anger rising.

My jaw clenched as I bit back my fury. "*Why*?"

Cannon reached into his pocket and pulled out a cell phone. *My* cell phone. With a glance at me, he looked back at the phone. "June fifteenth, fight tonight at eleven. Got two grand riding on your ass, pick you up at ten thirty. June twenty-first, two fights tonight, can you handle that? Could be good odds, but you'll need to bring the savage you. July eighth, pick you up at eleven, try not to break this one's leg." Cannon slowly raised his eyes to mine.

"You read them to Kris." I looked away from him, my gaze fixed on the ceiling, fighting back the tears. "You won't have *explained* anything. You read them in that *exact* tone, and he'll have overreacted."

"Or he just *reacted* to the fact a shifter was bringing more and more attention to herself with her reckless, *selfish* behavior."

"Damn it, Cannon! You know that's so much bullshit right there!"

"Your brother told you to stay safe. He trusted you to keep your head down."

"He sent me to seclusion," I muttered bitterly, still upholding the lie.

"Now who's bullshitting? I knew you were off that mountain before I was even in my packlands." Cannon stood, his agitation keeping him from remaining still. "I'm not stupid and neither is your brother. He knew I knew the moment he answered the phone."

Fear for my brother chilled me to the bone. "Are you going to tell the Pack Council?"

"That you ran back to the humans at the very first opportunity?" Cannon's scorn was scathing. "No."

"Why?"

"Because your brother was protecting his pack." Cannon rolled his head on his shoulders. "His misplaced trust is not a crime." Flicking a glance my way, he huffed out a sigh. "Plus, it kept you away from that other idiot."

I watched him as he spoke, my eyes getting wider and wider as disbelief coursed through me. "You think I can't be trusted? You *wanted* me to run?" I guessed, and when he didn't deny it, I stepped towards the bars. "You wanted me to run so I wouldn't be with Landon? You are the most arrogant fucker I have ever met!"

"I wanted you here, where I could keep people safe," Cannon corrected me. "Not being anywhere near Bale's son was a bonus."

"For who?" I asked, bewildered, and then I was pacing again. "I am *not* a danger!"

Cannon held the phone up. "These messages say different!" he growled.

"Those messages are common to any fighter who works that circuit. They don't go to fight for fun, they go to win!" I yelled at him. "You have to be brutal to win!"

"No, you don't!" he roared. "Not a shifter. Not against a human!"

"Oh my Luna, how the fuck are we still arguing about this?" I roared at him. "You'll never believe me. Why am I even trying?" I shook the bars in frustration. "You're never going to let me out." The despair caught me off guard. "I'm locked here forever."

"Your hysterics have poor form," he told me with a cold biting tone. "Put more energy into selling your sob story."

I spun quickly, grabbed the plate, and threw it at him through the bars. I missed. He didn't even dodge. The fact he stood still and unimpressed deflated my anger.

Royce chose that moment to enter the room, and I saw his smile fade as he looked between his alpha, me, and the broken crockery. "Bad time for this?" He half raised the bowl. "Should I put it in something non-breakable?"

His attempt at humor to break the obvious tension fell flat.

"What's happened now?" he asked cautiously as he walked towards me. He pushed the bowl through and nodded at my whispered thanks.

"Your alpha, the asshole, told my brother I was fighting. He told him I broke someone's leg in the ring, and he told him he went and collected me to keep people safe. From *me*." I didn't look at Cannon. "Did I get it all, *Alpha*?"

"Royce is aware of everything I do, pup. He also agrees that fighting in human fighting rings is too much of a risk of exposure to our people."

"I—"

Cannon cut me off as he spoke over me. "He *also* agrees that you are a lying, manipulative cheat, who fights unfairly for greed and gain."

"I didn't exactly say that," Royce mumbled awkwardly beside his alpha.

Cannon turned his head to look at him. "Which part did I get wrong?" he asked coldly.

"I never said she was manipulative."

Wow. "Just a cheat and a liar then?" I asked him bitterly.

"And a risk to our people," Cannon added blandly.

"Yay me." With a huff, I sat on the cot. "I should be locked up." I held Cannon's impassive stare. "But if I'm such a danger, why don't you go find a silver bullet and just shoot me in the head?"

Cannon shook his head slightly as he watched me before turning to Royce. "How can I work with this?" he asked him seriously. "She doesn't listen, she's self-absorbed, and she's fucking annoying."

"Back at you, asshole."

Cannon held his hand out to the cell as he continued to speak to Royce. "See? Impossible."

Royce looked between us. "Eat your stew, Kezia. I didn't sweet talk my wife into extras for you to let it go cold." He walked past his alpha and took the seat, moving it between us to sit, like he was an umpire at a tennis match. He fixed me with a hard stare. "Today, girl. Eat."

Grumbling about bossy bastards, I picked up my stew and started shoveling it into my mouth. However, it was so good that outright appreciation made me slow down to enjoy my food.

"All the crimes you've committed, and you can still eat," Cannon grunted.

"My only crime is that I know how to survive," I told him quietly. "Do you know how much it costs to live down there? Rent? Heating? Food? Clothes? The first time that I left, I left with nothing. *Nothing.* I have one thing that I'm good at, and that's fighting. I made money. I never, *ever* wolfed out. She was never present. I am probably all the things you hate about me, Cannon, but I *am* a survivor." I looked at them both. "I will never apologize for that."

"You had the money the second time," Royce spoke quietly. "You didn't need to fight."

"Money is not infinite. Do you know how much I eat?" I asked him as I patted my flat belly. "I'm always hungry."

Royce glanced at Cannon, and he let out a sigh. "The heat," he mumbled. "Her metabolism will be burning through every calorie as it tries to replace what she needs." He looked at me with a grimace. "My wife, around her heat, she binge eats. A lot. It's one of her signs we know her heat's coming, even before *she* knows her heat's coming."

Cannon was rubbing his jaw as he watched me. "It would explain the aggression," he said thoughtfully.

"The aggression is because I simply don't like you."

He ignored me. Color me surprised.

"The aggression added onto the hunger, and the anxiety—"

"Why am I anxious?" I asked them as I watched them talk about me as if I weren't there.

"You're a wolf without a pack down there; we're not meant to be alone," Royce said to me as he continued to share a look with his alpha. "It adds up."

"What adds up?" I asked in exasperation. "Why do I feel that I'm missing something?"

Cannon looked me over and then rubbed his forehead. "Shit." He looked up at the ceiling and then back to Royce. "I'll speak with Doc." With a nod to Royce, he left.

"Royce? What the hell is going on? Speak to Doc about what?"

Royce was suddenly very keen not to make eye contact. "Erm...well, you see..." He took a deep breath. "Your heat, it's never truly come to fruition."

"And?" I shook my head. "Says who?"

"Well, you did," Royce said with a flush to his cheeks. "And..." He looked at the door as if it were a lifeline and he was drowning at sea. "You may be more controllable—"

"*Controllable*?" My voice was like ice.

"Poor word choice," he mumbled. "You need a full heat. No interruptions. No anything. Just a full untampered with...heat."

"Okay?" I looked at him, taking in how flustered he was and not understanding why. He said he was married, so it's not like he was unaware of these things. "And that's bad, why?" He glanced at me. "You look like this is a bad thing, is this a bad thing?"

"Well. You're...you."

"Gee, Royce, I wouldn't say we were friends, but I thought we were past enemies."

"No, I don't mean it like that. I mean you're still, you know, untouched." He frowned suddenly. "You are, right?"

"It's really getting old how many people always ask me if I'm a virgin in this place. Is it a fetish? A cult?"

"Your heat is stronger when you're a virgin," he reminded me in exasperation. "Are you still...?"

"Yes. Thanks for asking," I snapped at him. "I know exactly what my heat is like. It is mine after all. I don't see why that's a *I need to talk to Doc* thing!"

Royce was looking at me like I was missing the obvious. Was I missing the obvious? And then I realized I was.

"Cannon," I said with understanding.

Royce was nodding and looking at me like he'd literally just seen the penny drop. "Exactly. Your mate."

My mate. "Shit."

"That's what he said," Royce muttered grimly.

"This could be bad." Worry gnawed at me as I looked around the cell. "Couldn't it?"

"Bad? It could be hell."

Awesome.

CHAPTER 6
Kezia

I spent the next two days waiting to speak to Cannon, but he was avoiding me again. However, Nikan was bringing me my dinner. His easy smile and good humor were infectious even if I was in a cell.

Royce had warned me that Nikan didn't know about the mate bond, and I was more than happy to have as few people as possible know about it. When Nikan was here, I could pretend I wasn't waiting anxiously for my heat or to see Cannon again. Royce had left the conversation very open-ended and ambiguous, using the "get out of jail free" card that Cannon was the alpha.

Cannon was indeed the alpha. He was also an alpha who was hiding from me.

Sitting on the cot, staring at the ceiling, I recognized Nikan's scent as he brought me dinner. Straightening up, I saw the small pack of cards on the tray and frowned at him in question.

"You play poker?" Nikan asked easily, pushing my tray through the cell door.

"Nope. I can play snap." Reaching for my plate, I enjoyed Nikan's easy laugh.

"You want me to teach you how to play poker?"

Uncovering my food, I grinned at the fat juicy steak and baked potato. "I think Royce's wife likes me," I whispered in a mock conspiratorial tone to the alpha's brother.

Nikan chuckled as he shuffled the pack. "Cannon cooked tonight. Royce and his family are camping."

I slowed in my chewing as I eyed the steak. "Alpha Dick made this?"

Nikan was grinning as he avoided eye contact. "You want him to take it off you?" he joked with a quick look over his shoulder.

"Pfft." I took a hearty bite. "That would involve him coming in here, and we both know he's avoiding me."

Nikan looked up at me with a slight frown. "Don't you *want* him to avoid you?" he asked, lowering his eyes again.

"I *want* him to let me out," I told him honestly. I took a bite of potato. "While avoiding me, if possible," I added with a grin, relieved to see Nikan's bright smile again. "So, how do we play poker?"

Nikan explained the rules to me as I ate, and when I was finished, I was too caught up in the rules and dealt hands to mourn the fact dinner was finished. I was sitting cross-legged on the cell floor, with Nikan across from me, learning to play poker when Cannon walked into the cell.

"What the fuck are you doing?" he asked Nikan, his jaw slack.

"He's teaching me to play poker," I answered as I saw the guilty flush on Nikan's face. "Problem?" I glanced at the large alpha male in front of me, and seeing his frown, I averted my eyes again. "What's a royal flush again?" I asked Nikan.

"Same suit and top cards. Ten, jack, queen, et cetera," Nikan mumbled.

"Oh, cool," I said with a forced smile, trying to ignore the heavy presence standing over us. "I have one of them." I laid my cards down on the floor of the cell. "Do I win again?"

My winning hand was enough to break Nikan's gloominess about his brother being here. "Luna, Kez! How?" he asked with a laugh.

"You keep dealing me the cards," I told him with a grin, handing my cards over to him, which were quickly swept up by the alpha. "Jerk." I scowled up at him to see him flicking through my cards.

"You have work tonight," Cannon spoke to his brother, holding his hand out for the rest of the deck. "You have to speak to Doc about that trip north too."

I watched as Nikan clenched his jaw but got to his feet. I couldn't recognize the tone the alpha was using. It was almost like a reprimand, but it held a softness that I'd never heard from him. That was why I was watching Cannon and not Nikan, so I missed the reason Cannon frowned at whatever look his brother shot his way.

"You leave her alone in here all the time," Nikan grumbled. "Why is she a prisoner?"

"I won't discuss this with you again," Cannon spoke sternly, *that* tone I was familiar with.

"I—"

"Quiet," Cannon commanded without looking at me, his attention on his brother. "You know why she's in here. Nothing's changed, no matter how charming she is."

Nikan opened his mouth to protest, but a flat stare from his brother, and he mumbled a goodbye to me before he left the room, closing the door behind him.

Cannon's bluntness had left me speechless, and instead of

fighting with him, I got up from the floor and went back to my cot. I sat on the edge of the bed, watching him expectantly.

Cannon's attention was on the door, a slight frown on his face. When he turned to look at me, I wasn't expecting the frustration.

"I didn't do anything," I blurted, hating myself for how defensive I sounded. "And I've never met one person who called me charming."

"*That* I can believe," Cannon grunted as he watched me. "Do you think you should be playing cards with him?" he quibbled gruffly, pulling the seat towards him.

"Why can't we play cards? He taught me poker. I was winning."

"Nikan was letting you win."

My eyes narrowed on the alpha, not willing to believe him. "Why?"

For the first time in a while, I saw an emotion on his face that wasn't stern disapproval. Instead, I watched him as he rubbed his forehead. "I want to say he has poor taste."

Scrunching my nose up, I squinted at the alpha. "Huh?"

Cannon fanned the cards out on his thick thigh and pointed at the slight discoloration of some of the cards. "This deck is old. It's the one I taught Nikan to play with. It has the high cards marked."

Leaning forward, I peered at the cards. Sure enough, I could see the discreet markings now that I knew what I was looking for. "Oh." Chewing my bottom lip, I looked up at the alpha. "Explains why I was winning," I told him with a playful shrug.

"Mm-hmm, doesn't it..." Cannon watched me carefully. "How are you feeling?"

The question took me by surprise. "Um...fine?"

Cannon raised an eyebrow. "It's not supposed to be a test, try again."

"You're horribly bossy," I told him instead. "Where is Vance? How is *he* feeling?"

Cannon stretched his long legs out in front of him, his arms folded loosely over his chest as he watched me. "He's fine. Doc's been with him."

I could scream and yell and fight, or I could try to have a conversation with the brick wall in front of me. "Why is he here?"

"Where else should he be?"

It was my turn to give him a flat stare. "Just answer the question," I told him with a roll of my eyes.

"You were with him. A group of males took you. People who get left behind ask questions."

I was already frowning. "You took him so he wouldn't ask questions?"

"You think I took him for his company?"

Sitting still was difficult when he was being such a prick, but we had a tender truce right now, and if I cursed at the asshole in front of me, he would walk away, and I wouldn't get any answers. "Of course not," I snapped with more bite than I intended. "You just made it...well...it doesn't matter. When do you let him go?"

"I made it like I was jealous?" Cannon asked, ignoring the latter question.

"I didn't say that."

"You didn't have to say it; it's obvious that's what you meant."

"No, it isn't. It's only obvious to your ego."

"So, it *is* obvious?" he challenged me with a smirk.

"No! It's obvious to you because you're delusional."

"Am I obvious or deluded? I'm confused."

"You're an ass."

"An obvious ass or a deluded ass?" Cannon cocked his head to the left, his eyes dancing with laughter, and I looked away from his playfulness.

"Definitely an ass," I mumbled, but I couldn't hide my smile.

We sat in a comfortable silence for a few moments, which was unlike us, and although I didn't want to ruin it, I still had questions.

"Cannon—"

"He's been with Doc. He got some tests, we asked him some questions, he's in holding."

Fear traveled down my spine. "Why?"

"Why what?" Cannon asked me, still in his relaxed, almost lazy pose.

"Why is he still here?"

A half-nonchalant shrug was my answer.

Getting to my feet, I made the few steps across the cell to look through the bars at the male on the other side. "What are you hiding?"

The easy, relaxed facade was gone, and in its place was the coiled tense alpha I knew, ready to spring. "Who says I'm hiding?"

"You don't fool me," I warned him quietly, my gaze searching his face for any clue as to what he was up to.

Cannon stood slowly, stretching widely, his arms high, his shirt exposing the golden tan of his abs. Lazily scratching his head as he settled back from his stretch, the alpha smirked at me as he caught me looking.

"Don't I?" he murmured as his green eyes met mine.

Goose bumps ran over my skin as I held his stare. He may be an ass, but by Luna, he had sex appeal by the bucket load. I saw the answering flare of lust from the alpha.

A foreign scent, floral and...*feminine*, wafted towards me. Confused, I looked past Cannon to look at the woman who had entered the room.

She was stunning.

I wished I was exaggerating, but I wasn't.

She was tall, maybe taller than me, with long, thick lustrous black hair, a healthy golden glow from head to foot, and curves that made men sit up and notice. Tight black jeans and an off-shoulder pink shirt, which was loose but still managed to cling to her breasts, made my eyes narrow as I watched her approach Cannon. Curious brown eyes met mine as she looked me over and just as quickly dismissed me.

A perfectly manicured hand rested on Cannon's forearm, and he looked down as she spoke.

"Alpha, Doc's asking for you." Her voice was deep and husky.

I watched Cannon's brief nod, I saw her hand remain on his arm, and I felt my back get straighter as she stayed close to his side.

"Who's this?"

Cannon glanced at me and looked back down at the female. "Tell him I'll be there shortly."

"What? No introductions?" I asked mockingly as the female started to move away.

"Enough," Cannon growled with a cautionary glare my way.

"Alpha?"

She was loitering with intent. I heard my back teeth grind and realized it was because my jaw was clenched tight.

"Go back to Doc," Cannon instructed tersely, his eyes on me. "Close the door behind you."

With one last lingering look over her shoulder at the man who had fixed his attention on me, she left us, pulling the door tight behind her.

"Who's she?"

"Pack."

"Pack...what? Mate? Buddy? Worker? Bedwarmer?"

Cannon tilted his head. "You jealous?"

"I'm jealous of the freedom she has, nothing else."

Cannon crossed his arms as he watched me. "You're a shit liar."

"Funny that. You're usually so quick to tell people I'm some criminal mastermind, except I can't seem to lie, but when it suits you, I'm a liar."

"It never suits me for you to be a liar."

We glared at each other, and I would let it go. I would. But I could still smell her. "She reeks."

Cannon didn't hide his laughter. It only infuriated me. I could feel my claws ready to unleash as I watched him laughing at me.

As suddenly as it started, his laughter stopped. Hard green eyes met mine, and if I hadn't been so pissed at him, I would have heeded the warning. But I was pissed at him, as usual.

"Your eyes are changing," Cannon warned.

"Yeah?" I felt my claws extend from my right hand. "My claws are feeling thirsty too."

He stood in front of me, shaking his head as he took in the sight of me. "How the hell did you ever last down there for that long when you're so very fucking unstable?"

"Don't you ever stop to wonder that it's only when I'm near you I feel violent?" With my voice tight with anger, I was ready to launch myself through the bars if I could.

Cannon gave me a low mocking bow. "I'm leaving."

"Good. Stay away."

"So now you want to be in the cell?" he taunted me as he walked away.

"I just want to be where you aren't!" I shouted after him.

At the door, Cannon looked back at me over his shoulder. "Liar!"

The door shut with a ringing finality that did nothing to quell my temper. He didn't come back, and in a way, I was pleased, but mostly I was pissed off because I still didn't know who she was or why she got to touch him so freely. I ended up being irrationally furious for hours.

When Royce came in later that night to ensure I had eaten supper, I couldn't answer his query of why it looked like I had been crying for hours, because I *had* been crying for hours.

And no wolf with any pride was going to tell the alphahole's beta she was crying because the alpha was a giant dickhead who deserved to get knob-rot for his whoring ways.

Instead, I told him I missed my brother.

Thank Luna Cannon wasn't in front of me right then. Royce believed me and I knew with no doubt Cannon would have laughed in my face.

Cannon had left the playing cards when he left earlier, and Royce, who was obviously a decent shifter, unlike his alpha, must have felt bad for me and offered to play cards with me to pass the time.

As I sat on the floor across from him, I felt silly for my tears. "You don't need to keep me company," I told Royce quietly. "I know you have a family."

Royce continued to shuffle the deck. "My girls are in their beds," he told me gruffly. "My wife is baking bread for tomorrow and then will relish the peace of the house without me in it to get under her feet." He looked up at me with a smile.

"I have time to teach you how to win at poker," he added with a wink.

"Cannon told you Nikan was letting me win?" I guessed with a small sigh.

"It was mentioned," Royce told me with a tight smile.

Watching him as he dealt the cards, I felt the sudden need to defend myself. "I'm not this horrible person he thinks I am."

"I know."

"I never, ever, not once let my wolf free when I was fighting," I told him, holding his eye so he could see I wasn't hiding from him.

Royce inhaled deeply, tapping the cards against his thigh before he looked at me. "When your fights were finished and you were alone, did you shift?"

Confused, I nodded. "Of course, only when I was alone, and no one could see me."

He nodded sagely. "Did the human men you fought shift too?"

What? I looked at him in confusion. "They weren't shifters."

His eyes gleamed in triumph. "Still think you were fighting fair, Kezia?"

I stared at him in surprise. "I never hit them with my strength. Not my true strength."

"But you healed the moment you left them, and you went back fighting others, with no scars, no wounds, no aches or pains, as soon as possible, didn't you?"

Swallowing hard, I nodded once.

"So, I'll ask you again, do you still think you were fighting fair?"

Blinking rapidly, I shook my head, looking away from the beta in front of me. "It's not the same."

"Tell that to the man who needed to feed his family that week and all he had left to turn to was a fight in a barn, but you broke his leg, so instead of a bruise and some aches, he has a broken leg and can't work for weeks. Or tell it to the man whose wrist you snapped even when he told you he conceded, but you snapped it anyway because Vance told you he'd give you an extra hundred."

"That's not fair," I whispered, barely audible. They had found out about me. How?

"And while you may have bled on stage, within an hour of clearing that ring, you'd shifted to your wolf and back to human form, and you felt no pain. Did you?"

"No." My eyes were fixed on the floor. I felt the tears building, and I couldn't hold them back.

"You may have never hit them with your strength knowingly, Kezia. But show me a human girl who can snap a man's leg in a clean break, who can break a man's wrist with the flick of her fingers, or who can walk back into the ring three days after a beating and fight like nothing happened." I felt his heavy stare on me. "Do you still think you were *just* human?"

"I...it wasn't like that." I couldn't look at him. I couldn't lift my head at all.

I heard Royce get to his feet, knowing he was standing over me, the cards on the floor forgotten. "Wasn't it?"

The question hung heavy in the air long after he had left me alone to face the ugliness of my reality.

Hours later as I lay on the cot and stared at the ceiling through the veil of my silent tears, I realized Cannon was right.

I belonged in the cell.

CHAPTER 7

Cannon

"Is she still sulking?" I asked my second bitterly, standing at the window of my office. I didn't turn to look at him as he closed the door behind him.

"Sulking is harsh," Royce muttered, taking his usual seat. "I don't think she's faking."

I licked my top teeth but said nothing as I stared out into the street of our town. Blackridge Peak Pack walked through the streets as they made their way to get to their days. Our town was slightly bigger than the one she came from, and far more organized and reasonable. Fair to male and female.

I watched two of the pack walking together, laughing as they made their way to the school where they taught the young. We had four teachers, who split the grades between them, and if any of the pack wanted to be taught in human school, I had spent several months setting that up for them.

My father had kept these wolves down for too long. They deserved freedom and they deserved to make their own choices, on the condition that it didn't come back and bite their alpha in the ass.

I was only half joking.

Kezia was a prime example of what happened when *free* became rogue. When carefree became dangerous. When her choices threatened us *all* with exposure.

"Are you going to go and talk to her?" Royce asked me, moving in his seat uncomfortably. "It's been a few days since you were last in there."

"I know how long it's been," I told him as I watched two of the pack walk their child to school, merely a few steps behind the teachers, and it pleased me to see how relaxed they all looked. It was a stark contrast to the pack I came back to over two years ago. "I also know if I go in there, I will either kill her or fuck her. Which one would you prefer?" I turned to look at my beta.

"Neither."

"Which is why I am out here, making sure my pack is well and has food and has order."

"Are you saying Kezia is chaos?" Royce asked with a small smile.

My eyes narrowed as I watched him, and with a groan, I pushed away from the window. "You too?" I asked him as I dropped into one of the chairs. "I thought you would hold out longer," I added harshly.

"I *have* held out!" He frowned as he heard himself. "I have not softened towards Kezia," he corrected. "I am still unsure of her, and a large part of me still thinks as I did the night you caught her: she is a young wolf who needs direction."

"She risked everything."

"To flee, she did."

My heavy stare didn't bother Royce. He had been my friend from birth. "I thought you weren't going soft?" I rebuked him.

"I thought you were willing to listen to the woe of your mate?"

"Can you please stop saying that?" I asked him instead.

"Can you please make up your mind?" he asked with exasperation. "She's your mate. You decided to let her go, then you hunt her, finding her after five months of, really, can I be blunt and say torture? It was all "find my mate," and then we found your mate, again, and *again* you become a complete asshole."

"She was kissing a human."

"You're no angel, Cannon, don't even pretend with me," Royce scoffed, tapping the arm of his chair.

"I've touched no other since I realized who she was," I corrected sharply.

"True," he conceded. "But...the people she *trusts* told her that distance would help her break the bond."

"The people she trusts are idiots."

Royce's eyebrows rose slightly, but he never argued with me. "She isn't doing well," he offered after a few minutes of silence. "You can be stubborn all you want, but she needs you."

I watched as he carefully avoided eye contact. "What aren't you telling me?"

"You judge so quickly," he murmured, but still my best friend was finding the groove of the wooden flooring very interesting.

"Spit it out."

"Nikan has been in her room every lunch and dinner."

My groan was loud as I slipped further down my seat, my head tipped back to look at the white ceiling. "Why is this happening?" I asked no one, pressing the heels of my hands into my eyes. "Why?" I asked again.

"You shield him from too much."

"My father beat him every day I was gone."

"And you have supported him every step of his recovery," Royce countered back quickly. "Nikan is a strong wolf. A good wolf. You shield him, and I can tell you that man's seen more than you could ever shield him from!"

I was on my feet, pacing to and fro as my friend's words rang in my ears. "I know! I *know* that when I left the Peak and my brother behind, I left him to the prick in charge. I foolishly thought it was only me my father hated." Pushing my hair off my face, I met Royce's stare. "I know what I did, I know what I have done, and I know what else I still must do. I have years of work to make up for all of that to this pack, not just my brother."

Royce rubbed his ear. "You don't have to do as much as you think you do," he said carefully. "The pack is good, strong."

"But?"

He smiled. "You know me too well," he joked before he let out a heavy sigh. "But your brother is infatuated with your mate, and you need to stop that."

"And she can't stop it?" I asked tersely. Royce's unimpressed look said enough. "She's not as innocent as you think she is," I reminded him sullenly.

"Her pack hates her. Her brother's mate's twin pretended to be her mate because he didn't like the idea of his sister having something he didn't. Her human *friend*, and Luna knows I use the term loosely, knows much more than he ever let on to her." Royce waved his hand in my direction. "Another thing you have yet to tell her."

"Your point?"

"The point is that your mate *is* innocent when it comes to people using her for their gain."

He was right. I knew it. He knew it. I just didn't want to admit it.

"You are an *alpha*, could you remember that? Or are you going to hide in your study from her forever?"

"She pisses me off."

"It's a trait you both possess."

I glared at him, and he grinned. "I'll talk to Kezia."

"Good." Royce stood up.

"But you can tell Nikan."

My beta looked down at me, and when I raised an eyebrow, he called me a very unpleasant name before he turned on his heel and left my study.

With a grin, I made my way to the bunker. If I was honest, I could handle all the venom Kezia threw my way. I'd rather deal with her temper than my brother's disappointment that the girl he liked was my mate. We had a good relationship, but I still left him for five years while I traveled the world, and my father took an already beaten pack and ground them to the dirt.

In the bunker, I avoided Kezia's cell for a little while longer. Instead, I detoured to Doc's room. He was in his lab coat, pouring over a slide on a microscope.

"Do I want to know?" I asked him as I took a seat out of his way.

"E-coli."

I nodded. He could have told me it was the bubonic plague, it wouldn't have surprised me. "Food poisoning in shifters?" I guessed.

He raised his head and looked at me. "I purposefully fed contaminated spoiled food to five of you—not even acid reflux. I licked the packaging, and I had the shits for two days."

"Thanks for the visual," I told him with a grin. "I was one of the five?"

Doc rolled his eyes. "As per our agreement, Cannon. You are *always* one of the test subjects."

"Her?"

"No." Doc stayed glued to his microscope.

"You too?" I asked him with a frown.

"She's got enough problems." He looked up at the far corner, where the other cage sat. "You told her about *him* yet?"

I looked at Vance. He sat on his cot, legs crossed under him, back against the bars, and he watched. He hardly ever spoke, but he watched everything, which is one of the reasons he was in here, away from my pack. His cage was encased in plastic, thin and almost delicate in appearance, but it was rigid and unbreakable, and it kept him enclosed in silence.

Sometimes, Doc opened the system and spoke to him, but most times, he flicked on the air and let him sit in his cocoon of silence.

He had nothing left to say anyway. Not to me. I had pried every lie from his tongue, and when I was done, I had gone back and cracked open every truth he ever kept.

Eyes filled with hate watched me as I appraised him. His hair was unruly, his skin pallor pale, and he had lost the cocky air he'd worn when he strutted around fighting rings.

It had taken five months to find Kezia. It had taken three months to find him. *Him* we had watched for a long time before we made our move, never realizing that he was the one who would lead us to my mate.

"How long has he been silent for this time?" I asked Doc. "Did you feed him spoiled meat?"

Doc looked affronted at the question. "I am a scientist. Not a torturer."

"Does it matter if it's him?" I asked honestly.

"Yes!"

"Fine." Doc was still staring at me in disapproval. "I said fine! Fuck, Doc, I didn't say feed him to the coyotes." I looked at Vance again. "But you know…"

"We are *not* feeding him to the coyotes," Doc said in exasperation. "I know he's scum, and I know he could have hurt her, but no."

My wolf grumbled and I agreed. Coyotes were too good for Vance Forbes. I caught Doc's pointed stare, and I couldn't hide my guilty grin.

"Out. Stop stalling," he told me. "Go speak to her."

"I am a grown alpha," I grumbled as I got to my feet.

"Then go alpha your mate and stop avoiding her."

I'd like to say that I left his lab with dignity, but I was pretty sure I was mumbling about the unfairness of it all. At the door to her room which housed her cell, I stood outside for a long moment, running it through in my head how I was not to rise to her brattish ways.

With a deep breath, I schooled my face into one of a calm mask of indifference and pushed open the door. I almost choked on my tongue.

Kezia was in a handstand, wearing only boy shorts and a bra that was too small for her. Every inch of her was on display, and she was perfect. Even upside down. Her hair pooled on the floor around her, and with her eyes closed, she didn't know it was me yet.

Closing the door gently behind me, I masked my scent and my presence as I approached her. When she let out a low controlled breath, I realized she was in cool-down exercises. Her legs parted into the perfect splits, and I watched in fascination as she brought her legs back together, then down to a crouch, and slowly dropped them to the ground in a controlled move before bringing herself up straight.

Opening her eyes, she jumped when she saw me watching her, surprise quickly morphing into anger. "Creepy much?"

"Your control was impressive," I complimented her. "Where is it the other ninety-nine percent of the time?"

Kezia flicked me the finger, stooping to the bed to pick up her discarded sweats. "Where have you been?"

"Miss me?" I taunted. I felt my wolf's disgruntlement at the fact that I was yet again acting like a surly pup.

"Can you miss a disease?" Kezia asked me with a pleasant smile.

"They told me you were feeling sorry for yourself," I told her, feeling a petty sense of victory when I saw her smile dim. Dragging the chair to the cell, I sat down. "Moved on already?"

Kezia said nothing while she pulled her T-shirt on. With a flourish, she sat on the cot and looked at me, resting back on her hands as she waited for whatever reason I was here for.

Whatever reason? Where did I start? "Royce tells me you understand now?"

She broke eye contact, looking away as she shrugged.

"Use your words, pup."

"Royce put forward an argument that was worthy of consideration."

I watched her as she sat in front of me. So slight. So fragile looking. That white-blonde hair would age anyone else, but on her, she looked youthful. Large pale blue eyes, as hard and almost as colorless as ice. She looked small and delicate. In reality, she was solid.

Unbreakable.

"It's not a history paper," I rebuked her softly. "It's serious. I was led to believe you now understand that." Kezia licked her bottom lip as she continued to avoid my gaze. "Kezia?" She didn't look at me, only nodded. With a sigh, I leaned forward in my chair. "Do not make me come in there."

That earned me a scowl. "I get it, okay?" she snipped at me. "I'm a heartless bitch who beat men up and didn't care. There. That what you were looking for?"

Standing, I ignored her startled yelp of protest. Walking to the cell door, I punched in the code.

"You don't need to come in here!" Kezia shouted, scrambling up from the cot and backing to the far end of the cell.

"For Luna's grace, Kezia!" I protested. "You're hardly in danger."

"How am I supposed to know that?" she demanded, her hands on her hips.

I fixed her with a flat stare as I pulled the cell door closed behind me. "You're my mate, idiot."

"Idiot?" Kezia looked more affronted than before. "You can tell why I struggle to believe your intentions are good!"

"I'm hardly going to fuck you against the bars," I told her grumpily. "Sit."

"I want to stand."

"Fine. Get comfy, I have a lot to tell you."

She watched me through narrowed eyes and then, with great reluctance, inched towards the cot, sitting on the very end. "What is it?"

"Patience."

"Have you met me?" Kezia scoffed. "It's not one of my virtues."

"I'm aware," I deadpanned. I looked her over as she sat rigidly in front of me. "You're losing weight."

"I'm used to more food."

"Your brother must have needed a store just for you," I joked.

Kezia grimaced. "Sometimes."

She looked away and I subtly inhaled her scent. Blood? Ah, that made sense. "Do you need anything?" I asked her, feeling like I was invading her privacy.

Kezia flushed but pointed behind me to the small toilet area. "Royce has me covered."

Turning, I saw the small box of sanitary products. "Good." Turning back, I caught her studying me but said nothing. "I'll add more to the plate tonight."

"Thank you."

The silence grew until Kezia had enough. "Why are you here?"

"I need to tell Nikan you're my mate."

She blinked in surprise. "Um...okay?"

"He may be attracted to you," I told her bluntly. "I don't want... Well," I faltered. "You understand."

Kezia was frowning. "He's just friendly."

"I understand Landon was *just* friendly once too."

That earned me a glare. "There's no need to be *you* about it."

"If Nikan..." I bit my lip as I looked away. "If he addresses you about it, will you be kind?"

"I'm not the monster you think I am."

I didn't meet her eyes, but I gave a sharp jerk of my head in acknowledgment.

"Is that why you're here? To tell me you think your brother likes me more than just a jailed rogue?"

I chuckled before I could stop the laughter. "No. And please, for my brother's sake, try not to be so flippant next time you see him."

"I won't."

"Vance suspected you're not human."

I was watching her and felt a thrill of satisfaction when her mouth dropped open in disbelief. "No."

"Yes." I didn't want to tell her how I'd extracted the information from him, but I would if I had to. "He didn't believe your story. Let's be honest, who would?" I ignored her wince. "A girl hunted by the police for a triple murder is suddenly a case of mistaken identity?" Pushing my hair back, I met her hostile stare. "It's a stretch."

"It doesn't mean I'm not human."

"No," I agreed. "The silver bullets in his gun did that."

I didn't enjoy the look of betrayal this time. Even though I wasn't the reason for it, it still stung. "Silver?"

"Yes. Four of them."

"Shit." Kezia stood, her hands pressed into her lower abdomen, and I watched as she bent slightly forward. "Shit."

Frowning, I looked at her. "Do *not* even *think* of shedding a tear for him."

She shook her head, but I watched her left hand reach up and flick the tear from her eye. "I'm not." She flicked another away, catching my glare. "Ugh! I'm not."

"You're doing a shit impression of someone who isn't crying."

"Fuck off. I'm angry."

"Good. You should be," I told her forcefully before I hesitated. "Why are you crying then?"

"What did he say when you questioned him?" She changed the subject. "Did you torture him?"

Was there a wrong way to answer that? "Are you on board for his torture?"

Fierce blue eyes glared at me. "Yes!"

"Then yes, I did. He sobs like a little coward by the way."

"Good," she said fiercely as she slowly sat back down again. "Do it all over again and let me watch."

I grinned. "Savage little wolf." I felt the knot in my belly loosen slightly when she shared the smile.

"Meditation was a waste of time," she muttered as she resumed her seat on the cot. "Nikan then Vance, anything else?" she asked dryly, obviously trying to lighten the mood. Whatever I tried to hide on my face, Kezia groaned as she lay back. "Really? Ugh. Just hit me with it."

"Hey, this is no picnic for me either." I saw her lift her arm from off her eyes to pierce me with a glare. "Fine, it's about your heat..."

Kezia watched me warily. "What about it?"

CHAPTER 8

Kezia

PROPPING MYSELF UP ONTO MY ELBOWS AS I WATCHED him on my back, I saw the tension return to his shoulders. It was strange that I noticed it, but was I ever oblivious to Cannon? He looked good today. He looked better than good...he looked delicious. Thick dark hair pushed back from his face, still slightly too long, he suited it. Those dark green eyes watched me guardedly as my gaze roamed over his face, appreciating the sharp cut of his jaw and the high cheekbones that should have made him look feminine, but somehow he remained one hundred percent masculine.

"Why are you staring at me?"

"What about my heat?" I asked again, unwilling to admit I was admiring his good looks. I sat up further, pulling my legs up and crossing them on the thin cover of the cot. "You said it's about my heat. What about it? I thought we went over this?"

"Went over what?" he asked, frowning as he studied me.

"My heat!" I said with an exasperated eye roll. "I haven't had a full one, or that's what *males* keep telling me. According to them, it's making me all..." I narrowed my eyes as I watched him when I

75

spoke the next word, challenging him before I'd even spoken to say one word out of turn. "Difficult."

The alpha missed the unspoken warning and burst out laughing. "*Difficult*? You think *you're* difficult?" He laughed louder. "You are so fucking far removed from difficult it's not even in the same word search as what you are."

Folding my arms tightly across my belly, I pierced him with a glare that even my brother, Kris, would back down from. "Is that right?" I asked him quietly. "And what word would you use, *Alpha*?"

"Catastrophe."

I blinked. "Catastrophe?" Was he kidding? "*Seriously*?"

Cannon wiped his eyes, watching me with a grin. "You are on the same level as a natural disaster."

"Okay," I said, pushing myself off the cot. "Likening me to an earthquake or a tornado or something, I think someone's overindulged in exaggeration. I get it, you think I'm a handful." I looked towards the opposite wall as I didn't want to see him laughing at my discomfort anymore.

"Should I make a list? Prove it to you?" he taunted from where he sat on *my* cot, relaxed and carefree.

"Nope. I get it."

"You know, your emotions are heightened because you are always riding the edge of your heat."

Throwing my hands in the air, I turned to glare at him once more. "You think you know everything, but the only answer you ever give me is my heat. *Why is she like this?* It's her heat. *Why is she eating so much?* It's her heat. *Why is she fighting in human underground fighting rings?* It's her heat. *Why is she making out with the alpha dick?* It's her heat."

"Making out?" Cannon's top lip curled upwards, still obviously amused by me. "I haven't *made out* with anyone since I was a teenager."

I mocked his use of air quotes as I mimicked him. "'I haven't made out with anyone since I was a teenager.' Oh my Luna, how old are you now? Fifty? Eighty? Ancient?"

"I'm thirty-three in human years. In real terms, I'm an adult."

"Aren't I an adult?" I retaliated.

His head cocked to the side as he ran his eyes in a slow, careful, almost lazy trail up my body. "Depends on what mood I'm in."

He locked his stare with mine, and I felt my mouth go dry. Goddess, why was he looking at me like that? More importantly, why did it thrill me so much?

"My heat," I blurted.

"I thought that was my excuse?" he gibed smoothly.

"Shut up." I turned away; I could never think clearly when he was near me. Maybe it *was* my heat, and I was protesting for protesting's sake. Turning back to ask him to expand on what he had been saying, I jerked back when I realized he had moved off the cot and was behind me. "How?" I swallowed hard. "How do you do that?"

"Do what?" Cannon reached out and brushed a strand of hair off my face. He didn't pull his hand away. Instead, his fingers trailed down the side of my cheek, tracing along my jawline and then back, pushing slightly into my hair as he cupped my cheek. "How do I do what?"

Frozen under his touch, I couldn't remember what I'd asked him. Licking my lips to tell him I'd forgotten the question, I sucked in a breath when he stepped closer.

"Did you enjoy kissing the human?"

"Um." I coughed at the dryness of my throat. "It was different."

"Was it indeed?" I felt his fingers tighten in my hair. "Different how?"

My wolf was silent within me, yet there was a very loud voice in my head telling me not to answer that question. "Just...you know, different."

"I don't know," Cannon murmured, his head dipping, and he skimmed along under my jawline with his nose. "Use your words, Kezia."

"He wasn't you." Where the fuck that came from, I had no idea, but my heart felt like it stopped, and my foolish, careless words seemed to have the same effect on Cannon, who went utterly still in front of me.

"Kezia..." He let out a low groan as I watched his eyelids flutter closed. "I'm so pissed you let him touch you, taste you. I'm still angry...so you can't say things like that." When his eyes opened, they were the mix of his green coloring and the electric blue of his wolf. "When you say stuff like that, I forget I'm angry."

"I'm sorry?" My voice was a whisper as I watched him. The pull towards him was undeniable, and the strain with which I was holding myself back was getting to be too much.

"For your words or your actions?" he asked gruffly, slipping one hand onto my hip and sliding it slowly onto the curve of my ass as he used the movement to pull me into his body so I was flush against him.

"I didn't mean to say it out loud," I admitted as I desperately tried not to touch him, but the palm of my hand was already resting on his pec, and I could feel his heart beating under my hand.

"Did you *mean* to kiss him?" Cannon's lips were at my ear, the gruff timbre of his voice causing my body to shiver while his fingers dug into my ass like he was kneading dough.

"No. I wasn't thinking. He was there, and I..." I moaned when his hand slipped under the waistband of my sweatpants and his big hand touched my bare skin.

"And you...what?" Cannon kissed softly down my neck. "You weren't thinking? He was *there*, and you?"

I didn't miss the bite to the word *there* when he spoke, but in my fevered state, I also didn't pay it the attention it deserved. "I wanted to know what it felt like to be kissed by someone else."

Cannon's hand stopped moving, his lips stayed soft but still against the pulse in my neck, and the room was so quiet that I could hear only my breathing coming in short pants. Slowly, the alpha drew his head back, looking at me in the eyes as he pulled away.

"By someone else?" he asked softly. "Who *else* has there been?"

"Landon," I answered immediately and saw his gaze harden. "Which you already know, and we both know what happened that night after it!" I reminded him, remembering what he'd done to me on my cottage's kitchen floor. How he'd made me explode as he worked me over with his mouth and tongue.

Cannon was watching me closely. Slowly, so slowly I almost doubted the feeling, he began to knead my ass cheek again. The rhythm of his strong fingers pressing in and out was both soothing and exhilarating.

"Was I your first kiss, Kezia?" he asked me, his eyes hooded as he waited for an answer.

"Yes," I croaked.

Cannon's eyes flared almost teal, and he pulled me closer. "First kiss on these lips," he murmured, his lips brushing mine, and I felt his hand move to the front of my sweatpants. "And first kiss on these lips too?" Fingers grazed against me, and I couldn't hide my wetness or suppress the groan that erupted from me. "Answer me," he commanded.

"Yes."

"Fuck, Kezia." Cannon pushed two fingers between my folds, gently teasing my clit. "Why did you have to tell me that?" he grumbled as his hand started to move, his thumb brushing over that tight bundle of nerves.

"You asked!" I tried to squirm away. "You can't be in there, I'm...I'm bleeding," I hissed softly in protest.

"We're wolves," Cannon answered between peppering kisses along my collarbone, his fingers rubbing soft circles over my clit. "I don't give a fuck if you're bleeding."

My hands were on his shoulders, fingers digging into the solid muscles as my back arched into him, and my hips ground against the rhythm of his hand, wanting his fingers inside me. "It may not look like it right now," I told him, my mouth tasting the skin of his neck, "but *I* care. So, I need you to move your hand away."

"Is that right?" I could feel his smile on my skin, his fingers picking up pace. "You want me to stop this?" He pinched my clit, and my knees buckled slightly.

"I..." Luna, I could feel my orgasm building. I didn't want him to stop. I might kill him if he took away my pleasure.

Cannon abruptly stepped back, pulling his hand from my pants just as the door opened and Royce walked in. Royce took one look at us, turned on his heel, and walked out, the door closing firmly behind him.

It was enough of an interruption to bring me back to my senses.

"Holy shit." With shaky hands, I pushed my hair back, my body burning from the last few minutes.

Cannon took another step back, his head down as he stared at his hand, his fingers rubbing together, when I realized it was my wetness he was rubbing between them.

Embarrassment flooded me. Pushing past him, I grabbed my washcloth and threw it at him in haste. "Wipe your hands."

Cannon let the cloth fall to the floor. As he finally looked up at me, I saw the mixed eye color and knew his wolf was still riding close to the surface.

"I don't want to wipe my hands. I want to wear your scent all day." His words contrasted with his expression. He looked angry at the thought of it, and with a frown, he pushed his hand into the pocket of his jeans. "Your heat is making us both reckless."

"I didn't do anything," I protested weakly. I didn't miss the flat stare as he took three more steps back.

"We need to let this play out," he told me, coming to a stop at the entrance to my cell. "Once your bleed is passed, the heat won't be far behind—"

"How do you know?"

"Because I'm a shifter and I'm several years older than you."

Both statements bothered me. "I'm a shifter and I know none of this."

"Because no one cared enough to tell you."

"Fuck you."

"It seems inevitable at this point." Cannon let out a heavy sigh as he nodded in agreement.

"That's not what I meant, and you know it," I grouched at him. With my legs still feeling shaky, I sat down on the bed, hoping he didn't know why I needed to sit. His smirk told me he saw right through my subtle ploy.

"You need me to finish you?"

"No!" I blurted louder than I intended. "It's not something that needs to be ticked off on your to-do list!"

He gave a careless shrug and turned to open the cell door. "We'll finish the conversation later."

"Are you running away from me?" I asked suspiciously.

Cannon let himself out, closing my cell door loudly, but the dark heated look he gave me made my heart rate pick up once more. "You want me to come back in, pup?"

I shook my head. I knew exactly what would happen if he opened the door right now. "I think you're better on the other side."

Cannon nodded, but he watched me carefully. "Once your first heat's past, it will lessen. The pull."

"Promise?" I stared down at my clasped hands.

"I think so."

My head jerked up at his honesty. "Think?"

He looked away briefly. "Never had a mate before. No idea if the urge to fuck you into oblivion dies down eventually."

His candidness sobered me, and I laughed despite the tension between us. "That sounds painful."

Cannon smiled despite himself and pointed over his shoulder to the door. "I'm going to go. I'll stay away as much as I can. Royce and Doc are ready for you to go into heat. Don't shift. Let your body experience it."

"And if I shift anyway?"

"Shift back." He saw my grimace and looked down to the floor. "I'll be here if needed to command you to stay human."

I could feel the color drain from my face. "If you come in here..."

"I can be in control. It doesn't mean we'll fuck."

My eyes got wider. "Have you seen us now?" I asked harshly. "Are you in control now?"

"I'm trying, Kezia!" Cannon snapped at me. "If I fuck you

when you're in heat, we're mated for life. No get-out clauses. No takebacks. The bond finalizes and it's me and you, pup. End of." He rubbed his hands over his head. "Do I want to come in there and fuck you over and over until this crazy fucking urge that makes me want to crawl out of my skin and into yours passes? Yes. Yes, I do. I want to slam so deep and so hard inside you that you won't know where you end and I start." He took a deep breath. "But if I do any of those things, the bond is set. We won't be able to break it. Ever."

I swallowed hard past the lump in my throat, fighting the tears back. "I know."

I did. I knew we still had a way of getting out of this stupid mate bond. He didn't want it. He didn't want me, and why would he? Look at me. I was a mess.

"I can be strong," I told him, remembering what my brother had told me the night my heat hit me. "I'm strong, I can fight it."

"I don't want you to fight it," Cannon said tiredly. "I need, *we* need, for it to hit you like a ton of bricks." Shoving his hands in his back pockets, he rocked back on his feet. "But we need you to remain in this form. Your wolf isn't helping you by letting your body put it off."

"I know."

We stood in silence for a moment, him looking past me, and me with my head turned slightly away.

"I'll see you in a few days," Cannon eventually spoke.

"Absolutely." I raised my hands, gesturing to my surroundings. "Not like I'm going anywhere."

"It's for the best," he murmured.

I met his stare. "For who? If you let me be, this wouldn't be happening."

"If I *let you be*, who else would be dead?"

That hurt. A lot. I gave him my back as I got onto the cot, keeping myself angled away from him so he couldn't see my tears.

"I'll see you when it's passed," I told him quietly. "For the love of Luna, don't come back in here until it's over."

"You can do this, Kezia. Just try to stay human."

I heard the main door snick closed, and I let the tears fall.

Just try to stay human. Why? When it was obvious he didn't think of me as a human at all.

CHAPTER 9

Kezia

HE STAYED AWAY AS PROMISED, BUT IT WAS POINTLESS, my heat didn't come. My normal human cycle passed, and then nothing else happened. I endured many tests from Mal, who insisted I call him Doc, and since he was piercing me with a needle regularly, I agreed.

I was in my cell, playing solitaire with the cards that Nikan left, when Royce came in with my lunch tray.

"Got a treat for you today, Kezia," Royce told me with a grin.

"Is it a proper shower with a side helping of freedom?"

He lost a little bit of his smile, but he continued with his positive attitude. He was so different from the man I met when they first took me here. "Rare roast beef, fried onions, thick mustard sauce, and my Hannah's fresh baked bread."

I squinted at him. I had already sniffed out the contents of my lunch tray. "A beef sandwich?" I asked him dubiously, not hiding my smile at his enthusiasm.

"No, girl. Not a beef sandwich, one of my Hannah's beef sandwiches." He saw my doubt and let out a sigh. "Just, trust me. Okay?"

It didn't surprise me when he opened the cell door rather than slide the tray through the opening. Royce had started coming into the cell more and more. It was nice that he had lost his animosity and treated me like an equal.

Sitting up, I held my hands out for the tray and laughed as he removed the plate cover with a flourish. The aromas hit me with full force, and I inhaled sharply.

"Yeah?" Royce asked me knowingly with a sly grin. "Not just a beef sandwich now, is it?" he mocked, taking a step back.

I wasn't answering because my teeth had already sunk into the soft, flavorsome bread, and the first taste of the delicately seasoned beef had hit my tastebuds. "Oh Luna," I breathed as I chewed slowly. "What is this? Is it just beef?"

He looked incredibly smug and proud at the same time. "Yup."

I think I groaned as I took another bite. Royce had taken a seat at the end of my cot, but he was on his feet again, looking behind my makeshift privacy curtain that housed my toilet, sink, and hose that I used to rinse myself with. Royce looked between me and my bathroom, then resumed his seat.

When I was licking my fingers and lamenting my sandwich was finished, he was on his feet again.

"You know why you're in here, don't you?" he asked me suddenly.

The question surprised me, but I nodded slowly. "I fucked up. I killed people. I fought humans and I didn't think of the consequences."

Royce was a big guy. Not as big as his alpha, but still, he had to stand around six three, maybe four, and he was broad. Brown eyes fixed on mine, serious as he considered me.

"If you were to get free, if you were to leave here, would you return to the ring?"

"No." I shook my head vehemently. "I would work the bars and stuff and make do. I would be more careful, but…"

"But you don't want to go back to them?" he guessed slowly.

Lowering my eyes from his, I fixed my gaze on the floor. "No."

"And where would you go?" Royce folded his arms across his chest in a move very similar to his alpha.

"My brother?"

"You telling me or asking me, Kezia?" Royce gave me a small smile as he waited for the answer.

I smiled in return. "I don't know. Kris is my pack…"

"But those backward mutts at Anterrio are not," he finished for me, watching me shrug in answer.

Royce eyed me for a moment and then looked over his shoulder to the door to the room. Looking back at me, he nodded, his lips tightening into a thin line, and he looked me over from head to foot.

"What?" I asked warily as the silence stretched.

Royce suddenly grinned widely. "Up."

"Huh?"

"Up. On your feet, Kezia, let's move it." He gestured impatiently with his hand, and I shuffled to my feet, wondering what the heck was going on. He turned his back to me and headed to the door of my cell. "Put those socks on," he instructed, and I did as I was told. "Come on."

What? "Huh?" I asked blankly.

"You want a shower, an actual shower, or do you want to stay in here with that hose?" He was through the cell door and walking across the room now, seemingly ignorant of the fact I was rooted to the spot as I gaped after him in astonishment. "You forgot how to walk, Kezia?"

I was out of the cell at a run as I hurried to catch up to him. At the main door, he waited, his look hard once more as he assessed me when I came to stand beside him.

"I have a wife and two girls at home. I will not hesitate to take out any threat to them." His eyes were hard and his expression grim. "I am older, stronger, and I've killed more than my share of men. Human and shifter. Are we clear?"

"I would never." The words came out in a whisper. "I can go back to the cell," I added. "If you doubt me."

He watched me, his eyes flicking over my shoulder to the cell. "I don't know if I trust you yet," he acknowledged. "But I don't doubt you either." Royce pushed the main door open. "Come on."

The corridor I had only glimpsed until now was bright and cheerful looking. Cream walls, large round suspended ceiling lights, and a heavy-duty vinyl floor that was immaculate made me wonder how often it was used. Peering out into the corridor, my feet stayed rooted to the floor inside the room.

Gnawing my bottom lip, I looked up from the floor to Royce. "Royce?"

The hardness vanished almost immediately, taking in my hesitation, and he held his hand out to me. "Come on, Kezia. You got this."

I took the offered hand, feeling a sense of stability as his big hand wrapped around mine. "There's showers in the facility," he told me gruffly, walking me down the corridor, ignoring the frequency with which I looked over my shoulder to the open door to my cell room. "I think some fresh air may benefit you first, what do you say?"

My head jerked up to look at him in surprise. "Outside? Like, in the open?"

Royce's jaw clenched but he nodded. "Under the blue sky."

Tears flooded my eyes, but I quickly dashed them away with my free hand, not quite willing to let go of the lifeline that was Royce right at this moment. "I'd like to go outside," I admitted softly.

He made a soft noise but said nothing. Together, we walked hand-in-hand past several doors, and then Royce took me up a short flight of stairs, and I caught the first scent of freshness as we neared two large heavy iron doors.

I watched as his hand rested on the handle, and I spoke before he could. "I will cut my veins wide open before I ever bring harm to your family."

"I know."

He pushed the door open and stood back. I took the invitation for what it was, hurrying past him into the fresh afternoon air. Breathing deeply, I walked a few yards from the door as I took in my surroundings. This area of Blackridge Peak was wide and open space, but there were plenty of trees to be seen too. Turning in a half circle, I saw the roofs of the buildings in the town. They were a short distance from where we were but definitely within hearing range. Curiosity had me rising on my tiptoes to try to see more, but the hint of wildflowers on the breeze had me turning away from the town and taking in the huge clearing.

My wolf was close to the surface, eager to test her legs out on the soft inviting grass.

"Shower first, shift later," Royce suggested from behind me.

My wolf glared his way, but the need for an actual hot shower was trumping running in the grass. "Is hot water limited?" I asked him, hurrying to catch up to him, hesitating when he started to walk away from the place where I'd been captive.

Royce didn't bother hiding his smile. "The girls are in school, and Hannah is out. You can use all the hot water if you need to."

"You're taking me to your home?" I asked softly.

"I am." He cocked his head slightly. "You want to go back into the bunker, or do you want to shower in a home?"

Giddiness overcame me, and I beamed up at him. "A home." He nodded once and resumed walking. "All the hot water?" I looked up at him, pulling my braid over my shoulder and examining the ends. Royce grunted a yes, and I felt like I'd just been given the best present ever. "I think I need to use it all," I confessed with a huge smile.

The walk to Royce's house was quick. We passed several of the pack, and not many of them looked our way too long. The pack went on with their day, a few hellos or nods of acknowledgment, and we were forgotten. I was with their beta, and even I knew I would be hard put to beat the male beside me. Plus, I didn't want to. If anyone was in danger of staring, it was me. No one knew me here, and whether it was that or the fact I was with Royce, I felt free. There were no hard distrustful stares, no whispers, and no judgment.

"Your pack seems friendly to strangers," I commented quietly.

Royce scanned the few pack he could see. "Mm-hmm. Plus, every single one of these shifters could wipe the floor with you." He saw my startled stare and winked. "All pack fight in Blackridge Peak. Every able shifter trains in the art of combat. Some have served their time in the military."

"Like you?" I guessed. "And Doc?" It made sense for the pack to have found a half-breed in the military. Doc was too human to have been born in this pack.

"Yeah." Royce led me up a short path set amongst perfectly maintained gardens, pushing the door to his home open. "Our alpha too."

I gave a huff in acknowledgment. "Explains so much," I muttered, following Royce inside and down a hallway.

The room he led me to had a pale pink coverlet on a double bed. Thick plush carpet that my sock-covered feet sank into caused me to ooh as I looked down at the cream flooring. The walls were cream, the drapes a heavy material that promised to cut out any light, and overall the room was comfortable looking and welcoming. Royce gestured to a door, and I walked into the adjoining bathroom.

"Clean towels are under the sink. Everything you need should be in there."

"Whose room?" I asked, watching him walk to the door.

"Guest bedroom." Royce jerked his thumb over his shoulder. "I'll be in the living room when you're done. I'll get some clean clothes for you and put them on the bed." He looked me over once more. "When the water runs cold, come out," he added teasingly just before he shut the door behind him, leaving me alone.

I didn't explore the room. I didn't run to the window to escape. I was already pulling off my clothes as I headed straight to the bathroom. Flicking the lock, I dropped my clothes in a pile on the floor. Finding the towels, I took two and was relieved to find the shower was a simple setup. Turning it on, I adjusted the temperature, and then with lightheaded anticipation, I stepped under the spray and didn't pay any heed to how loud my moan of appreciation was.

The simple pleasure of a hot shower soothed something within me. As I washed my hair, a proper lather, rinse, and repeat, and then smothered it in conditioner, I found myself humming a tune. Using the towels as floor mats, I went back to the cabinet in search of a razor. Using the creamy body wash, I was soon smooth in all the places that mattered. The water turned tepid, and with great reluctance, I exited the shower. In the bathroom cabinet, I found a comb in its packaging, along with a new toothbrush and toothpaste. I'd already brushed my teeth today, but I was feeling so clean I wanted the whole package, and that meant a clean mouth too.

Drying my hair, I luxuriated in the simple pleasures of feeling normal.

In the bedroom, Royce had left me a pair of black cotton shorts that came to mid-thigh, a black tank top, and plain underwear. The underwear was folded too neatly to belong to anyone, and I suspected they were new.

Feeling like my old self again, I left the room to find Royce.

I found his wife first. Her back was to me as she busied herself setting up a tray of what looked like lemonade and sugar cookies. Her light brown hair sat on her shoulders in soft waves. A plaid shirt and shorts like mine, but white, complimented the golden tan of her skin.

Not wanting to alarm her, I took a step into the kitchen. "Hello."

She turned to me with a friendly smile, quickly running her gaze over me from head to toe. "He always forgets boots," she muttered, wiping her hands on a towel and walking to the back door of the house. "What size are you, Kezia?"

"Size?"

"Feet?" She was already walking back in with a pair of slippers.

"Eight?" She handed them over and I nodded. "My children also never wear shoes, thanks to their father, but I think you may feel better with something on your feet." Light brown eyes watched me. "Hannah." She offered me her hand.

"Um, Kezia." I shook her hand, the slippers held tightly in the other.

"They don't wear themselves you know," she admonished, pointing at them. "Shower good?"

"The shower was amazing."

"I can't believe they've had you in that bunker without one for so long." Her frown was directed over my shoulder. "Come, you must be thirsty." Picking up the tray, Hannah walked past me out of the kitchen.

"I used things," I blurted. "A razor, toothbrush, toothpaste, a comb..."

"It's why they're in there...to be used."

"Thank you."

Hannah walked in front of me. "You coming?"

Leaping forward, I followed her to an informal living room.

My eyes landed on Cannon's immediately as he stared at me from the comfy-looking couch. "Ah, shit," I grumbled, awkwardly lingering as I waited for his anger.

"Good afternoon to you too," he snarked back at me, looking me over, his face giving away nothing as he took in the borrowed clothes.

"Take a seat, Kezia," Hannah instructed. "No one stands on ceremony in my home." She was sitting in the only other chair, and with great reluctance, I made my way over to the couch, perching at the edge of the seat as far away from him as possible.

Cannon snorted at my lack of subtlety. "I don't bite."

"Liar." My eyes flew to Hannah's as my face went bright red. "Sorry."

Hannah was chuckling, looking between the two of us. "No

need to apologize to me," she said with a laugh, turning to pour the lemonade. "Royce said you were fun to watch together, just let me get comfy."

Looking at Royce in confusion, I jumped when Cannon reached forward, causing me to sink back into the couch, rolling clumsily towards him as the seat dipped.

He looked at me, pausing in mid-reach for his glass of lemonade. "What are you doing?"

"Getting comfy," I lied, shuffling backward.

Narrowed green eyes watched me for a long moment, and then he was sitting back himself, effectively ignoring me as he took a bite of his cookie.

"Kezia?"

Looking at Hannah, I took the offered glass and sugar cookie. "Thank you."

"Manners?" Cannon snorted. "Since when?"

"Since always," I bit out, trying to remain polite so Royce's wife didn't think I was everything horrid Cannon claimed.

"Bullshit."

Giving him a wide-eyed stare, I flicked my glance to Hannah. Cannon grinned at me.

"What? I don't need to impress her. I've known her a long time."

"You could *try* to impress me," Hannah grumbled good-naturedly. "Luna knows, it's long overdue."

"You know what's long overdue?" Cannon retaliated as he popped another cookie in his mouth. "Your husband explaining why my prisoner is out of her cell."

While my stomach dipped with anxiety, Royce merely sipped his lemonade calmly. "Your *mate* is out of her cell because she was filthy. And, Alpha, you should have let her out weeks ago."

"You told Hannah?" Cannon asked flatly.

Royce rolled his eyes. "I'm not answering such an inane question." He set his glass on the tray. "Kezia," he spoke to me, ignoring his fuming alpha. "Hannah works with Doc here in town. She's been studying your bloodwork and has some insights into your heat—"

"You've been doing her bloodwork?" Cannon demanded. "Since when?"

"Since Doc took the first vial," Hannah answered with a wicked grin. "You know I'm better when it comes to blood."

Cannon looked between them. "You," he said, pointing to Royce. "Outside. Now."

The speed with which he got up and left the room made me worry for Royce, but the beta merely sighed loudly before getting up and following his alpha.

I watched him leave the room and looked at Hannah. "He'll be okay?"

"Cannon?" She reached for a cookie. "Nothing a good punch in the dick won't sort out."

"I heard that!" Cannon shouted from outside.

"You were meant to!" Hannah shouted back playfully.

I didn't correct her that I was asking about Royce. I kind of wanted to see Cannon get punched in the dick, to be honest. He deserved it.

"Now, Kezia, while they're out there being silly peacocks, why don't we talk about you?"

Shifting slightly in my seat, I looked to the open door, wishing Royce would come back. Or Cannon. Right now, I wasn't fussy. "What do you want to talk about?"

"Everything."

CHAPTER 10

Kezia

"Everything?" I asked Hannah. "I don't understand?"

She smiled at me with encouragement, both of us turning to look at the door when we heard a grunt from outside.

Hannah waited a moment, listening until she heard a louder thump and rolled her eyes. "I wish they would act like alpha and beta more," she muttered. "All joking aside, what example do they set to the pack if their leaders are punching lumps out of each other?" Scowling at the wall behind me, she made a carry-on motion to me. "*Everything* means tell me it all. You're not originally Anterrio Pack, Royce tells me. What pack do you come from?"

"I..." Licking my lips, I shifted nervously. "I don't remember." My time with Kris had been so short I hadn't had a chance to find out if he had been looking into the Blackridge Peak Pack for the murder of my parents. The whole mess with Landon claiming to be my mate, with Cannon *actually* being my mate, and finding out that my brother was an alpha...I hadn't had time to learn anything else.

Hannah squinted at me, most likely sensing the lie, but her slight nod let me know she was letting me keep the lie. "Nikan said that the pack didn't let you shift?"

Clearing my throat, I changed my focus to my hands. "When my brother approached Pack Leader Bale, it's because he couldn't get me to shift."

"You were a child; children don't shift until they are of age."

"I shifted as a babe," I told her quietly. "When my parents were gone, there was no one to..." I coughed to clear the dryness of my throat. "There was no one to force the shift to human."

Glancing up, I saw her looking at me with wide eyes. "How long?"

"A couple of years. We were young, so we don't know how long exactly."

Hannah watched me carefully. "And in Anterrio?"

"The shaman believed I needed to know the girl as much as the wolf," I told her, smiling slightly as I thought of the old shaman.

"How long before you shifted?"

"Eight years."

Hannah's mouth dropped open. "But..." She took a deep breath. "The pain? The pain must have been so hard," she said sadly.

Shrugging, I looked away once more. I didn't want to see the sympathy in her eyes. I didn't want to acknowledge that any shifter would have known how much pain it caused me to stay human and keep my wolf closed off. The fact my pack knew what agony they had forced me to endure through my younger years reminded me how little they cared for me.

"I'm sorry," Hannah said. Reaching over, she held out her hand, offering it to me in sympathy. Automatically I took it, feeling a warmth in my chest when she squeezed my fingers. "No wolf should be denied that long," she murmured with a final squeeze of her hand.

"It's in the past." I shrugged it off. It was a long time ago, and I had moved on.

"It's why your brother was sure you could fight your heat," Cannon spoke from behind me.

I hadn't heard them come back into the house. Turning, I watched them both watching me. "A trick?" I asked Hannah, turning to look at her.

"I don't play games," she told me firmly. "I genuinely want to know about you. You are my alpha's mate after all." She looked at Cannon as he and Royce resumed their seats. "And I care very much for my alpha."

"The thing with the blood," Royce asked me. "The shaman tests you, all the time?"

Straightening my back, I flicked my gaze between the three of them, avoiding looking at Cannon directly. "Is it any different than the vials that Doc takes?"

"Yes!" Cannon answered with a snort from beside me. "Doc is trying to track your heat so we can finally move past this...this... deadlock we're at."

"Deadlock?" I demanded, feeling my irritation rise. "You're so focused on my heat you're blind to everything else!" I snapped at him.

"Blind? To what? The fact you're an untrained, reckless fool?"

I was on my feet, heading to the door. "Royce, I'm ready to go back to my cell. I'm done here." Looking over my shoulder, I looked at Hannah. "Thank you for the hospitality and the hot water."

On the path, I noted the flattened grass and an overturned

plant pot. It looked like things had gotten rougher than I thought out here.

Hannah came out of the house and tsked when she saw her lawn. "They've been doing this since they were kids," she muttered, stepping lightly over the grass and fixing her plant pot. "You'd think they would grow out of it."

"They are male."

She grinned at me as she straightened up. "You're not going back there." When she saw my confusion, she pointed up towards the bunker. "I won't have it. You are no threat to me or my girls. You'll stay with us."

"Sweetheart?" Royce asked from the doorway.

"Abso-fucking-lutely not," Cannon said at the same time. "She stays in the cells."

A passing pack member, who'd been in the process of offering up a greeting, stopped short at Cannon's words and looked between all four of us with wide eyes.

"Vic," Cannon greeted gruffly. "How are you today?"

"Good, Alpha." His attention flicked to me. "Hello?"

"Hi." I took a step back, feeling the warmth of Cannon at my back. "Nice day." I heard the huff of laughter of the alpha behind me as I attempted small talk.

"It is," Vic said, taking a step forward. "Are you visiting long?"

I waited for someone to answer, and when it was clear the older shifter had thrown them off their game, I smiled widely. "I haven't decided yet," I told him pleasantly. "I like to travel around."

"Ah, wanderlust," Vic said with a wistful look, leaning casually on the fence. "Had the travel bug myself when I was younger, cured myself of that real quick."

"Really? How?"

Vic held his arm up, which had been hidden from me with the way he was angled. "When you start leaving body parts behind, it's time to come home."

I took in the arm that ended at the elbow and back to the shifter. "War?"

"Two tours," he said with a nod. "Saw a lot, lost a lot, found a lot more."

I'd never seen a shifter with a permanent injury before. I was fascinated. I moved closer to the older male. "You can still run?"

He bellowed out a laugh. "I can run just fine, girl," he said with a wide smile. "Never seen an injured wolf before?"

I was already shaking my head. "No, I haven't." I stared at the smooth skin.

"You want to touch it, don't you?" he said with a grin.

"He means the arm," Cannon added gruffly right behind me. "He *better* mean the arm."

"Ew, don't be crass." I dug my elbow into the alpha's ribs, ignoring the laughter around me, moving forward to the older shifter. He held his arm out, and I touched the skin gently. "Pain?"

Vic shook his head. "Still get an itch in my palm now and then, but the pain has gone."

"Fascinating." Bolder, I gripped his limb. "I know this is rude of me," I told him as I continued to explore. "And I know I am probably causing your alpha a coronary at my lack of manners," I continued, "but I've just never seen this on a shifter before. I've seen it in humans, but I thought it would feel different."

Cannon's large hand covered mine as he pulled it away from Vic. "You're right, your lack of manners is, as usual, astonishing. Vic allowed you a courtesy, don't overdo it."

Vic didn't seem perturbed by my curiosity, but he didn't

contradict his alpha. "So, are you staying here?" he asked me, nodding towards the house.

"Yes—"

"No," Cannon spoke over me. "Kezia is my guest."

Guest? Ha.

Vic's eyes widened in surprise, but I saw a mischievousness in his look as he flicked his attention between us. "In *your* house, Alpha?"

"Yes," Cannon said firmly, drowning out my response.

I stiffened in surprise, careful not to draw attention to myself, feeling very conscious of all the attention on me.

Vic whistled low. "Well, Alpha, you're a braver man than me, that's for sure."

Startled at the implication that Cannon wasn't safe with me, I reassessed my opinion of Vic. "He has nothing to worry about with me," I said, sharper than I intended.

Vic laughed and I looked over to the doorway where Hannah and Royce still stood. Hannah was grinning and Royce was trying to keep a straight face.

"You?" Vic wheezed. "Oh, I ain't worried about you, girl, you seem lovely." I ignored the huff behind me. "I just hope you're ready for Koda."

I realized Vic was talking to Cannon, causing me to half turn to look up at the alpha curiously. Cannon was watching Vic, and I recognized the look all too well.

"Kezia is my guest." I didn't miss the emphasis on the word *guest*, but he continued. "I can have visitors."

Royce coughed out a laugh, and when I looked, Hannah had her head turned away completely, her shoulders shaking.

Vic pushed off the fence, grinning openly. "Let me know how

that goes." He winked at me. "Lovely to meet you, Kezia. I'll see you again."

I watched him walk off, whistling to himself, and when I was sure he couldn't hear me, I turned to look up at the bane of my existence.

"With you?" I demanded. "Are you insane?"

Cannon was looking around his town, noticing more people paying attention. "Shut up." Taking my arm, he started to lead me back into the house.

We were halfway to the front door when two high-pitched yells sounded, and I spun in surprise as two little girls ran up to the gate, Nikan hurrying after them. I jumped back out of the way as they hurried past me and threw themselves at Royce.

"Daddy!"

I watched him scoop them both up, his laughter at their excitement at seeing him causing me to smile.

"Kezia," Nikan greeted me as he approached. Running his hand through his hair, he nodded towards the two girls. "I swear they get faster every day," he told me.

"Why aren't they with their class?" Cannon asked him.

"I met them on the way here and told their teacher I'd take them home. Wasn't expecting to see Royce." Nikan gestured to the front of the house. "Neither were they."

"He hasn't been gone?" Royce had been in my cell room every day, so I assumed he'd been home.

"He's been working long days," Cannon told me gruffly. "He's missed a few bedtimes."

I felt immediately guilty. "Oh. Me?"

Nikan reached out and rubbed my arm soothingly. "Not your fault," he told me sympathetically.

Cannon looked at his beta with his family and then at his

brother before finally resting his attention on me. "Why'd you have to come out of the house?" he muttered. He was focused on Royce before I had a chance to reply. "Royce?"

The big man turned, his smile fading a little as he seemed to remember we were here. "Two minutes!" he shouted to us, getting ready to put his girls down.

But Cannon was shaking his head. "Come to the house later," he said, waving the small family inside. "We have things to finish."

Royce hesitated, looking between us and Nikan. "Alpha?"

"Just go," Cannon said with a weary sigh. "I doubt even Kezia can cause any more trouble today."

When the cottage door was closed, I looked up at Cannon. "I resent that."

"I don't give a fuck," he muttered. "Come on."

"Where are we going?" Nikan asked me as we followed him.

"Kezia is my guest," Cannon bit out, and I could see the tight clench of his jaw.

Nikan leaned in toward me. "He let you out?" he whispered.

"Royce did," I whispered back. "It was only for a shower."

"But now that people have seen her," Cannon interrupted our whispered conversation, "she has to stay out. Or we'll have too many questions to deal with."

Nikan grinned at me behind his brother's back, and I returned his smile. "Cool."

"No. Not cool," Cannon corrected. He turned to face us. "You fuck up, you go back."

"What am I going to do?" I asked him in exasperation, my hands on my hips.

"With you?" Cannon looked me over. "It could be anything." He turned and walked away from us, and I almost turned and walked in the other direction, but Nikan grabbed my arm and pulled me after his brother.

Cannon's house was in the middle of their town, it seemed. It was a two-story house with a nice wraparound porch and looked well-maintained. He said nothing as he opened the door and led us inside. I looked around but couldn't see any guards. His door hadn't been locked—could anyone just walk in here? How strange.

He opened a double door, and I looked around as we entered a study. It was full of books and had several comfy-looking chairs and couches. There was no desk, and I wondered if it was a library instead.

"Close the doors," Cannon instructed Nikan.

I felt the difference in the room when he did. "Soundproof?" I asked.

"Yes, take a seat." Cannon pointed at one of the chairs as he dropped onto a sofa. "Why'd you go outside?"

"Why are you a dick?"

We held each other's stare. "Did you want my pack to see you? Force my hand?"

Dropping my head into my hands, I groaned. "I wanted *away* from you." My hands muffled my voice, but I knew he could still hear me. "I wanted away from your arrogance and your attitude." Looking up at him wearily, I shook my head. "You're a lot. I can't..." I took a deep breath. "You're a lot. Okay?" Looking at the shelves, I tried to read the spines of the books, realizing some of the books were modern thrillers.

"What did you do to her?" Nikan asked, and I could hear the protectiveness in his tone, and if I could, that meant his brother could too.

"Didn't we discuss this?" Cannon sounded as weary as I felt.

"Yes. You said Kezia is your *mate*." Nikan held his brother's stare. "You also said you would be nicer to her."

"I *also* said," Cannon said, standing up, "I would kick your ass if you gave me any shit about this."

"So?" Nikan had an outright challenge in his eye. "You *also* said you were trying to break the bond. Is this how you do it? By moving her *in*?"

Cannon said nothing but turned his attention back to me. "There's a guest bedroom upstairs. It's beside mine. I'll know if you try to leave."

"Beside yours?" I felt a surge of uncertainty as he held my stare, and it didn't get any better when he nodded once in confirmation. The weird fluttering in my tummy didn't ease my reservations about this whole plan either.

We both ignored Nikan's snort of derision.

Standing slowly, I looked around the room. "I need clothes. Toiletries. Can I get my backpack?"

"Sure." Cannon's fingers drummed off the back of a seat. "I'll get them from the bunker."

Nikan, who had been watching us closely, muttered something about getting it instead and left us. The heavy thud of the door swinging shut behind him was the only sound in the room as we both watched each other warily.

"Is this the best plan?" I asked Cannon quietly. "Me and you? Here? Together?"

I saw the uncertainty within him as Cannon flicked his gaze away before looking back at me. "Yes."

"And my heat?"

"We'll deal with it."

"Right."

This had disaster written all over it, but the alternative was a return to the cell, and I would do anything other than that, even if it meant staying here...with him. I could do it. How bad could it be? I took a step towards the study doors, remembering something the older shifter had said. "One more thing?"

"What?" he asked with controlled patience, and I knew he was barely holding onto his temper.

I smiled sweetly, or what I hoped was sweetly, and Cannon's gaze narrowed in response. "Who's Koda? And why did Vic think me being here would be a problem for her?"

CHAPTER 11

Cannon

SHE WAITED FOR ME TO ANSWER, AND I DIDN'T HAVE any idea what to say to her that wouldn't have those ice-blue eyes judging me the minute I opened my mouth.

"Speechless?" Kezia scoffed. "You?"

"No." It sounded more like a growl as she watched me, one eyebrow raised in question.

Kezia's gaze dipped to the floor. "I see," she murmured. With a deep breath, she returned her gaze to mine. "A lover then? Girlfriend?"

"A pack member," I corrected.

Kezia looked more relaxed as she smirked at me. "Bedwarmer then?"

I didn't have a defense to that, but it seemed I didn't need one as the woman across from me shrugged.

"You don't need to be all you about it," she told me easily. "You're like fifty years old, and I'm not stupid. You have experience, a lot of it, I bet, and you don't get that just from your right hand." Her smile was fake as she gave me a quick once-over. "I mean, some would think you're okay to look at, and as I said, you know what you're doing in the bedroom department, I'm sure. Just because I'm a virgin in the room doesn't mean everyone else is, right?"

Her tone was mocking, her expression derogatory as she spoke about herself like she didn't matter.

I didn't like it.

"Fifty?" I asked her, folding my arms across my chest as I regarded her. "Really?"

Kezia cocked her head to the side as she looked me over from top to bottom once more. "Forty-five?"

"I've paddled your ass once before, pup. Don't make me do it again," I warned her, my wolf huffing his amusement as she rolled her eyes at me. "Koda is someone I've had a casual agreement with before," I told her honestly. It was easier to say it to her now she'd made the joke about my age. "No feelings, no relationship. It was just…" I thought of the right way to say it without offending her. "A mutual agreement."

"Sex, you mean?"

Kezia was trying to look casual, but I could see the tenseness in her shoulders, the way she didn't quite meet my eyes when she spoke. However, she was being blunt, and I offered her the same courtesy. "Yes."

"Often?" She looked at her right hand, suddenly interested in her nails.

I relaxed my arms, shoving them into the pockets of my jeans, even though I felt anything but at ease. "Often?" I parroted. "What do you mean?"

A narrow glare was sent my way. "I'm not asking how often you banged her in one night. I mean was it a regular thing? I mean, like once a week, once a month, daily?"

Fuck this. I was not answering that. We may be against the whole thing, but Kezia for all intents and purposes was my mate. You did *not* tell your mate how often you banged your casual hookup.

"Are the details necessary?" I asked instead.

"I wasn't asking what her favorite position was," Kezia muttered testily.

"Thank fuck for that," I mocked and was rewarded with another glare. "Are we done with the interrogation now?"

"You're awfully defensive," Kezia commented, assessing me once more. "I have one more question."

"I haven't fucked her since I learned you were my mate." Her eyes widened at my candor. I watched her lick her bottom lip, looking away from me, a flush reddening her cheeks. "I haven't been with anyone else either before you ask." Those blue eyes returned to mine, brimming with curiosity, but she kept her silence. "It's not in my nature to fuck around on my mate," I added with more bite than I intended. "I don't kiss others when I am bonded to another."

Kezia's face paled at the reminder of Vance, and she broke our stare off.

"You have any more questions for me, or can I show you to your room?" She didn't answer but pulled the door open instead. She moved to the side, letting me pass her to lead her up the stairs. My house was simple in layout. Living areas downstairs and four bedrooms upstairs. I walked past the small room that I was using for storage and pushed open the next door. "Here."

Kezia walked past me, taking in the room quietly. It was simply decorated in neutral colors.

"Bathroom's across the hall." I saw her look and I eased her worries. "I have my own; guests have to share." Rubbing the back of my neck, I looked away from her. "I'll get you towels. What else do you need?"

She was looking out the window, watching the street below. "Your house is so central."

"It is."

She glanced over her shoulder at me before turning back to the window. "You have no guards."

"Why would I need guards?" Then I remembered her pack leader's house. "I am the alpha of my pack," I told her with more heat than I intended. "My pack need not fear me nor feel like I am not here to serve them."

Kezia turned to face me. "Serve?" she asked curiously. "Don't you mean protect?"

"Am I not serving them by protecting them?" I countered. "I am not inaccessible. My doors are always open to any of my pack."

"And your bed?" Her gaze didn't waver.

"I told you I've been with no other since I learned who and what you were."

"I don't believe you," Kezia said simply, turning back to the window. "If you had been...without"—she took a deep breath—"then an old shifter in the street wouldn't be teasing you about your *bedwarmer* being pissed you were hosting a female in your private residence." She looked at me again. "Is she the female from the other day, when I was in the cell?"

I chose to answer the easiest question first. "Yes." Stepping further into the room, I could hear her heart beating rapidly as she fought to remain calm. "Vic is an old gossip who likes to cause mischief and make my life difficult."

"Difficult?"

I couldn't stop my smile. "He hated my father. He's been a strong advocate for me since my return. But...he's also a pain in the ass, especially when it comes to causing me trouble. He took one look at you and knew exactly what it would look like to my pack, and I've made no secret of the fact I have an understanding with Koda." I considered my next words carefully. "Koda has also made it no secret that she thinks we may be more than...casual."

"You mean more than fuckbuddies?"

I winced at the harshness of her tone. "Yes."

"So, she thinks you're in a relationship?"

"No. Koda is very aware of what we are."

Kezia was frowning. "I don't understand." She held up a hand to stop me from speaking. "Do not dare tell me it's because I'm too young."

I fought the eye roll. "I wasn't going to say anything of the sort. You're, what? Nineteen now?" She nodded. "You know how it all works, you're not stupid. What I was going to say was that while Koda knows *exactly* what she and I are, and more importantly what we are *not*, she makes sure that anyone else in the pack thinks differently."

Kezia's eyes were wide. "You mean you fuck her, tell her it means nothing, but know that she's telling your pack something completely different? And you're okay with that?"

I suddenly felt uncomfortable. This judgment from this slip of a girl was unsettling me. "You're making it sound more than it is."

"Am I?" Kezia scoffed. "You mean like Koda?" I didn't have a reply to that. "By letting her let your *pack* think that you may as well put a ring on it, dude."

"Don't be ridiculous."

"She may *know* what you have between you," Kezia said scornfully, air quotes and all, "but that doesn't mean she doesn't *want* more." Cold blue eyes looked me over slowly from head to toe and back up again. "You've led her on. I'm not getting involved in some stake of claim she has on you. Make sure she knows that you want to break this bond. I have no intention of fighting over you."

She was facing me now, her back to the window so the afternoon light behind her made it difficult to see her well. "There will be no claim from Koda," I told her, firmly walking further into the room. Reaching out, I caught her arm, pulling her towards me, catching her by surprise until I had her right in front of me. Looking down at her, I saw a flash of confusion before she cleared her expression.

"What?" she asked me, her voice wavering slightly.

"Koda has no claim on me," I repeated. "And if she thinks she does, I will correct her very quickly. Mate or no mate." Dipping my head, I spoke in Kezia's ear, relishing the sharp intake of breath, the way her heartbeat picked up, and the soft scent of her body as I moved closer. "Do you want the bond broken?" I asked her quietly, my lips skimming the shell of her ear.

Kezia jerked her head away from me, looking up at me, her eyes searching mine questioningly. "Don't you?"

We stayed like that for a long moment, neither of us committing to an answer. I could feel her heart as it beat against mine, our chests pressed together. Kezia was average in height, and I loomed over her, but still, the way we were standing, I could feel her, and I knew she could feel every part of me.

Every hard part of me.

"This will never work," Kezia breathed as she held my stare. "Me living here. We've not been alone for more than twenty minutes and already you look ready to devour me."

"You do taste good," I murmured, moving closer, our lips almost meeting. "Can you blame me for wanting more?"

I felt her hand travel over my bicep, and I wasn't sure she was aware she'd moved, leaning into me more. "It was good," she admitted a little breathlessly, a hint of vulnerability as she watched me. "I...I don't think this is the best idea."

"Terrible idea," I confirmed, my hand slipping around her waist to the small of her back, pulling her in more. "Twenty minutes?" I asked. Moving my head down, I skimmed my lips along her jaw. "That all?"

"Maybe less." Kezia tilted her head back to give me better access to her neck. A small moan escaped her when I tasted her skin.

"Your heat's back?" My hand moved from her back down to the curve of her ass, squeezing the plump cheek.

"No. I don't think so." Kezia's fingers were on my belt.

"You smell..." My head was buried in the crook of her neck. Inhaling deeply, I felt my cock get harder. "Delicious."

Her hand pushed the hem of my shirt up before fingers traced over my skin tentatively. "You feel..." she whispered, almost too low to hear. "Amazing."

Fuck me if that didn't make my cock swell more.

"Cannon...we need to step back...right?"

My hand was now under her shorts, fingers on her skin, tracing circles over her bare ass. My other hand was buried in her hair, holding her head exactly where I wanted it. Both of her hands were under my shirt, running over my chest, skimming down my sides. She was right, this was dangerous.

Reckless.

Stupid.

We knew better.

I knew better.

Pulling my head back, I looked down at her and saw the need

and desire I was fighting reflected in her eyes. "We need to step back," I confirmed.

"Okay."

Neither of us moved. My wolf rode close to the surface. I could feel his need to claim the woman in front of me. She was his mate. Our mate.

Ours.

Mine.

"Fuck." I closed the distance between us.

She tasted so good. Our mouths moved urgently against one another, hands running over each other as we frantically grabbed at each other. Lifting her smoothly, I felt her legs wrap around me as I turned us and pressed her against the wall. She had nowhere to move to, and as our kiss deepened, I realized she didn't feel trapped at all. Kezia tightened her legs around me, urging me closer, and I moved my hips, forcing her legs wider to accommodate me.

Her top was on the floor. I didn't know who removed it, but I knew I was pleased it was gone. Her skin was soft, and her scent of vanilla and spice was addictive. Pulling the cup of her bra down, I murmured my approval as my lips covered her hard nipple.

"Oh, fuck," Kezia moaned, burying her hands in my hair. "You're so good at that," she praised me, moaning in protest when I lifted my head before she realized I was only moving to her other breast. "Yes, there."

Pulling my head up, she claimed my mouth again. Turning us, I took a few steps and lowered us to the bed. Leaning back slightly, I grabbed the waistband and pulled the shorts off her, the plain underwear following. Pushing her legs open, I felt greedy satisfaction as I saw how wet she was for me.

"This for me?" I asked, kissing up her inner thigh. I didn't wait for an answer. Fuck, she could have told me, but I heard nothing over the racing of my heart. My mouth covered her, and the first taste of her sweet pussy erased any sense I had left.

She was divine.

I couldn't get enough. I needed it all. Dimly, I was aware of Kezia's moans, her cries of pleasure, her fingers tight in my hair, her hips rocking against my mouth as she writhed under me. When I pushed a finger inside her, I felt her walls quiver around me, clutching at me, needing something much more. I slid another finger inside her. Her pussy was so tight and untouched, resisting the stretch I was demanding but welcoming the rhythm of my fingers as I rubbed them against her walls.

The knowledge I was the only one to ever do this to her made my pulse spike. My cock was straining against my jeans. I'd never been this hard, never been this desperate to get inside someone.

Moving my hand down, I fumbled with my buttons, pulling my cock free. I ran my hand over the length, working myself.

Opening my eyes, I looked up at her. Her eyes were closed, her head thrashing from side to side. She was muttering *yes* repeatedly. Her legs spread as wide as they would go, giving me all the access I needed to fuck her with my tongue. Hands fisted the sheets as her body sought the release she was begging for.

Curling my fingers inside her, I picked up the rhythm, watching when her eyes flew open, her gaze meeting mine. Instinctively I sucked her clit into my mouth, and Kezia screamed out in pleasure, and as my mate flooded my mouth with her climax, the sound hit me right in the balls, and I knew I was going to come all over the sheets like an inexperienced youth.

I couldn't breathe. I don't remember ever having been that turned on. I hadn't even fucked her. Moving up her body, trailing kisses as I listened to her panting under me, feeling proud that my mate was pleasured, I pulled Kezia into my arms as we both fought to regain our breaths.

I kicked my jeans off, quickly putting my cock back in my underwear, wondering what the hell either of us was doing.

Kezia moved onto her side, leaning into me, her forehead pressed into my chest, struggling to regain control.

"Thirty minutes?"

Looking down at her, I saw her looking back up at me. "What?" I asked.

"Twenty minutes to argue, ten minutes for...that...." Her face was flushed, her eyes still dilated and glazed. "Thirty minutes."

"Didn't know you were counting," I muttered, returning my gaze to the ceiling.

"I wasn't." She snorted. "Counting? You think I had any coherency during...that?" I heard her embarrassment and under-lying satisfaction. I grinned, feeling smug. "I'm guesstimating," she continued.

"The point of the guesswork?"

"We've been alone, say thirty minutes," she murmured. "I'm not in heat."

She wasn't? Huh. "Okay?"

Kezia propped herself up on an elbow as she looked at me. "This happened after thirty minutes," she said. Seeing my look, she rolled her eyes. "Fine, give or take thirty minutes."

"It did," I agreed solemnly.

"So?"

"So..."

"How can I sleep here, Cannon? If this is thirty minutes, what will hours together be like?"

Nirvana.

Rubbing my eyes with the heels of my hands, I understood

what she was saying. We wanted to break the bond, not cement it. The bond wanted us to mate. Being this close was the worst idea possible. "Fuck."

"I should go back to Royce."

My wolf roared. Moving quickly, I had her pinned beneath me, hand around her throat, not tight, but enough to let her know she was mine.

"While I can still taste your pussy, pup, I advise you not to let another male's name past your lips," I warned softly.

Kezia watched me, her eyes hooded with desire. "That was hot," she told me, fingers running up my forearm. "I mean, the speed, the strength, the dominance..." Her gaze dipped to my lips, and she swallowed, eyes flicking back up to mine. "Dammit...this isn't helping."

"You're not leaving," I told her, brushing my lips against hers. "Unless it's back to the cell."

"Does the door lock?" she whispered, lifting her head off the pillow, pushing against my hold on her neck, reminding me my hand was still wrapped around her throat.

"No."

"Get a lock?" Kezia suggested. Her tongue flicked out, tracing my bottom lip.

"I'll get two." Catching her mouth with mine, I kissed her, losing myself in her once more.

I never heard the footsteps on the stairs.

I never sensed the presence of another in the room.

I was only aware of Kezia and how right she felt underneath me.

"Who the fuck is this slut?"

CHAPTER 12

Kezia

THE FEMALE IN THE DOORWAY OF THE BEDROOM startled me, but not as much as the speed with which Cannon leapt off the bed and confronted her. I saw her cowering as he towered over her, and despite being as naked as the day I was born, I jumped off the bed to grab him.

I sensed no violence coming from him, and something told me that this wasn't the kind of alpha he was. He wasn't the kind of alpha that ruled by fear. I knew that as well as I knew my own name.

Cannon was in his underwear only. I don't remember taking his shirt off, and it was completely the wrong time to appreciate the man's physique, but hot damn, he was droolworthy.

"Shirt!" he barked at me without looking, and while he couldn't see my exasperation, I knew he expected it because he let out a huff of amusement, and with relief, I saw his shoulders lose some of their tension.

I pulled the shirt over me, realizing too late it was his and not my own. Catching the hem, I went to lift it off when I heard his low growl.

"Leave it."

My eyes caught the narrowed stare of the woman who had walked in on us.

Us.

My heart skipped a beat. There was an us? Shaking my head, I shoved all weird and confusing thoughts to the side as I focused on the situation in front of me.

"Koda?" I guessed, coming to stand beside Cannon. He didn't look at me, but I felt him relax as I moved closer to him. "Hi," I offered the other woman.

Well, this wasn't awkward at all.

"Who are you?" she asked me, her gaze flitting between Cannon and me.

"She's not a slut," Cannon growled, anger once more riding his emotions.

"I'm Kezia," I offered, reaching out and running my hand down the alpha's arm. "I understand what that must have looked like." I had no idea what I was doing. I'd never been in this situation before. *What it looked like?* It was *exactly* as it looked, me and her alpha—lover—naked on the bed, wrapped up in each other after a really, *really* good make-out session. "I'm a...guest?"

Koda was beautiful. There was no other word to describe it. She was perfect. Dark hair, dark chocolate brown eyes, perfect bow-shaped pout, perfect figure, perfect height, perfect curves. She was perfect. I wondered how many times my brain could use the word *perfect* to describe her... She was also shrewd, because the look she was giving me told me she knew I was full of shit.

"You're the prisoner from the cells."

"*Prisoner* seems extreme," I mumbled, taking a step away from Cannon, who reached out and tugged me back to his side. "Nice to meet you?"

Koda looked me over quickly. I was disheveled, wearing her alpha's shirt, which reached mid-thigh, and she'd have to be unconscious not to scent the smell of sex in the room. I shifted to my other foot as I was weighed, measured, judged, and dismissed in the space of five seconds.

Koda moved her attention to Cannon. "Alpha?"

"Why are you here?" Glancing at him, I winced at the coldness of his gaze as he waited for an answer.

"I saw Nikan." There was a beat of silence before she continued. "He came in here with a backpack and left so quickly I thought you were..."

"I was what? Busy?" he scoffed.

Backpack? *My* backpack? My face flamed. Nikan had come back while I was rolling around the bed with his brother, heard us, *me*, and rushed out the door just as quickly as he probably entered it.

Shit. This was embarrassing.

Cannon glared at me so briefly that I thought I imagined it. "What do you want?" His tone was still cold, and I felt bad for the female in front of us.

"I...nothing." Koda straightened her back, holding her head high. "I'll leave you to it."

I didn't miss the inflection on the word *it*, and I couldn't help but take offense, although I tried not to react. Cannon also heard it and didn't hide his disapproval.

"Koda," he warned. "Your petty jealousy is beneath you," he told her bluntly. "We fucked. You knew it was nothing more than scratching a mutual itch. If you made it more, that's on you."

"Shit." I hadn't realized I had spoken out loud. This was uncomfortable as hell. Eyes filled with hurt and loathing met mine. "Sorry." Focusing on the open doorway behind her, I wanted to leave the room, but I knew I had nowhere to go, and it was unlikely Cannon would let me leave.

"You have nothing to apologize for," Cannon scolded me.

"I'm apologizing *for* you," I retorted sharply. "You're being a dick." He huffed in displeasure but said nothing in his defense.

Koda was back to looking between the two of us, her confusion clear, her questions bubbling under the surface just waiting to burst free. "I should go."

"You should," Cannon confirmed.

Ouch.

I elbowed him not so subtly, and he didn't even budge.

Koda watched the interaction, and I saw a flash of pain before she turned and hurried down the stairs. We heard the door close, and only after a long moment of silence, I turned to the alpha dick of the century.

"Dear Goddess, you are a heartless dick," I snarled at him. "It may have just been an itch to scratch for you..." I took a deep breath to calm my temper and push away the weird pang of jealousy. "Also, who *says* that to someone? That was brutal. But whatever it was for *you*, it was *obviously* more for her."

"She's a good actress," Cannon said carelessly, picking his jeans up off the floor.

"Know that from experience?" I snarked back at him.

Hooded green eyes full of smugness looked me over slowly. "Trust me, pup. I know when someone's faking underneath me."

Asshole.

"Happen a lot?" I asked, one hand on my hip.

"Never." He looked far too confident. "Don't try to lie to me with whatever bullshit you're about to spout."

I bit back the response he predicted as he spoke. Could I say I faked it? Sure. But what would the point be? He knew it wasn't true. You couldn't fake the sounds I'd made for him. Well, if it was possible, I didn't think *I* could.

"You were still cruel."

"She called you a slut." He fastened his jeans. "Unacceptable."

"She doesn't know me!" I protested, following him out of the room as he jogged down the stairs.

"Exactly."

Throwing my hands in the air, I followed him into his study. "I mean, for all she knows, I could be a slut!" Cannon looked at me, an eyebrow raised, causing me to blow out a breath. "I'm not. Obviously," I mumbled. "But she doesn't know that. She doesn't know I'm not some bedwarmer of the pack. I could be new."

"We don't have *bedwarmers* in my pack," he growled. "Every male, female, and child in my pack is treated fairly and with respect," he bit out tersely. "Pack bedwarmers are a disgusting, archaic practice, and packs that still use those methods of sexual exploitation should be ashamed of themselves."

I was speechless. I'd seen Cannon pissed off lots of times, usually at me, but he was more than pissed off right now. He was angry. Yet still my stupid mouth couldn't keep itself closed, even though I admired his stance on an outdated practice still held in many packs.

"You didn't show much respect to Koda."

He didn't so much as wince. "She called my mate a slut. She's lucky I didn't rip her throat out."

Fuck.

I swallowed.

Cannon arched a brow at me. "What? Speechless? You? Surely not."

"Har har." Flicking him the finger as he flung my words back at me, I took a seat, pulling his shirt over my legs, very conscious of my nakedness beneath it.

Cannon lowered himself onto a couch, his look assessing, his gaze returning to my bare legs more than I think he realized. "Locks on the door is a good idea."

I hadn't expected him to come back to that, but I nodded in agreement. "I can go somewhere else," I suggested again, careful not to trigger his unreasonableness. "It would be easier."

He nodded thoughtfully. "And when you see Koda or another single female enter my home, how will you feel?" My wolf snarled viciously, and I wasn't aware I'd growled until I saw his smug-as-fuck grin. "So we agree? We stay together?"

"It's a stupid idea."

"The bunker?" he countered.

"But I can stay in my room if you can stay in yours."

He laughed out loud before becoming serious again. "The pull is getting stronger," he admitted quietly.

I nodded, avoiding his penetrating stare. "We're not helping either." Pointing to the ceiling, I felt myself blush. "I think the more we do things like that up there...the harder it is to stay away."

He was nodding but frowning. "I agree. You stay here, you stay out of trouble, and we try to stay apart."

"I can't believe I am saying this," I muttered. "Maybe I would be better back in the cell?"

He was already shaking his head. "Too many of my pack know about you now. Vic isn't the town gossip for nothing." He looked amused and annoyed at the same time. "Why do you think Koda was slinking up my stairs when she's never been in any of the bedrooms before?"

She hadn't?

"Vic will have told people, Royce's girls saw you. Koda saw you," he continued. "Too late to put the spilled milk back in the bottle."

"I'm milk?" I asked, my lips twisting at the analogy.

"You're definitely creamy."

Fire scorched my cheeks at the innuendo. "That was cringey," I protested weakly, looking anywhere but at him.

"It was tacky, I agree, but still true," Cannon chuckled. He got to his feet. "I need to go find locks."

"Locks? Two, right?" I asked him softly. I wouldn't put it past him to cage me inside the room.

The way he looked at me, I had to sit on my hands to stop myself from pulling off his shirt and laying back on his couch and telling him to climb on.

"You want the bond broken?" he asked me quietly, his face clear of expression.

Did I? I wasn't sure. "It's maybe for the best."

Cannon nodded curtly. "Agreed. I'll put locks on my door too."

I barked out a laugh of surprise. "You think you need to lock me out?" I asked him incredulously.

"I know I need to lock me in." Cannon's eyes darkened and I felt my laughter die in my throat.

The tension built between us, and I was helpless to fight it. He crossed the room in two strides, and I'd already risen off the seat to meet him. He kissed me so deeply that my toes curled, and it wasn't long before I was climbing him like my own personal tree.

"Fuck," Cannon cursed, pulling his shirt off me. "You're like a drug."

His hands ran over my nakedness, and I arched into his touch, hungry for more. "It's crazy, the need that I have," I admitted, gasping in pleasure as his fingers stroked over my sex. Pulling his belt free, my hands unfastened his jeans, one hand slipping inside, touching him for the first time.

I didn't expect the feel of his cock. Silk and steel at once. My fingers wrapped around his length, and the feeling of pride as he groaned in pleasure when I started to move my hand was also unexpected. He was thick and long. While his mouth claimed mine, I let his cock go to push his jeans down and then used both hands to take hold of him again.

I had no idea what I was doing, but it seemed the alpha didn't care how inexperienced I was. The whimper of pleasure when I squeezed his length slightly made me moan in return.

The banging on the door made me jump, both of us springing apart. The door to the study opened fractionally.

"I can't hear you," Royce said gruffly, "but I can *smell* you both. Unless you want the mate bond to be permanent, I suggest you move apart."

Cannon and I watched each other, and in an unspoken agreement, we both took a further step backward.

"You have two minutes to be decent," Royce told us both. "Then I'm coming in."

Cannon fixed his jeans, and I once more pulled his shirt on. I was wet, I could smell it, Cannon's wolf could smell it, his eyes flashed turquoise, and I knew I needed to get out of the room.

Knowing Royce had already seen too much of me for it to be an issue, I pushed the door open and ran up the stairs to the room I had been given. Looking around frantically, I grabbed the clothes from earlier and darted across the hall until I found the bathroom.

Locking myself in the bathroom, I started the shower. I

needed his scent off me. That's what it was. I could smell him, his scent clung to me, so my wolf craved him and made me act all *wanton*.

Scrubbing myself clean, I finally got out of the shower and realized I had no towels. Opening the bathroom door a crack, I found two towels outside the door. Snatching them up, I dried myself and put on the clothes from earlier. Taking a deep breath, I headed back to the study.

Royce was sitting on one of the couches, reading a book. He looked up when I entered.

"Hey," I greeted, knowing my face was red.

"New plan," Royce told me, closing the book.

"Bunker?" I asked with a sinking feeling in my belly.

"No." He grinned but it had no mirth. "You stay here. You *must* give me your word, Kezia, that you will not run. You will stay here and *try* to fit in."

I nodded. "I can do that."

He stood. "Good. You hungry?"

I blinked at his sudden change in conversation. "Where is, um, the alpha? Cannon, I mean. Where is he?"

Royce scratched his cheek as he watched me. "New plan, like I said. You stay here, he stays with me."

I knew my mouth dropped. "What? He's leaving me? Here?"

"No, he is *not* leaving you here. I am taking him *from* here. You two..." Royce shook his head. "You can't be together. Alone." He frowned at the contradiction. "You cannot be alone together," he clarified. "You're incapable of keeping your hands off each other." He looked annoyed. "Cannon told me the locked door idea." He snorted his contempt. "For two intelligent shifters, you're both dumb as a bag of rocks."

"He's okay with the fact I kicked him out of his house?" I asked dubiously.

"He's adaptable," Royce said grimly. Pinning me with a hard stare, he tilted his head. "Can I ask you a question?"

No? I felt nervous. "Sure."

"Do you want to be his mate?"

"Um. I..."

"If you want the bond, tell him."

Did I want the bond? Did I want to be mated to the alpha of the Blackridge Peak Pack, the pack that may have murdered my parents? The alpha who kept me caged and a prisoner? I knew nothing about him.

"No." I looked at Royce. "I don't want the bond." The unspoken *yet* echoed in my head, and I chose to ignore it.

Royce's face gave nothing away. "Then you stay here, he stays with me. Your next heat, we put you in separate states, countries if we must, and then we find a way to break it. Right?" When I said nothing, he sighed long and loud. "*Right*, Kezia?"

"Yeah. Right."

With a nod, he walked out of the study. "Come on, let's eat. Time you met the pack, and I don't have to tell you not to mention the murders, the blackouts, or the fact you're the alpha's mate, do I?"

"Nope. I don't need to be reminded not to say anything."

Royce led me out of the house, and we walked in silence as I looked around the town. Royce stopped outside a large community building.

"Mess hall," he confirmed. "You ready to be the new girl?"

"No." I smiled at his laughter. "I don't blend well, and I don't mingle well either."

"Shocker. You're so approachable." He led me to the double

doors that were pinned open, and the sound of laughter and cheer came from within. "You're a piss poor liar too," he said with a careful look over his shoulder. "You don't want the bond?" He huffed out a laugh. "Delusional, both of you."

Both of us? I stood frozen as he entered the hall. Did Cannon want the bond? Did he want to be my mate?

"Kezia! Food doesn't get eaten by itself!"

Jumping into action, I pushed all thoughts of the bond aside as I hurried after Royce and entered the hall of a pack I didn't know.

I had bigger problems to focus on right now. Cannon could wait.

CHAPTER 13

Kezia

I MAY HAVE BEEN EXAGGERATING, BUT IT FELT LIKE every head in the room turned to look at me. I was, unfortunately, used to being the center of attention for the wrong reason, and I suddenly felt a very familiar sense of unease settle on my shoulders.

Royce was oblivious to my discomfort, and not to make the shifters in the hall stare at me even more, I quickly followed the beta of the pack.

The mess hall, as they called it here, was slightly different to our canteen at the Anterrio Pack. Here, the serving area was in a large semi-circle, and all the seated areas sat within it. It was as if the food area were enclosing the pack in a hug. I frowned at myself at the weird analogy. Maybe I'd lost brain cells after my last orgasm from Cannon...

Looking at the benches and tables, I noticed there was no other option than to sit *with* someone, or at least have the opportunity to have someone sit with you.

Royce handed me a tray absently as he started making his way around the serving dishes. I almost lost my grip as he started piling things on my plate and his, and soon I was no longer focused on the pack staring at me—I was too busy wondering where he thought I was going to put all this food.

"Um, Royce?" I whispered urgently. "I don't need more food."

The shifter turned to look at me, his mouth open in shock, his eyes wide. "Are you saying you can't eat it all?"

I felt my face warming at his teasing. "You've given me a week's worth of food!" I hissed at him, conscious that some of the pack were still watching.

"You'll need it, your training starts tomorrow."

Training?

"What?" I hurried after him as he continued to the end of the line. "What training?"

"You want water, coffee, or soda?" He looked at me expectantly.

"Water's fine, thanks. What training?"

"Hey, Kezia."

Turning halfway around, I saw Nikan, and by his slightly awkward wave, I knew we were both thinking about what I'd been doing with his brother earlier. "Hey," I greeted weakly.

Nikan eyed my tray. "Dear Goddess, are you feeding the pack?"

"No, Royce is feeding me for some kind of marathon," I told him testily as I saw a large glass of water placed on my tray.

"Training," Royce corrected. He looked around the benches, and much to my horror, he pointed towards the fullest one smack in the middle. "There."

I never thought I would miss the solitude of the cell so much as he led me amongst the curious to sit at the almost crowded table.

Royce sat down beside me, tearing a roll in half, using one half to point at me. "Everyone, this is Kezia of the Anterrio Pack. She's here for a while to learn our fighting techniques. You know how backward the thinking is over there. Thankfully, her brother had the sense to seek better for her."

I gaped at him, but the murmurings and welcomes from those around me meant I had to look away from the shifter casually eating a mountain of food.

"Kezia is a nice name," an older female said to me. She had light brown hair, a warmth in her hazel eyes, and a friendly smile. "Is it a family name?"

The truth was I didn't know. So I did what I do best in all uncomfortable situations, I went with it. "Yes, but I prefer Zia."

I didn't miss the slight stiffening of surprise from Royce, but he flung me into the deep end of this social pool. It was his own fault if he forgot to ask if I could swim.

"Zia's nice too," the woman told me. "I'm Willy."

"Willy?" I knew I blurted it out, and I got a few laughs for it too. "Sorry."

She wasn't in the least bit offended. "My mom, and her mom before her, and her mom before *her*, they're all called Willomenia. I have seven brothers; there was no way I was being called *Willomenia* just because I was a *girl*. Oldest brother called me Willy before I learned to speak to tell him not to, and by that time, it was too late!"

"Seven brothers?" I knew my eyes were wide. "All to—" I stopped, catching myself in time, but Willy knew where I was going with my question, and thankfully, she and several others were all laughing.

"All to the same momma? Yup, there's eight of us." She leaned forward. "And we're one of the smaller families in the pack."

My eyes were as round as saucers as I listened to several of the pack boast about their family sizes. Midway, Royce handed me my fork, and I ate and listened, and laughed, to the stories of the pack and their families.

"Do you have much training?" a male further up the table asked me.

"I can fight," I told him carefully as I ate my third chicken leg.

"Every shifter can fight," another male spoke, "but do you have any training?"

Royce kept on eating, and I was unsure how to answer. "My brother trained me," I told them honestly. "He's the pack leader's head of security." I saw several sneers and immediately defended Kris. "He doesn't agree with Pack Leader Bale's position on keeping the females from fighting." I hoped I didn't get Kris in trouble for this, but I wanted these shifters to know my brother was decent. "Kris let me train with him. He taught me everything he knows, and I also trained sometimes with Pack Leader Bale's son, Landon."

Some of the shifters nodded, and others exchanged knowing looks. I wasn't entirely too comfortable about what they *thought* they knew.

Another male turned to me slightly from where he sat on another bench. He had told me his name, but I'd forgotten it already as there were too many to remember at once. "Our training is a little more rigorous than what they teach over at Anterrio." His eyes flicked to Royce's, who sat silently beside me, drinking his water, his meal finished. "A lot of us are military trained," he continued.

Looking around, I saw several of the conversations had stopped, and many of them were just watching me. "Okay? Um... that's...nice?"

The male grinned widely. "You have no clue what's in store for you tomorrow," he said with a laugh, which caused others to laugh. But I got the feeling they weren't laughing *at* me, and somehow, that made me relax more.

"Should I be laughing?" I whispered to Royce under my breath. I saw his wide smile, and I guessed that was a *no*.

"So, Zia," a female asked. "Are you staying with Hannah, Royce, and the girls?"

"Zia's staying in the alpha's house," Nikan spoke for the first time since sitting down, and I felt my cheeks burn as friendly stares turned into more speculative looks.

"With Cannon?" a voice asked from further down the bench.

"Well—"

"Yes," Nikan spoke over Royce. "That's where the alpha lives too." His laugh sounded forced, or maybe I was paranoid, but I was once more very conscious of the fact I was the center of everyone's attention.

Clearing my throat, I tried not to look at Royce for help. "Well, the alpha was kind enough to offer me a room, but he won't—"

"And why wouldn't he?" Royce said, leaning back, looking completely at ease with everything. "Our alpha is generous and welcoming."

Was that rhetorical or was he telling them? Looking at the shifters gathered, I wasn't sure. An older shifter was watching me, deep in thought.

"Was at your pack a few weeks ago," he said thoughtfully. "Some murmurings about that Bale's son having a mate that ran away..."

I felt Royce straighten beside me as the shifter continued.

"Think they said something about her being in seclusion..."

He spoke slowly but his gaze was sharp, and I couldn't stop my hands tightening into fists under the table. "That you, Zia? Did you run?"

My eyes met Royce's and I wasn't sure I was concealing the panic I was feeling.

"Is that why you're here?" Willy asked sympathetically. "Are you having some time before the mating ceremony?"

My mouth opened but no words came out.

"Curious bunch tonight, aren't you?" Cannon said good-naturedly as he strolled into the mess hall. "A visitor to the pack, and you all become interrogators." He looked around with a smile. "Taught you well," he added with a wink, causing most of the pack to laugh and the weird tension to leave the room.

Cannon dropped onto the bench opposite us, and I didn't miss the tight look in his eyes as he looked towards Nikan, but it was gone quickly.

"Is that leftovers on your plate?" he asked me teasingly, and Royce chuckled beside me. Cannon shared a conspirator's look with several pack members. "This girl can eat. I don't know where she puts it. That's why I'm here, to tell Cook and the others they'll need more food while she's here."

"I'm not that bad!" I protested loudly, which caused more laughter.

"You are," Royce confirmed.

The shifter who had asked if I was Landon's mate hadn't laughed with everyone else. He was still watching me. "Nikan says the girl's living with you, Alpha? That right?" he asked, his head cocking to the side.

Cannon shared a look with Royce before turning to address the older shifter. "She is. You have a problem with that, Tev?"

Tev looked at his alpha, and the blatant dislike he had for him was plain to see. "I've many problems with you, *Alpha*."

I flinched at the open hatred in Tev's voice, but Cannon snorted loudly in the sudden deadly silence of the mess hall. "And I you. I've also told you that you can leave anytime you want, old timer."

"This is my home," Tev sneered.

"And it's *my* pack," Cannon reminded him sharply. "You're the last one, Tev." Cannon's voice was quieter, a warning in his tone. "I let you live out of respect for your kin, but don't push me." He stood slowly, an alpha male uncoiling with deadly calm. Cannon turned his head slightly to look at me, Royce, and Nikan. "We need to discuss Kezia's schedule." He looked over his shoulder to the shifter who had mentioned the military training. "Leo, you free soon?" When he nodded, Cannon gestured to the three of us. "Join us at the house in about fifteen minutes, and we'll discuss this one's training?" When Leo confirmed he would, Cannon turned to leave.

Royce and Nikan were on their feet, and as I hastily clambered to mine, I was showered with farewells and see-you-soons. The brief tension with Tev was smothered in the blanket of kindness that was extended to me as I left the hall.

Outside, I didn't miss the tension in Cannon's shoulders as he led us back to his house. Royce and Nikan followed silently, and I decided the best thing to do was follow their lead, although I was burning with questions.

We filed past the alpha into the study, and as the doors slid shut, I turned in time to see Cannon punch Nikan right in the jaw.

"Do you think this is a game?" Cannon snarled at his brother. "I'm sorry your crush is my mate, but what did mouthing off in front of everyone gain?" he demanded angrily. I felt Royce pull at my arm softly, and I took a few steps back from the two pissed-off siblings. "Did you even think, or were you so consumed with pointless jealousy you didn't *think* about Kezia at all? Or how your careless words would affect *her*?"

Me? I went to speak, but Royce not so subtly dug his elbow in my ribs.

Nikan was rubbing his jaw, but I caught the look of regret he sent my way. "I didn't think," he admitted sourly.

"We were going to stay apart," Cannon told him bitterly. "I was going to stay at Royce's place, but you fucked that up."

"How?" I asked. "You can't stay there anymore?" My blood raced with excitement, while my stomach dipped with dread. It was a weird combination that made me feel slightly nauseous.

"No," Royce said with a sigh. "It was never foolproof," he offered to Cannon with a sympathetic look towards Nikan.

"I didn't know that," Nikan said grudgingly. "Is it bad?" He looked between the two of us, and I had no clue what he meant.

"Is what bad?"

"It's worse than bad," Royce answered him. "They can't be left alone."

Oh. "Right, *that*." I avoided looking at all three of them but caught sight of Nikan's face as it paled.

"I heard, um, earlier."

"I could move?" I blurted, because I did not want that conversation right now. "Out, I mean. I could move out?"

"You can't." Cannon was still furious. "Tev putting you and that imbecile together from Anterrio, and the pack thinking you're here on seclusion from your mate, there's no other place you would go *except* to the alpha's house. It's the safest place to be for a female soon to be mated," he added scornfully, once more glaring at his brother. "A female *not* mated to me, that is."

Nikan mumbled an apology and Royce let out a loud sigh.

Rocking back on my heels, I looked around the room. "So? Locks on the door?"

Cannon grunted but a smile hovered over his mouth at my attempt to ease the tension, and Royce let out a low chuckle.

"I could stay here," Nikan offered. "You know, act like a... buffer?"

"It might work."

I turned to see what the alpha thought, but Cannon's eyes narrowed to slits as he regarded his brother. "Was that your plan?" he asked him. "To be where she is?"

Nikan's cheeks reddened and I wasn't sure if it was with outrage or embarrassment at being caught. "No! I was just thinking out loud!" he protested, but I noticed that Royce was also watching him closely.

"She's mine."

I wasn't prepared for the rush of satisfaction and pleasure that coursed through me in response to his low, possessive growl. My hand pressed against my lower belly, a movement so slight, but it wasn't missed by the alpha across from me.

Royce shoved to his feet, stepping purposefully in front of me. "And this is why they needed to be separated," he muttered grouchily. "She's not even in heat, and they're like two sex-crazed bunnies."

"I think *bunny* is deceptive," I murmured as I stared at his back.

A slight knock on the door made all four of us look as it slid open, and Leo stepped inside. He faltered once, looking at all of us warily. "Was I not supposed to come in?"

I couldn't help it, I giggled at his wide-eyed expression, and Royce let out a low rumble of laughter.

Cannon shook his head as the tension in the room lifted. "You're right on time," he told Leo. "Take a seat, there's lots to discuss."

CHAPTER 14

Kezia

"You've seen me fight!" My back teeth ground against each other as I tried to keep my temper in check as the overbearing oaf in front of me explained to Leo how much I needed *basic* training. "I do not need *basic* training."

Cannon flicked his hand casually as if he was swatting away my protest like I was an annoying fly. "Her stamina isn't where it should be, so she'll need to build that first before any real combat training," he continued.

"My stamina is fine!"

"Hmm, what else?" He looked at Royce as he thought. "Stealth! Honestly, humans can move more quietly than she can."

"Really?" I snarled at him. "That why it took you five months to find me, *Alpha*?"

Leo, whose attention had been on his alpha the entire time, despite my interruptions, turned his head to look at me. "Find you?"

Shit.

I ignored the pointed glare that Cannon was sending my way and decided to go with a half-truth. "I ran away," I told him with a shrug. "The whole mate thing, you know, it's a lot. And I wasn't expecting it, and yeah, it's a lot. And I didn't need the pressure, and I don't exactly blend in my pack, so I—"

"Panicked."

I met Cannon's eyes. "I didn't panic," I murmured. "I just needed to clear my head."

His snort spoke volumes.

Leo was looking between us with consideration. "Alpha? The search teams?"

There were search teams? I felt a little smug. They had *teams* looking for me, and he wanted to say I wasn't stealthy? "Teams?" I asked, struggling to keep the smirk off my face. "As in more than one?"

"North America is a vast search area," he told me coldly. "Your trail is easy to pick up when you are human."

I lost my smugness at his not-so-subtle reminder my wolf was difficult. Or that *he* found her to be difficult.

Cannon returned his attention to Leo. "Stamina first. Then combat. Then tracking."

"I can track."

"No, you can't." His brow furrowed as he looked at me. "Pup, just...shut up. I know what's best for you." At my indignant gasp and Royce's mumbling, he groaned out loud. "I don't mean it like *that*. I've seen you fight, yes, you can beat the shit out of a human. Well done. But if you want to fight or defend yourself against a *shifter*, you need to relearn everything you *think* you know. And trust me, from someone who has seen you fight, as someone who has been in the same ring as you, you need *basic* training to hold your own against a fully trained shifter."

My focus on him became narrower and narrower as he spoke, until I was sure that my eyes were barely slits in my face.

"Glare at me all you want, Kezia, but I put you in a one-on-one fight tomorrow with one of my pack, even one of my half-decent fighters, and you'll be on the ground in less than ten minutes."

"Challenge accepted."

Leo coughed to cover his laugh, but Nikan was shaking his head. "Zia, listen to him. You're decent, we've seen you, but let's try it this way first. When you fly right through the basic training, you can tell us you told us so. Yeah?"

Royce was nodding in agreement, and as I looked between the four of them, I wondered what I was missing. "You all really think I am so bad?"

"Not bad," Royce corrected. "You're just not shifter trained."

"Kris trained me," I reminded them all. When I saw Leo frown, I explained, "My brother."

"Your brother is a beta in a pack that doesn't treat all of its wolves equally." Cannon's scorn was clear in his cold tone. "He may have indulged you by showing you some fighting skills, but he has not taught you fully. To do so risked you both and his position in the pack. He already has a lot to lose in that pack, right?"

I knew he meant Cass and the fact my brother was an alpha living as a beta, and I knew Cannon was protecting Kris by not saying that in front of Leo, but that didn't mean his words about my fighting ability stung less. "The Anterrio Pack has given us much," I answered demurely.

"And a mate for you," Leo added in helpfully. "Who agrees for you to train, which is some forward-thinking for that pack." He looked at the others. "I mean, they're so stuck in the past it's a shock to know you trained there, if you know what I mean?"

Cannon gave me a knowing look. "Yes, you're very fortunate

that your mate is so open-minded. About so many things you've done recently."

"Right, well," Royce said as he stood. "That all sounds like we've made some real progress." His expectant look at Leo caused the other shifter to stand. "What time do you want Kezia at the training yard? Six?"

"Six?" I blurted.

"Problem, pup?"

"Shut up." I looked at Leo, who was failing to hide his shock at the way I spoke to his alpha. "Six?"

"I can make it later if you like, six thirty?"

That was his idea of later? "Six is fine," I told him with a smile. "I love six in the morning. Almost my favorite time of day."

At the door to the study, Royce looked over his shoulder at Cannon. "You good here?"

Cannon nodded. "Doc's coming soon with his daily report."

Royce hesitated but, conscious of Leo beside him, he gave us all a wave and told us to have a good night.

Getting to my feet, I stopped when Cannon cocked his head at me. "Where are you going?"

"My room?"

"Doc will be here soon, stay."

Nikan was doing his best to blend into the chair, it seemed, rather than get involved. "Why do I need to stay? Do I need to know about the daily report?" I asked the overbearing giant.

Cannon huffed in irritation. "The report *is* you, so I would say yes. Wouldn't you?"

"Why am I a report?"

"Why are you so difficult?"

"I'm not difficult! Why is there a report on me? And what do you mean daily? There's a daily report?"

"Oh, good Luna, why did Royce ever let you out of that cell?" Cannon growled.

"Hey, you wanna ask her questions, why not ask her why I got lumbered with you?" I snarked back at him.

"Trust me, pup. I ask her every fucking day."

"You conceited—"

"So, Royce wasn't exaggerating," Nikan spoke loudly. "You really are always at each other's throats or you're screwing."

I stared at him. "We don't *screw*!"

"Yet," Cannon grunted, kicking his feet out as he slouched down in the chair.

"Not from the lack of trying either," Nikan said gruffly, slumping back in his seat. "I agree," he said with a rueful look at his brother. "What was Royce thinking?"

"I am right here," I reminded him with a sharp kick to his shin. "He let me out so I could get clean."

"He let you out because he's a softie," Cannon grumbled. "I should demote him," he mused.

"You won't hide this from the pack," Nikan said to him as he looked between us. "It's so obvious it's more to you than she's nervous about a mate bond. A mate bond to someone else," he added with a scornful huff.

"I know," Cannon snapped. "Which is why we were trying to keep us separated, but you and your big mouth ruined that."

"I said sorry."

"And do you think *sorry* fixed it?"

"Are you always this moody?" I asked. "Do you need to eat or something? Chocolate? You're like Cass during her bleed. Or Kris when he's hungry."

Nikan leaned back, groaning out loud, his hands covering his face. "Of course, it makes so much sense."

Bewildered, I looked at him. "That he's a moody shit when he's hungry?"

"No." Nikan dropped his hands and looked at me. "That his wolf isn't happy you're so close and he isn't with you."

"I'm right here."

"*With* you, with you."

What was he talking about?

"He means not fucking you."

I blinked. "Wow. The way you try to woo me"—I batted my lashes—"it just leaves me speechless."

Cannon stood quickly, the frown creasing his forehead. "I need a walk. Tell Doc to wait until I'm back."

The front door of the house slammed shut, and I blew out a breath. "I should go back to the cell."

"Wolf's out of the bag," Nikan said with a small smile. He shrugged his shoulders. "It's my fault, I was a jealous dick. Sorry."

Right, so we were doing this. "Um, it's fine. You didn't know." I walked to the window and watched the street.

"You knew though," Nikan spoke softly behind me. "Didn't you?"

Half turning, I looked back. He was focused on the floor, his hands clasped together in a tight fist, elbows resting on his knees. "That we were mates? They'd mentioned it. I didn't believe them, well, kind of...

"You could have said." He sat up straighter, turning his head to make eye contact.

"I didn't know you liked me, you know, like that." Nikan's incredulous look was almost comical. "Don't look at me like that. I come from a pack where hardly anyone talks to me, and one of my two friends is male, and you're just like him."

I didn't expect the sudden anger as he pushed to his feet. "Do not compare me to that fucker."

Sure, Landon and I may have a rocky relationship right now, but growing up, he was my friend. "Landon's not—"

"Landon is an ass, and the only people who don't call him out on his bullshit are that pack because he's the pack leader's son. Trust me, that little weasel has been playing the daddy card all his life."

"I didn't know you knew him so well," I said coolly.

Nikan scoffed. "I know him better than he realizes. Don't compare me to him."

I walked back to the chair I'd been sitting on. "There's a lot I need to know, it seems. But what I meant was that my two friends, one of which was male, how I was with you, is how I was with him. A friend."

Nikan didn't look like he believed me, and then the more he looked like he wanted to say something, he shook his head. "Well, now I know why he said you're his mate."

"I never said he was clever," I muttered, which made Nikan smile. Sitting down, I thought about the conversation this evening. "You know, I *can* fight. I fought Landon. And I won."

Nikan shrugged. "From what we learned when we were there for the Luna Ball, you were already in heat."

"No, it hadn't started yet."

"Did you shift?"

"No." I shook my head in denial. "I started to, I won't lie. But I pulled her back. We fought as equals."

"Then he's a shit fighter."

"Nikan!"

His look was unapologetic. "You'll understand tomorrow."

The doors opened and Doc came in. "Ah, my favorite test subject, free in the wild," he greeted with a warm smile.

"Not free in the wild," I corrected him. "But I guess I'm free. If being stuck here with Alpha Dick is termed *free*."

"Alpha Dick?" Doc asked with a grimace. "Is that anatomy-specific or..."

"His personality!"

"Right, well." He took a chair across from me. "It's going well?"

"They fight even more out here than they did in the bunker," Nikan told him.

"Should make for lively evenings," Doc said with a grin. He pulled a jar out of the satchel he carried. He held the jar out to me. "One level teaspoon, every morning and night, in half a cup of warm water."

"Why?"

"It's the only question she knows," Cannon remarked as he walked through the open door. "Keep these doors closed when we discuss her," he admonished his two pack members once he closed the door.

"Told you he's a dick," I muttered under my breath as I felt the magic seal the room.

"My bad," Doc shrugged off Cannon's gruffness. "One level teaspoon, every morning and night"—seeing that I was about to speak, he hurried on—"because it will or should control the onset of the next heat. Or the first heat. I need to run some more tests to determine the exact status."

"Did the shaman give you this?" I asked, unscrewing the jar and sniffing the contents.

"No. Science gave me this."

Looking up, I considered him. "Smells a lot like what the

shaman gave me."

"I'm sure it's a coincidence." His sneer was barely concealed, and it rubbed me the wrong way.

Tilting my head, I ran my eyes over Doc. "You don't believe in Luna, right? All medicine and science and no faith?"

"Everyone is entitled to their own belief."

"And your belief is science. Not in our Goddess."

Cannon muttered something about this not being the time, but I was focused on Doc. He rolled his head on his shoulders as if he was uncomfortable. "I see results with medicine. I don't see results in healing people using only prayer."

"I get that." I did, totally understandable for a man with a restricted view. "Then how does science explain shifters? And our advanced healing abilities. And our immunity to some diseases, and our longer life spans."

"A mutation in the DNA."

"Hmm, and my wolf calls you the mutant."

"Your wolf would be correct." He gave me a humorless smile.

"And when the doors close in this room, and it becomes soundproof, what science is that?" I watched his Adam's apple bob. "I know it isn't technology; a shifter's hearing is too sharp not to notice human technology. I know it isn't science; there is no machinery or technology of any kind present in these walls. The doors are simple wood. Yet when they close, I feel the magic. *You* can feel the magic. Your alpha felt it in the shaman's home when he performed the same spell to give the same privacy. He watched him learn from my blood through simple taste, while you perform tests to get the same results he does with a simple lick of my blood. The same results which called for the same remedy." I smiled at Doc as I shook the jar. "I have faith in science, and I have belief in Luna. I don't have to write one off to have the other."

"Did you miss your calling for the priesthood?" Nikan joked, trying to ease the tension.

I looked at him, my face betraying my irritation. "No. I spoke an untruth earlier. I didn't have only two friends in my pack. I had three. The shaman has known me, and cared for me, for a long time. He has given his life to Luna, his sight too, and it pisses me off when his work, his dedication, and his faultless service are so casually written off as a scam. We're not a mutation of DNA. If we were, there would be more of us. Shifters were born of magic. By Luna's grace do we survive. I for one am not going to piss my Goddess off by throwing her gift back in her face and telling her science will care for my children and their children after them." I stood and handed the jar back to Doc, who took it wordlessly. "I'm tired," I told Cannon. "I have an early start. I want to go to bed."

He gave a slight nod, and I dipped my head in thanks. At the door, I turned back to Doc. "I'll tell you the same as I told the shaman, the herbs don't work. Had you simply asked me instead of you all thinking I'm a clueless fool, I could have saved you the time."

Closing the door behind me, I went upstairs. I wasn't one for religious outbursts, but I also wasn't comfortable having my belief, my existence, tossed so carelessly aside by a half-shifter who thought the answers lay at the end of a microscope.

Maybe I overreacted. Maybe Cannon would tell me I had to apologize in the morning. Maybe it would be one more thing they could blame on my heat.

With a snort, I headed to the bathroom to brush my teeth. Now I knew how human women felt when men always blamed their mood swings on PMS. The fact I'd done the very same thing to Cannon earlier didn't escape me, nor did the fact that I was pissed off with them all. Even myself.

Rinsing my mouth, I stared at myself in the mirror. My white-blonde hair was pulled back tight, and I pulled the hair tie free, letting my hair fall free down my back and around my face. Even with my hair loose making my face look softer, I still looked tired.

"The sooner this heat comes, the better," I told the mirror with a heavy sigh. "I need some control back."

I felt her come forward, her amber eyes full of wisdom that I did not have.

Surrender and you will rest.

"No." Inhaling deeply, I shook my head. "If I give you control, I don't trust where I'll end up." I met her stare boldly. "*When* I'll end up. Three months later? Six? A Year?"

I am not the enemy, child.

"I know," I whispered. "You're not my enemy...I no longer know if you're a friend though. I don't know if I can trust you."

She held my stare for a long moment before she melted back, and when I was sure her presence was faded, I headed to bed. Another night with only a light sleep was better than no sleep at all, especially when I had to prove to all these doubters tomorrow that I was not a weakling.

One day, just one day, where I didn't have to prove myself or be in control, that's all I wanted. Climbing into bed, I stared at the ceiling. "Is it too much to ask, Luna?"

Turning on my side, I closed my eyes. For all my defending of the Goddess with Doc, no matter how many times I asked her my questions, she never answered.

CHAPTER 15
Cannon

"She seems extra feisty," Doc muttered as I closed the door behind Kezia.

"The only pack decent to her in that fucked up Anterrio Pack were Bales's twins and the shaman," Nikan defended her as I knew he would. "She's loyal. I mouthed off about that prick Landon, and she bit my head off too."

That got my attention. Curious, I asked him, "What did you say?" My brother's head dipped, and I exchanged a look with Doc. "Nikan?"

He shrugged. "I brought up the whole, you know, she-knew-you-were-mates thing and I didn't, and she knew I liked her—"

"Did she?"

Nikan snorted. "No. She told me she thought I was just like Landon." He sighed. "I wasn't very complimentary about him, and her protective side kicked in."

"For Landon?"

Nikan gave me a wry smile. "That's what I said."

"Huh." I thought about it. They were friends before he lied about her being his mate. When she went into her heat that day in her pack, he had tried to claim her, but it wasn't as a mate. It was like he was a spoiled child wanting to play with a toy first before anyone else. Every male knew sex with a female during her heat was wild. Idiot youths who didn't know sex was *just* as good and could be as wild with any woman if you knew how to please her, wanted to bed a female in heat for the "experience."

Seems Landon was as much of a dick as I thought he was.

I turned my attention to Doc. "I told you the herbs the shaman gave her made no difference."

He shrugged. "It was worth a try."

"She doesn't need to be wound up and agitated about things we can't control," I told them, finally taking a seat. "I need her to relax. I need her to let the wolf out so I can find out what the fuck is happening inside her and to let her wretched heat finally surface and move her out of this constant limbo that she's been in for months." Glaring at a bookshelf, I thought of all the things that needed to happen for Kezia to finally let control slip. "I can't help her if she keeps fighting herself."

"You could try telling her that?" Doc suggested.

"She's impossible to talk to." I pointed at the doors where she had just left through. "You've spoken to her." Shaking my head in exasperation, I looked at them both. "I've interrogated terrorists across enemy lines more easily than trying to have a conversation with her."

"You should maybe try talking rather than trying to get her clothes off," Nikan snarked.

"Her clothes come off easily," I bit back at him. "It's getting them to stay *on* that's the problem." I saw his cheeks flush and kicked myself. It wasn't my intention to rub it in his face that she was mine. Honestly, it would be better if she wasn't.

Would it?

I ignored that question. I'd *been* ignoring that question for a very long time, it felt.

"We could drug her?"

I gaped at Doc, my wolf prowling closer to the surface. "What the fuck?"

Doc rubbed the back of his head. "She's highly strung, you said it yourself. She's spinning too many plates. To get her to relax, properly relax, we could drug her."

"The humans call that assault," I snarled at him, shoving off my seat. "They'd be right."

"Be serious, Cannon." Doc's exasperation was riding close to the surface too. "You have her in your pack. Her brother's informed the Pack Council that she killed three men, human men, and we know she doesn't know how she did it. She's immune to *silver*. We need inside her head, and if you are right and she is somehow separate from her wolf, we need to know *how* and why."

I watched my friend as he spoke, seeing the gleam in his eye at the possibility of studying something new.

Only Kezia wasn't a project.

She wasn't a science experiment.

She was a nineteen-year-old wolf who needed protection. Protection *I* could give her.

"Leave it alone for now," I told him. Casting my eyes to the ceiling, I let out a low exhale. "It's enough for now. I'm going to go to bed. You can see your way out."

Nikan rose, saying nothing about the fact I was retiring so early. "Will you lock the door?" he asked. "It's not just you in the house anymore."

My door had never been locked since I was alpha. Not that my pack had a habit of walking into my home in the middle of the night. But...Kezia was under my roof.

"Yes. Probably best."

Doc misinterpreted completely. "At least a lock on the front door will wake you if she tries to run."

Nikan opened his mouth to correct him, but I shot him a warning look. "Absolutely," I agreed.

"Although if she ran, at least we'd have a chance to catch the wolf," Doc speculated as he headed to the door, and I knocked my brother's arm to stop him from grabbing Doc and probably punching him. Or maybe I was the only one who wanted to punch him, and reaching out to my brother was the way to stop me from following through.

I waited until they were gone and locked the door behind them. The simple act of securing my house seemed against everything I stood for since I killed my father to free this pack from his tyranny. I could practically see the sneer on his face at the fact I was changing my ways for a female.

"It's not a constant change, it's an adaptation while she's here," I reminded myself.

I made a quick round of the house, making sure it was secure before I climbed the stairs. The phrase *while she's here* repeated like a mantra through my head. We both said we wanted to break the bond. I knew putting distance between us was bullshit. Luna created mates for her alphas to bring balance to the pack. To balance the alpha, the strongest and best provider for the pack, he needed an equally strong female to support him. A mate to produce strong heirs and keep the alpha line going.

It was survival of the species at its most basic. Shifters needed alphas, and alphas needed a mate.

Outside her bedroom door, I hesitated. I could hear her

breathing, light, uneven, restless. In the cell, she had slept the same way, her mind resisting the lull of a deep sleep, keeping her on edge. Keeping the wolf from taking over. I needed her to surrender, but I also feared it.

With her guard down completely, how was I supposed to keep away from her? Knowing she was vulnerable.

Pushing the door open, I stood in the doorway, watching her sleep. Kezia's hair was splayed out over the pillow, and her face turned away from the door towards the window. The blanket was at her waist, her arms free, one raised over her head.

Even though she wasn't in a deep sleep, she looked peaceful. Closing the door behind me, I went to my room. She didn't need to wake up and see me leering at her like that fucker Landon would.

I needed her to feel safe here. I needed her to learn to *trust* me.

Taking a seat at the edge of my bed, I dropped my head into my hands. How did I fix this? I could try talking to her. She was prickly, but she was intelligent. Too smart sometimes, but she knew what was at stake more than any of us.

She was also nineteen.

"Age means nothing. We're not human; stop hearing Royce in your head," I berated myself. A good half of my pack served overseas. Royce was one of them. Female shifters had their heat to contend with, males had their aggression.

There was no better way for a male shifter feeling restless and aggressive to get that driven out of him than by fighting in the military.

Discipline. Hard work. Training.

It alleviated the spikes of aggression. However, too much time spent among humans also skewed perspectives. With two daughters of his own, Royce fixated on the age difference. There were two years between Hannah and him, and he viewed my age difference with Kezia as an issue.

It was only an issue if we made it one.

A mate was a mate. Luna chose them for a reason.

Getting to my feet, I pulled my shirt off. "It's not like I'm going to make her call me daddy," I grumbled and then groaned as my cock perked up. "No," I growled. "You're not jerking off in the shower again."

Five minutes later, I was jerking off in the shower, remembering the sweet taste of my mate as she squirmed under my tongue. With more self-disgust than usual, I got out of the shower and was toweling myself off when I heard the creak in the hall.

Throwing open my bedroom door, I startled Kezia, causing her to jump.

"What the fuck are you wearing?"

She looked down at her tank top and panties. "This is what I sleep in."

"No." My blood was heating again. Pinching the bridge of my nose, I forced my mind to unsee her dressed in so little. "Why are you up?"

"I heard water running," she mumbled. "It made me want to pee."

I looked at her over my fingers, seeing her looking me over, her teeth caught on the bottom corner of her lip.

"You're in a towel." A finger pointed at the towel on my hips. "You can't bitch at me for wearing this...at least I have clothes on."

"You have underwear on."

"It's more than you."

"This is your first night here. We can't do this if we intend to stay away from each other," I reminded her. "Get more clothes."

"Same."

We glared at each other.

I saw the minute her glare turned from heated to something much worse. Desire. "Kezia…"

"I know," she whispered, backing away. "Did you get those locks?"

"Do you see them?" I bit out in irritation. "Just…just close the door." Her door closed quickly, and back in my room, I counted to five to stop myself from following her into hers. Making the decision, I dropped the towel, pulled on a pair of sweatpants, and shoved my feet into my sneakers. I needed to get out of the house, or we'd never make it through the night.

With a shirt in hand, I opened the door and found her in the middle of the hall, wide-eyed and her cheeks flushed. Had she been heading to my room?

"I didn't go to the bathroom," she told me apologetically. She frowned when she saw what I was wearing. "Are you leaving?"

"I have an errand to run." If I clamped my jaw any tighter, my teeth may break. I could smell her arousal. She was killing me.

"At night?" Suspicion entered her eyes. "An errand or Koda?"

"Don't insult both of us with stupidity, pup."

"Then where are you going?"

I looked at her in bewilderment. How did she not know? "I can smell you, Kezia. You're aroused. I'm aroused. I want to fuck you so badly that I can't be here. Not if you want to wake up tomorrow still a virgin."

Her eyes were like saucers. "Sex completes the bond."

"Mm-hmm."

"You don't want the bond." She looked at me and then I felt the pain as her heart rate spiked and something caused her to double over. "Argh!"

Leaping forward, I grabbed her. "Kezia?"

And I scented it.

All around us.

Suffocating my senses.

"Your heat." *Fuck, not now.*

Kezia clung to me. "Cannon! Oh Luna, it hurts."

Cradling her closer, I tucked her head under my chin. "I know, I feel it." She'd just become the wolf equivalent of catnip. Lips pressed to the crown of her head. My alpha senses picked up the sound of movement from outside. "Is your window open?" I asked tersely.

"Yes."

Fuck.

Kezia pushed herself away from me as another wave of pain wracked her body. "Take me to the cell," she commanded. "You need to protect them."

"From you?"

"From *you*, Alpha." Slowly she got to her feet. "They're in more danger from you now that the mate bond is waiting for us to complete it."

"It means I'll need to take you through the town." She stumbled and I reached for her to steady her. The contact was electrifying. "Or..."

Kezia looked up at me, both of us reaching for the other at the same time. Our mouths melded together as I pushed her against the wall, dipping slightly to grab her ass and hoist her up, relishing the feel as her legs wrapped around my waist.

Kezia tore her mouth away from mine as another cramp surged through her. "Cannon," she whimpered.

Pressing my forehead against hers, I tried to fight the urge to claim her. "Tell me what to do." My fingers dug into her skin. "I can't think, pup. I need inside you." My muscles tightened as I strained against the pull to give in to the call of her body, my head burrowing into the crook of her neck. "Tell me what to do," I whispered against her skin.

"The cells. Get Royce. You said we need this to pass." Kezia pushed against me. Her legs lowered as she tried to stand. I moved back slightly to give her room and watched as the beads of sweat formed on her brow as her limbs shook. "I'm fighting the urge to shift." She inhaled deeply, her hands reaching for me before she stopped herself. "I'm fighting a lot of urges." She took a deep breath to calm herself. "We get this one out of the way, we'll be better. Right?"

I had no idea. It sounded good at the time, but now, seeing her in pain, I was no longer sure about any of it.

Royce. My alpha power called to him. He was alert instantly. *It's happening. I need you.*

I heard his reply, and I wrapped my arms around the woman in front of me. "Hold on. Can you hold on?"

"Yes." She took a deep breath, inhaling my scent. "No?"

I chuckled as we both sank to the floor. "I can't let you go," I explained. "I want to, I know we need to, but...it's like...I can't not touch you," I murmured, holding her tighter.

"You're not in control," Kezia whispered, her lips pressing into my chest. She let out a whimper. "It hurts."

"I know." I took a deep breath. "I can feel it."

Kezia's head tilted back as she looked up at me. "You can? That's...freaky."

"Tell me about it." I winced as her body curled up in agony. "It's okay," I soothed her, stroking her hair. "It's okay."

"I don't understand how sex works."

I hesitated. "Is this the right time for a birds and the bees conversation?" I teased, latching on to anything that distracted me from *her*. She elbowed me.

"Asshole. I mean, everything hurts." She moved further onto the floor, curling up in a ball, and I was curled around her. "How would it even happen when I'm being a human pretzel?"

"How would what happen?"

"You know—" Her whole body tensed as more pain erupted within her. Kezia was gasping. "Penetration," she ground out.

"Now?" I tried to joke but it fell flat. "You're not focusing on the fact that you would be feeling other things." My voice was gruff. Heavy with want and need. Every part of me wanted to not be fighting the pull to her.

"Is it hard for you?"

"I'm sure you can feel that it is," I muttered.

Kezia gasped as another bolt of pain went through her. "I want a deer."

"I'll get you one."

"Two."

"Greedy." My lips skimmed her neck, my tongue flicking at her scar.

"What if we half did it, would it be better?"

Her naivety made me chuckle. "I don't do things by halves."

"Selfish."

My fingers traced over her stomach, and her moan caused my body to erupt in goose bumps. "Don't moan, I'm barely hanging on," I pleaded, my body pressing into hers.

"I'm sorry." She moved her head to look at me, and I saw the tears on her cheeks.

"Not much longer," I promised.

"She could come out, make it stop," Kezia whispered.

"No. You need this. I know it's a dick thing for me to say, but you need to get through this." Did she? I hoped Doc was right.

"I'm here," Royce said as he approached slowly. "Hannah too."

I snarled at the male coming for my mate, and my wolf took over. The shift was so sudden I had no control over it.

"Alpha," Hannah spoke as she stepped in front of the male. "I need to take her. She's in pain."

Looking down, I saw her on the floor. My head dipped, and I nudged her head softly.

"You're really huge," she said through chattering teeth. "Of course, you would be. I knew you were, but up close, you're stupid sized."

Help her.

Hannah rushed forward, and Kezia used my friend's support to get to her feet. When Royce stepped forward to help, I blocked his path.

"I'm not touching her," he assured me, backing off.

Leaping forward, I blocked the female coming up my stairs, my teeth bared.

"Easy, Alpha," Willy said. "Girl's in heat, towns going into a frenzy, you need another female here."

Forcing myself to change, I turned away from them all. "Royce!"

"Get yourself some new pants," he suggested, and I took the out he gave me, barricading myself in my room on the pretense I was covering my nudity from a shifter who had helped raise me.

Kezia cried out and my fist went through a wall.

"She's fighting hard," I heard Willy say softly. "It's because she's mated," she told them as I heard them begin to move away.

"Won't be easy for her to go through this alone, without her mate here."

She wasn't without him.

I *was* here.

Hiding.

Because we didn't want this.

Another jolt of her pain had me on my knees. "Fuck," I hissed as I fought off the roll of agony in my gut.

We didn't want this. This was the right thing to do.

The next wave of agony rolled over me as I fought the mating call, bringing me low to the floor. Flames of pain lashed across my body as the need to be with her grew stronger.

"Luna!" Curled in a ball on my bedroom floor, my hands over my head to protect myself as it felt like blow after blow kept raining down on me. "Goddess, *please!*"

The next stab of pain made me see stars.

"Alpha?"

I recognized Royce's wary call. "She's in the cell. You need to come, keep her in her human form."

Lifting my head, I looked at him. "I can't," I said through gritted teeth. "I'll be too close."

"Her brother?" Royce suggested, but I was already shaking my head.

"Too far." With a groan, I pushed myself to my feet. "Keep everyone away. No one can see it affecting me like this." With stilted movements, I pulled on a shirt. What felt like a punch to the stomach had me staggering. "How the fuck is she standing through this," I muttered.

"She isn't," Royce told me, frowning. "She's in agony," he added, realizing too late that he shouldn't have spoken so carelessly.

The need to protect her and be with her nearly overrode the control I had of my wolf. Barely hanging onto my human form, I bolted down the stairs and across town with complete disregard for what my reaction would look like to my pack.

I heard Royce shouting behind me, but I didn't pay any heed.

All that mattered to me was my mate. She needed me, and I wasn't there.

CHAPTER 16

Kezia

I was in the dark, on the familiar cot, my body folded in on itself as wave after wave of pain washed over me. Under the excruciating pain, almost as prominent as the agony I was in, was the hunger.

Hunger to hunt.

Hunger to eat.

Hunger to fuck.

The need for the latter was almost as unbearable as the pain. *Everywhere* was pain. As we had raced through the town, the light had stabbed at my eyes, and too many smells overwhelmed my senses. Now in the cell, I had only one thought.

Where was he?

I needed him. Luna, I *needed* him.

The throb between my legs was unlike anything I had felt before. I needed his hands on my skin, his clever fingers stroking between my legs. I needed that wicked mouth on me, lapping and licking...feasting on me.

I was aware of the others in the room with me. I'd heard one of them comment on my familiarity with the cell, but they'd been hushed quickly.

There was a male nearby. I could sense him. He wasn't the male I needed, and it was pissing me off that he wasn't.

My body only wanted one male.

"Where is he?" I gasped between the mix of pain and longing. A familiar scent moved forward. "Hannah?"

"It's me," Royce's wife confirmed. "Landon is with your pack," she spoke softly.

"I don't give a fuck where Landon is. Where is he?"

Hannah moved closer. "*Landon* is with your pack."

This time through my pain, I heard the slight emphasis on Landon's name. He was my pretend mate. My cover story for the fact that the mate I *did* have didn't want me.

"I need..." I groaned as the need in my core intensified.

"I know," Hannah murmured sympathetically. "We're going to leave you—"

"Why the hell are you leaving me?" I demanded, my head lifting. I wasn't meant to be alone, was I? "I have to be watched." Didn't I? Wasn't there a reason I was not shifting?

"We thought you may need some alone time." I could hear the small quiver of embarrassment. "We understand the urges, but we're not, um, mated. I can only imagine how bad it is for you."

Had I not been rocking from side to side in pain, curled up in a ball, I may have blushed at the realization that they were giving me privacy to take care of some of my more urgent intimate desires. Rolling onto my front, I pressed my head into the thin mattress, groaning when it did nothing but remind me of the few times the alpha—*my* alpha—had been close to me on this cot. Kissing me. Touching me. *Wanting* me.

"I *need* him, Hannah!"

I heard movement, and when I looked, I sensed that Hannah was as close to the bars as possible. "I know," she whispered quickly. "I'm so sorry, Kezia, but you know why he isn't here."

I did.

I knew.

He rejected me.

With a roar, I was on my feet. Anger laced my already heated veins. My claws broke free of my skin, but with effort that caused me to scream out in more hurt, I pushed my wolf back.

No! You will not come forward.

You are in pain, child. Amber eyes watched me. *Let me heal you. Like I always do.*

No. I will do this. I can get through this.

She shook her head at me, a look full of reproach as she faded back. *You cannot fight me forever, child.*

"I can damn well try," I muttered as everything I had been feeling previously ratcheted up tenfold.

His scent covered me. Wrapping around me like a warm blanket, dampening some needs and hunger, intensifying others. Wildly I looked for him, sensing him near the doorway, grateful for the momentary lapse in the agony I'd been fighting.

"Cannon," I breathed his name in relief.

"Everyone out." His command was one of an alpha. His pack wouldn't go against it, but I knew one still lingered. "I won't go in, Hannah," I heard him assure the female.

Won't go in? Into my cell? He was here and he wouldn't come in? Anger rushed back.

"Because I'm not good enough?" I snarled, hearing the door close.

"You know why, Kezia." I heard him walking towards me, and then he was in front of the cell. I could make out his silhouette in the darkness, wolf sight so much more powerful than human's.

"Why are we in darkness?" I inched forward, eager to be closer.

"They said the light was causing you discomfort."

"Everything right now is causing me discomfort." I huffed. "You're doing it right now by being on the wrong side of the bars." My fingers grazed his, and I heard his sharp inhale.

"Kezia." He said my name with a groan. Like he was in pain. Did it hurt that he wasn't in here? Inside me? Fucking me. Claiming me?

"I need you." I pressed forward, the bars immovable but with enough space that my arms slipped through. My hands were on his chest, touching, stroking, exploring. "I need you so badly."

"I know," Cannon sounded as desperate as I did. "I can't get in."

My fingers stopped their exploration. "Can't? Why?"

"I made them change the code," he told me, one hand reaching through and taking hold of my hip, pulling me tighter into the bars. "I also made them lock the door to the room. On a timer. It's just you and me, pup."

"No." I stepped back, jerking out of his hold. "*No!*" I yelled. "You're here but you're not here!" I screamed in fury. "I need you *in* here! *With* me." I felt him reaching for me, and I jumped back, out of his limited reach. "You don't get to fucking touch me," I seethed in anger. "You bastard. You fucking bastard, I *need* you."

"I'm here." I could hear the pain in his voice, the devastation of the hurt he was causing me.

I didn't care.

"You're not here," I snarled. "You're a coward." I ripped my tank top over my head, throwing it to the side. My panties followed, and with no regard for modesty, I plunged my hand between my legs. The groan at touching myself made Cannon whimper.

"Kezia." The strain was there.

Good.

If I was suffering, so was he.

"I'm soaked," I told him, rubbing against that small bundle of nerves that was ruling my body. "I've never been like this."

"I can smell you," Cannon ground out. I heard a thump.

"The bars are impenetrable," I mocked him. "You can't get in." I smiled with malice when I heard the thump again. The sound of an alpha trying to get into a cage to be with his mate.

"Your scent." The need in his voice almost brought me to my knees. Sitting on the cot, I spread my legs wide. My fingers stroked me with easy familiarity. "Fuck, Kezia."

"You can't *fuck Kezia*, though, can you?" I sneered, tipping my head back against the bars as I played with myself. The fact I was making Cannon ache as I was aching only heightened my pleasure.

"Put your fingers inside yourself." His voice was guttural with desire. "Let me hear how wet you are."

I did as I was told, the moan I let out causing another thump against the bars.

"Get over here."

The command was dominant. The alpha's Will pressed around me, and I was on my feet. Strong hands grabbed my arm, and bringing my hand to his mouth, Cannon licked my fingers clean hungrily.

"Spread your legs and don't fucking move," he growled, kneeling in front of the bars. His hands reached through the bars, restricted in movement due to the horizontal bar that ran across the cell. He tilted my pelvis forward, almost causing me to lose my balance, but I grabbed the bars quickly, crying out in relief when I felt his tongue sweep over my flesh.

"This will get uncomfortable quickly," I told him, pushing myself into the bars and using my strength to manipulate my body so Cannon's mouth could reach as much of my center as possible. It wasn't enough, the strokes were light and limited because he couldn't fully reach me the way he wanted to. The bars restricted so much of our movement, and it must have hurt like hell against his face, but still, none of it mattered when the first orgasm rippled through me.

I sagged slightly in relief, but although the need abated slightly, I could feel it already coming back.

"We're not finished," Cannon assured me, his hand on my right hip gripping me tightly. "I'll eat this pussy all night, Kezia. I *am* here for you."

I could have wept as his mouth and fingers went back to pleasuring me. It was so good, and I needed so much more, but it was enough to stop the relentless craving that had been inside of me.

What must have been hours later, my sexual desires for the moment dulled. I lay on the floor of the cell, with Cannon lying beside me, as close as the bars allowed. Our fingers were touching. It wasn't enough, but we were making it be enough.

"You promised me deer," I said, breaking the silence of the last few minutes.

"I promised you two."

"You broke your promise."

His low chuckle made me smile. "The deer are here," he told me. "I just forgot to take them in with me. You mess with my head when you smell like this," he admitted. His hand moved from mine, and I heard him grip the bar. "Not sure how I would get them through this either. Probably best if they're not here."

"I thought I would be hungrier," I admitted. "Like the other times, when all I want is to eat."

He moved slightly. "Me being here satiates the other needs."

Sniffing, I wished I could elbow him as I recognized the truth in his words. "No need to sound so smug." I heard movement. "What are you doing?" I asked curiously.

"Massaging feeling back into my jaw," he told me lightly. "And my nose. Cheeks. Face."

Embarrassment flooded me. "Sorry."

"Don't be, it's the least I can do."

You could have done so much more.

It hung unspoken in the air between us.

"Do you think the Pack Council knows about me yet?" I hurriedly changed the subject. "Do they warn us before they arrive?"

"They're not the enemy, Kezia."

"Not to you, they're not." The sullenness of my tone betrayed my inner fear.

"Nor to you."

"Says the man who hasn't killed three humans." I moved onto my side, facing him in the darkness through the bars. I heard him do the same, my wolf sight making out some of his silhouette in the dark. "You have nothing to fear."

"Not true," he murmured. "If they take you…"

Unexpected tears welled at his admission, and I sniffed them back. "You don't want this bond," I reminded him, my voice barely a whisper.

"Nor do you," Cannon muttered.

"I don't know what I want," I admitted, the darkness giving me a sense of security.

"Why am I not surprised," he replied lightly. His hand was near mine again, and he tugged on my fingers. "Come closer," Cannon whispered.

I maneuvered myself as close as physically possible to the bars. Lips brushed mine, and I longed for more. His tongue traced over my bottom lip before he kissed me lightly once more, the bars impeding anything more. I could smell and taste my scent on his mouth, and my wolf grumbled with satisfaction.

"She's happy you smell of me," I confessed against his lips.

"I wish you smelled of me."

I whimpered as the desire returned.

"Shh," Cannon soothed me, his lips searching for mine once more. "This is what we want."

Pulling away, I once again fought back tears. "I know. Why be mated to a killer, right?" Sitting up, I pushed myself to my feet, retreating to the cot.

"Kezia—"

"I'm in control," I spoke over him abruptly. "Still in heat. The needs, the hunger, they're still here. But if you needed me weakened, like you have before, it's now. Do it now. My control is weak. She may be able to answer your questions."

I felt the change in him as he moved swiftly to his feet. "We can wait."

I knew he was offering me a kindness. "She's ready to come forward." My hands formed fists on my thighs. "If..." I swallowed hard. "If I don't come back, make her give me control back."

I heard his sharp intake of breath, my admission catching him off guard. "I will."

"Promise me," I whispered in the darkness, my head turned

away from him. Even though he couldn't see me, I didn't want to admit anything with him facing me. "I don't want to be lost, Cannon."

I heard him move forward, hands gripping the bars tightly. "You will never be lost," he told me. "I will always find you."

A few tears spilled over, and I let them fall. Cannon couldn't see me, and I no longer cared enough to hide them. "Her name is Moonstar."

~

THE CHILD FINALLY SLEPT. With care, we sank into her body, rose from the bed, and stretched. It had been so long since we stretched.

"You're still human?"

"Are any of us in this room human, Alpha?"

"I thought you would shift," he admitted.

We could hear his heart racing. "Would it please you more if we were on four legs rather than two?"

"I don't know," he told me, and we could scent his honesty.

"We will shift when your questions are done. Or when we no longer wish to answer."

"Who is we?"

We smiled. "We are."

"Where is Kezia?"

"She sleeps." We shrugged as we sat back down. "Is this why you prowl so close to us, to know where she is?"

"Who are you?"

"Who are any of us?" We heard his huff of anger, and we smiled. "If you do not like our answers, ask us better questions."

"You are separate from the wolf spirit?" he asked carefully.

We nodded. "We are. The wolf is strong though, much stronger than you think."

"Moonstar?" His words were hesitant. Unsure. "That is your name?"

"It is a name we answer to." We lifted our hair from our shoulders, a finger tracing the scar that burned. "It burned."

"What burned?" We heard him moving closer. We heard him muttering about lights, and we watched with amusement when he stepped back at the ball of light that appeared in our hand. "How?"

"You shapeshift so easily," we teased, sending the small ball of energy into the air above us, "but a little magic frightens you." We looked him up and down, admiring his strength. "You are worthy of her. Strong, like she is."

"What are you?" He looked confused and then fearful. "Luna?"

We laughed. "We are no Goddess, Alpha." We stood. "The little she thinks you reject her." We narrowed our gaze on the male. "It hurts her."

He licked his lips, understanding the warning. "And you do not like it when she's hurt."

"She has felt enough pain in her life. She will feel more."

Anger filled him, he stepped forward automatically to protect his mate. "If you hurt her—"

"We've protected her for a long time." Our hand moved to the back of our neck.

His cleverness watched us from behind his eyes. "How long?"

"The burn came first," we told him. "The pain we felt with the imposter, Bale." We shuddered. "The burn came again from the humans who beat us, used us," we spoke and met his stare. "We killed them too quickly for what they did to us."

His face was pale. We could smell his panic and fear. "She said they never got that far." The male looked wary once more. "She said they never raped her." Eyes wet with softness looked at us. "Did they?"

"We took them before they did," we answered fiercely. "Bones they had broken, cuts they made on our flesh. Knives stuck so deep they lodged in our bones." We remembered the pain. "You should thank us they are dead. We killed them too quickly."

"Does she know? How bad it was?" he asked, and we were pleased with his fury. "What those fuckers did to her?"

"We keep it from her."

"Thank you."

We watched the male curiously. "You are grateful she does not know?"

"Yes." He inhaled deeply. "I am more grateful than I can tell you."

We sniffed the air once. "We can tell."

"The burn?" he asked, moving forward. "You mean the silver bullets?"

Anger flared within us. Our fingers wrapped around the bars and pulled, the bars bending easily. We saw the male's shock, but we did not care. Crossing the distance to him, we lifted him off the ground by his throat. "You burned us."

"To see what would happen. I knew you would not die. I needed to know if she could survive silver."

He was not panicked. He was not scared. Curious, we dropped him. "It burns. Do not do it again."

"It kills others," he said, rubbing his throat. "It kills our kind. Not you."

"Or the brother," we confirmed. "We made both survive."

Looking around, we wanted to leave. It was time to run once more.

"How long?" the male asked. "How long did it take for them to come back? From the burning that first time? Months? Years?"

We thought about it. "We do not know months or years."

"How many snows came?"

We understood. "Three? Four?"

"What do you want from her?" he asked as we crossed to the door.

"Everything."

"She's mine," he told us, anger riding him. "You cannot have her."

Arrogant. Entitled. Foolish.

We turned to him. "She's always been ours." With a sharp pull, the door opened, and we changed form. The familiar wolfskin made us quicker.

Moonstar!

The command was strong, almost strong enough to stop us. But we remembered from before. The male would not hurt his mate. We ran towards the exit, eager to be free.

Moonstar! Stop.

The alpha's Will commanded us. Paws no longer ran. We fought for control. Pain as we fought him draped over our skin.

He was behind us. His voice in our head.

Let her go, he spoke. Stay in this form and let *her* go.

An alpha's Will pressed down on us. Not any alpha. An alpha mate.

Turning, trapped in this form, our teeth bared in a growl. Ready to fight.

The black wolf approached us, eyes full of the power of his kind.

Sleep now, Moonstar.

CHAPTER 17

Kezia

I FELT HIM BEFORE I WAS FULLY AWAKE. CANNON'S hand smoothed over my hair, and when I opened my eyes, I was surprised to see he was smiling. "Hey," he greeted.

"Hey." Wetting my bottom lip, I wanted to ask him what happened, but when he leaned forward and kissed me lightly, I forgot my questions. Cannon drew back and I looked at him, my eyes searching his. "What was that for?"

"For trusting me," he spoke softly. "To bring you back."

Immediately I looked for her presence, but she was absent. "How long?"

"How long what?"

"How long have I been asleep?" Pushing myself into a sitting position, I reached for the glass of water he handed me. Taking deep gulps, I quenched my thirst. "One? Two days?"

"Five."

"Oh. Wow." Putting the glass down, I pushed my hair back. "Sorry."

Cannon moved forward in his seat. "Why?"

"You'll have had so many questions to answer from your

pack." Breaking away from the intensity of his stare, I looked out of the open window, the sky a cloudless blue. It looked like a beautiful day.

"You want to go run?"

My head snapped back to face him. "Really?"

Cannon stood, extending his hand towards me. "Yes. We can run together."

I put my hand in his, and he pulled me to my feet. Standing so close to him, I remembered how selflessly he had pleasured me in the cell. "You're being really nice to me."

"I know." Cannon smirked. "It won't last, so relish it while you can."

"There he is," I teased, stretching a little. "Can I go to the bathroom first?"

Cannon shook his head in pretend exasperation. "Of course you can go to the bathroom, Kezia. You don't need to ask that."

He shoved me playfully when he saw my grin, and with a carefree laugh, I headed to the bathroom.

After I took care of my bladder and washed my hands, I splashed my face with cool water. Looking in the mirror, I examined my face. I looked the same. I felt the same. Why was he being so nice? Or was I just a suspicious cynic?

When I opened the bathroom door, he was waiting. "Ready?"

"Um, yes." I followed Cannon down the stairs, and he led me to the back door located in the laundry room. "If we're quick, we can miss most of them."

"Them?"

"I'll tell you if we make it without being seen." Cannon pulled his shirt off. "Get undressed."

I turned my back when he started to unbuckle his belt. My

heat had passed but that didn't mean the attraction was gone. Cool hands ran over my shoulders.

"You okay?"

"I'll, um...take these off," my voice came out in a whisper.

"You need help?"

My knees felt weak at his touch. I needed to get a grip on myself. "Or you can turn around?"

I heard his low laughter. "I'll turn around," he said with amusement, and I knew I was being silly. The man's mouth had been on most of my body. My naked body. The modesty train had left the station a long time ago. My cheeks flamed as I remembered us together in the cell.

I'd never taken my clothes off so quickly before, calling my wolf forward, alert for any sign of her being difficult. When I turned, the black wolf was waiting.

Let's run.

Cannon had already opened the door slightly before his shift, and once more, I followed his lead as the alpha of the Blackridge Peak Pack effectively sneaked out of town.

The black wolf set a fast pace, and my wolf rushed to catch up with him. We ran far from the town, stopping to drink from a small stream and share a rabbit. High up the mountain, the alpha slowed until we were trotting side by side. He'd told me on the run here that I had a group of people waiting for me to wake, all worried about me. It caught me by surprise how much it meant that the shifters of his pack cared about me.

Me.

Apart from my brother, the shaman, and perhaps Cass and Landon, I'd never had that before.

A familiar scent caught my nose on the breeze, and I would have stopped had the alpha not nudged me to keep moving. In a carved-out alcove on the face of the mountain sat two bundles of clothes and two backpacks. A small clearing was in front of it, and my head lifted in the summer breeze, sniffing out the scent I knew as well as my own.

Shift.

I followed his command, hastily reaching for clothes familiar to me. Pulling down the T-shirt over my bra, I let out a squeal of happiness when my brother rounded the alcove, throwing myself into his arms. "Kris!"

My brother squeezed me tight, and when we separated, my jaw dropped when the shaman stepped forward. "Holy shit," I exclaimed.

"I have missed you too, pup," he greeted me with a warm hug.

"You shifted?" I asked incredulously.

"You think I cannot run, pup?" he said as Kris guided him down to the ground.

I'd never thought about it, but as I thought about it now, I realized I'd been ignorant. "I assumed you couldn't," I admitted, my eyes lowered in shame. "I don't know why..."

"I am hindered by poor sight," the shaman spoke easily. "My impairment does not hinder my speed or my sense of smell. My poor vision does not define me."

"You're right, I'm a dick." Kris let out a sharp laugh but quickly smothered it. "There's a wolf at the pack, he's missing his arm, and he can still run," I told them as I sank to the ground.

Kris looked towards Cannon, who had settled close to me but not too close. "He is welcome?" he asked curiously. "To stay in your pack?"

"You think I will cast out a shifter because he doesn't have four legs when he shifts?" Cannon asked, reaching for one of the backpacks and opening it. He handed me a protein bar, passing one to the shaman also. He held out another to Kris. "I assume, like us, you ate on the way, but she gets hungry. I figured you would too." Cannon met Kris's gaze. "I cast no shifter from my pack or their home. Unless they are a threat to my pack or me." He grinned with no mirth. "There is little that is a threat to me." Once more, he held out the snack to my brother.

Kris took it hesitantly. "Thanks." I watched my brother as he turned the simple protein bar over in his hands before he looked up at the alpha. "Seems it's not only Kez that's a dick in the family."

"Kez?" Cannon was watching me, but I resisted the pull to meet his stare. The run had been nice, better than nice, but in this form, I could still feel the lingering effects of his touch on my body. Madness, of course. Five days had passed, but I felt like I could feel everything.

"It's just a nickname," I muttered.

"Mm-hmm, you seem to have many." His gaze swept over me. "Interesting."

Opening my snack, I took a bite, hoping no more questions were coming my way. But my brother was far too familiar with all my diversion tactics and saw right through me.

"You speak with your mouth full all the time," he teased lightly, but he was once more regarding Cannon. "But this time, my questions are for you."

They were? I looked between the three of them. "What did I do?" I asked fearfully, proving Kris right by speaking while chewing. "Have the Pack Council come already?"

Cannon reached over, his large hand rubbing my lower back soothingly. "You did nothing," he murmured. "And no, they haven't."

His touch confused me. *He* was confusing me, and what was perplexing me the most was the fact I liked it.

Cannon kept his hand near me, his fingers near my hip, but his attention was on my brother. "I know about your history," he started bluntly, causing me to stiffen in surprise. "Your parents were killed, you tried to raise this one alone, but you were too young for such a task."

Kris had stilled, his eyes alert and watchful, while I was more aggrieved at his terminology. "This one?" I muttered. "Really?"

Cannon, in familiar Cannon behavior, ignored my protest. "I know you were young," Cannon continued. "Do you know how young?"

"Are you asking me what age I was when I watched my parents get murdered?" Kris snarled.

"I was being more tactful, but yes."

"Why?" my brother asked, and I could see his anger. "Need an alibi?"

"Kris!" I warned. "Cannon isn't that old." I glanced at the alpha behind me, taking the opportunity to mess with him and hopefully defuse the situation before it began. "I know looks can be deceiving, but he's only thirty..." I paused. "Four?"

Cannon gave me a rueful look before fixing his attention back on my brother. "My father was a bastard," he spoke clearly. "Murdering shifters was a crime of his." His hand moved closer to me, his fingers pressing slightly into my thigh. "Murdering your parents wasn't one of them."

"And how do you know?" Kris scoffed. "You have his buckle."

Cannon looked genuinely baffled for a moment. "I have his what? My father's buckle?" Shifting his weight slightly, he scratched his jaw. "There is nothing left of Rek's in my pack," he told us. "Except me and my brother, if you want to be technical."

"You were wearing my father's, *our* father's, belt buckle the day we met you." Kris was on his feet, angry accusation burning in his eyes.

Cannon looked thoughtful. "Another piece of a puzzle," he mused. "If you could listen and answer some questions, I will do everything I can to answer yours."

Kris hesitated. I saw the glance at the shaman, and I knew he was communicating with him. "Make it quick."

Cannon nodded briefly. "How many years between you and your sister?"

Kris huffed, ready to say something smart, and I flicked my leg out and kicked him. "Just answer, it's easier, trust me." I turned to look at Cannon. "Five years."

"And Kezia was a baby when your parents were attacked?"

Kris shrugged. "Yes." He thought about it. "She was one, maybe younger," he added hesitantly.

"You went to Anterrio when she was what age?"

"Five or six," Kris said irritably. "Why?"

"So, you were ten? Eleven?"

"If you add five years on, that's the answer," Kris mocked.

"Kezia is nineteen now, making you twenty-four."

"If you dragged us out here to wow me with simple math, then I wished you'd called instead. It took a lot of bullshitting to get the shaman outside of the pack with just me as his companion."

"Kristoff," the shaman chided. "The alpha has a point."

I'd been following Kris's train of thought, so when the shaman implied there was more to the questioning, I turned to face Cannon more. "I'm also missing the point of the questions," I told him honestly.

Cannon looked between the two of us, and then straight at the shaman. "You've never told him?"

"Told me what?" Kris was really pissed off now.

Cannon met his furious gaze calmly. "An alpha is born," he said, holding his hand up to stop Kris from interrupting. "But we come into our alpha power when we are mature." He didn't blink as he spoke, holding my brother's gaze. "An alpha is mature when he is in his mid-twenties. It's why I couldn't challenge my father until I came back to the pack. I needed years to learn to master my power."

"Maybe you're a late developer," Kris spat out.

"I am one of the youngest alphas in North America," Cannon corrected him. "I came into my alpha power when I was twenty-four."

"Kris is twenty-three," I reminded him. "Almost twenty-four."

"He is, and he has been getting taught by the shaman for three, maybe four, years?"

"Three," the shaman confirmed. He didn't seem surprised by any of Cannon's vague questions or thinking.

"The point?" Kris griped.

"You're older than you think you are," Cannon spoke clearly. "As is my mate. It's why it's so impossible to stay away from her. We've been apart for too long, and the bond is keen to make up the time."

"What?" I moved slightly away from him. "I'm nineteen."

"It's why her heat began as soon as I was near," Cannon continued, unbothered by my protest and Kris's slack jaw. Cannon looked at me. "Your human bleed started when?"

"Fuck off, I'm not answering that."

"She was eight."

I looked at my brother in disbelief. "Dude!"

"I remember it well. It caused a lot of talk between the females." He rubbed the back of his neck. "Caused a lot of confusion for me too. Didn't know what the hell I was supposed to do with a kid who was suffering PMS."

The shaman spoke to Cannon. "How many years do you think they lost?"

"Four."

"Lost?" Kris and I demanded at the same time. It was the term I used when I succumbed to the control of my wolf. It bothered me that they were using it now.

Cannon nodded, his eyes on the shaman. "They both have scars at the base of their necks." He reached out, taking my hand, entwining our fingers. "They were both shot with silver. I think it's probable that it was at the same time their parents were killed." His fingers tightened on mine. "Whoever it was thought they had killed you all."

"You think we were shot in the back of the head with silver?" I asked him, trying to pull my hand free.

"I spoke to her, like you wanted," Cannon told me, tugging my hand back towards him. "She told me the burn happened first," he told us quietly. "She wasn't clear, but she said three or four winters passed before you were *both* healed."

"You're full of shit," Kris said angrily.

"I think it is four years, like we thought," Cannon continued to speak. "It puts Kezia at ten and Kris at fifteen when they went to Anterrio. It is common for a child of twelve to enter puberty." His attention flicked to Kris. "It is uncommon for an alpha to come into his power at twenty-four, but not unheard of," he added with a slight grin.

"You think we'll believe this shit?" Kris scoffed.

"It makes more sense," the shaman said thoughtfully. "I knew they were older than they said they were, but blood does not narrow it down so precisely." He unwrapped his protein bar. "The heat came from nowhere," he added after taking a bite. "I wasn't expecting it. When I tested Kezia's blood that day, the scent was so strong, when there had been nothing only the day before. But you would have been getting closer to the pack." He looked right at Cannon. "How many days did you stay on the edge of the packlands, watching us first?"

Cannon grinned. "Five."

My head was reeling. I couldn't take it all in. "What is going on?" I demanded. "He's the reason I went into heat?" I demanded.

"Are you believing this?" Kris asked the shaman.

"You are too young to be holding your alpha power," the shaman said bluntly. "Which is why I urged you to keep it quiet. I have never spoken directly to the other." He took another bite of his bar. "I am envious she spoke to you, Alpha Cannon. But a mate bond is more powerful than an old shaman."

"I'm not nineteen?" Somehow this was the detail my brain was stuck on.

"Twenty-three, I think, if I'm right," Cannon said. "I'm sorry."

"Why?" I huffed out a laugh. "Unless you were shooting me with silver when you were, what? Eleven? You weren't...were you?"

He looked pained at the reminder that he *had* shot me with silver. "Only twice, pup. Never again."

"Twice too many," I grumbled.

"Agreed," Kris snapped. "So...let me get this right. Kezia and I were both shot, to be killed, but we both survived a *bullet* to the brain, no, not a bullet, a *silver* bullet. We stayed, what was it? *Lost?* For four years. And we went to the Anterrio Pack, who didn't know by *looking at us*, that we were older than we claimed?" He pointed at the shaman. "And a *shaman* who didn't suspect?" He was practically vibrating with rage. "But *you*, a rival pack alpha, you spoke to my sister's wolf, and she told *you* all the secrets?"

Cannon looked so calm, so casual, and I was sure my jaw dropped when he coolly nodded. "She told me what she wanted me to know."

"Why?" Kris barked.

"Because he's my mate." I felt sick. Pushing myself to my feet, I turned away from them, taking a few steps to put distance between us, taking more than I probably should have, but no one stopped me, and I kept walking until I was alone. "Oh Luna, he's really my mate."

I felt him behind me. "Disappointed?"

Sneaky, stealthy alpha. "I don't know."

I heard his huff and his warmth as he moved closer. "Do I need to ask again?"

I felt him lower his head, his breath moving my hair. "No. Maybe?"

"Are you disappointed?" he asked again, and I could hear his smile despite the seriousness of the question.

Was I disappointed? I realized that I wasn't. Not about Cannon. It took me by surprise that I was now so sure, but him being my mate, I no longer had any doubts that it was true. "No, I'm not." I don't think I had doubted it for a long time and that realization was just as shocking.

Strong arms wrapped around my waist, and Cannon pulled me into his body. "It's a lot to take in, I know."

"She told you all this?" I asked, not masking the hurt that I felt that my wolf, *my* wolf, would talk to Cannon about things she never mentioned to me.

"This isn't the first time I have spoken to her, remember." His breath stirred my hair. "You need to hear more," he told me, his arms tightening around me. "Can you handle it today?"

Tilting my head up, I met his gaze. "I don't know."

Cannon dropped his head to mine, his lips brushing mine. "You're strong, and I'm right here."

"You did a lot in the five days I was out. Getting Kris and the shaman here...what else did you do? More tests?" The accusation was clear.

"No," he assured me. "But I do need your shaman."

Moving closer, I pressed my forehead into his chest. "I'm scared what else you have to say."

"I'm right here, with you," Cannon said again, arms holding me securely.

"I'm twenty-three?" I asked, looking up at him.

Cannon grimaced. "I'm sorry." A sly smile played about his lips. "Royce will be happy I'm no longer corrupting a teenager."

Smacking him in the chest, I pulled back with a sigh. "I'm a twenty-three-year-old virgin?" I wailed. "Luna, I am *never* living this down with Cass."

I saw Kris come around the side of the alcove with a scowl. "You dragged us out here, Cannon. Finish this."

Cannon turned to go back to the others, but I tugged at his hand, causing him to look back over his shoulder. Closing the distance, I reached up on tiptoes and kissed him lightly.

"Thank you," I whispered against his lips.

He drew back slightly, green eyes searching mine. "What for?"

"For making sure I had my family with me when you told me."

Cannon brushed my cheek with his thumb. He looked like he was going to speak, but instead, he gave a small nod and turned to return to the others. With a deep breath, I followed him back with my stomach in knots at what else he had to tell us.

I only hoped it wasn't worse than what he'd already shared.

CHAPTER 18

Kezia

As I sank onto the grass across from my brother and the shaman, I didn't realize how close I had chosen to sit beside Cannon until I literally knocked elbows with him.

"Sit on his lap, why don't you," Kris grumbled, and I flipped him the finger in response.

"You would prefer Landon?" Cannon asked quietly. When I looked at him, I recognized he was serious, and it struck me then that while he was my mate, he had not only gained me for his mate, but he had also gained Kris. Worriedly I looked at my brother, who seemed to have reached that understanding long before me.

"No. It's bad enough he's *my* mate's brother." Kris cricked his neck from side to side, a sign he was uncomfortable. "But I can't say I'm overjoyed at you either."

"We're still trying to break it," I blurted, ignoring the sharp stab of panic I felt at the thought. "Remember?"

"Are we?" Cannon looked at me with a raised eyebrow. "Maybe at one point, but are we still?"

"We're not?" Had they changed the script? I no longer knew

188

what was happening. I glanced at Kris, who was avoiding making eye contact. "You told me distance helped?" I accused the shaman.

"From revealing too much to your enemy," he answered simply. "Breaking the actual mating bond? I think death is the only way to break it."

My jaw slackened as I regarded him. "You sent me away to break it!"

"No, I sent you away from the Anterrio Pack," he corrected. "You are not safe there, child, you never were."

"Yet you let her stay there," Cannon spoke softly. "Knowing they would never accept her."

The shaman turned his head to face the alpha at my side. "And what would you have me do, Alpha? Turn two powerful children into the wild for the elements or rogues to take them? Luna sent a strong alpha male to me, and his equally gifted sister. I have served my pack and both Kris and Kezia since the day Bale took them in. I have protected them both, and now I am here, protecting them still. I didn't need the pack to *accept* her, I just needed them to keep her, keep them both, close."

"Why?" My voice was a whisper as my whole entire being felt like I was receiving blow after blow.

"The spirit inside you." Cannon rubbed his forehead. "Your wolf spirit is not separate from you, Kezia. Have you ever spoken to anyone about their wolves?"

"Yes," I scoffed. "I'm a shifter, we talk about our wolves all the time."

"Do we?" Cannon looked at Kris. "Do you?" My brother shook his head. "Why is that?" he asked him, and when Kris didn't answer, Cannon turned back to me. "Because when we are in our wolf form, we are not as aware as we are as humans. We *shift*, Kezia, into wolves. We *become* the wolf."

"I know."

"But you *don't* know," he said with frustration. "For you, it is always you *and* her. It is never you or your wolf. How many times have you been lost, pup? How many times have you shifted and never known and have no memory of it?"

"He's right," Kris said grudgingly. "I'm me, or I'm my wolf. I'm never separate. My thoughts are my thoughts in this form or wolf form. My wolf does not talk to me like yours does," he added gently. "Because he is not separate from me. I carry the spirit and the power from the magic of Luna to shift, but whatever I am thinking, it's me. As man or wolf, it's always me."

Frowning, I considered all of them, even the quiet shaman. Three males of varying ages. Two alphas and a shaman, three powerful males. All I would trust with my life, even Cannon. That startled me but was something to dissect another day.

None of them had a reason to lie to me.

"You don't talk to them?" I asked uncertainly.

"Not really," Cannon answered firmly, but I was watching my brother who shook his head sadly. "But you know I speak to her." Rising to my feet, I looked across at Kris as I started to pace. "You were the one who named her!"

Cannon turned his attention to Kris. "Named her or were told her name?"

Kris swallowed. "She told me her name."

"How many times have you spoken to her?" Cannon asked Kris while I stood against the wall, my fists curled at my sides as I tried to process.

"A handful." Kris stood too. He liked to move when he was thinking, a trait we both shared. "I don't believe you about the four-year missing gap," he added bluntly. "But"—his head dipped —"I do agree I am probably older than I thought. Some of the things don't make sense. Some do. I don't recall much after our parents were killed. Kezia was stuck in her wolf form. I could talk to her while she was a wolf. I know now that was an alpha ability."

"Very young." Cannon's voice held respect. "You will be very powerful when you are done with your training," he told him, admiration lacing his tone.

"Yeah." Kris rubbed the back of his neck, uncomfortable with the praise. "But I couldn't make my sister shift back, no matter how much I pleaded. Kezia was a child, her speech limited, then one day, a voice, not my sister's, spoke to me."

"She guided you to the Anterrio Pack?" Cannon guessed.

"She did."

"She told me there was pain with the imposter," Cannon said carefully. "Bale as pack leader cannot force a shift."

"A pack can," the shaman interrupted. "A pack leader has power from his pack. He can pull energy from them if they allow."

"And if they don't allow?" I asked warily.

"It hurts."

Staring at the ground, I closed my eyes briefly. "Now I know why they hate me so much. I caused them pain." I could hear the bitterness of my voice as I spoke.

"A long time ago," Cannon reminded me. "The truth is they're just dicks."

That made me smile and I looked up gratefully. "So, Bale can make us do what he wants if he uses the pack?"

Kris nodded. "Everyone but us," he confirmed. "And the shaman, obviously."

"Obviously?" I muttered. "There is nothing *obvious* about any of this to me."

"He didn't get you to shift," Kris said hurriedly, looking

guilty. "I did." Even Cannon looked surprised at that. "I mean, I didn't command it, but I knew the pack were hurting, and I knew he couldn't be an alpha. Dad had told me about alphas, and I knew..." He cleared his throat. "I knew Pack Leader Bale wasn't one. You were in pain. Whimpering. I can still see you lying on the ground, your back legs kicking as you struggled." He was pale as he recalled that day, and I felt a little of my resentment ease. "I hated that you were in pain, so I asked her to let you shift. She fought it, but...eventually, she listened. Then Bale used the pack to keep you in human form until you stuck in one form and wouldn't shift back."

There was silence for a long moment, but as I pushed myself away from the rock face, I met my brother's stare. "What did you promise her?" If possible, he got paler. "I know her, remember. She's spoken to me almost every day of my life. She likes to bargain." I refused to look at Cannon. "What did you promise her?"

"A secret." Kris sighed. "I promised to keep it a secret from you that your wolf was different."

"But her wolf *isn't* different," Cannon spoke into the silence that followed. "Kezia's wolf is like every other wolf spirit, but it's the *other* spirit that lives within her, *that's* the problem."

"*Other* spirit," I muttered bitterly.

"A passenger within your soul," the shaman spoke for the first time in a while. "There are many legends of them. A guardian of sorts, they can be good, evil, both, or neither." His hands rubbed together as if he were cold. "I do not think she means you harm. I think she protects you, but I also think, in doing so, she will in time harm you."

"She has always protected her," Kris argued. He looked

worriedly between the two of them. "Why would she harm her now?"

"She wants her body," Cannon spoke bluntly. "Each time she takes over, Kezia takes longer to come back. When Kezia shifts to her white wolf, she is like any other shifter. But when the other spirit takes over, Kezia struggles more and more to come back." He turned to the shaman. "Did you know she could do magic?"

"I can?"

"No, *you* can't," Cannon clarified, not breaking his gaze from the shaman. "She created a ball of light. Her strength is like nothing I've ever seen. She bent bars of steel like they were made of paper."

"How did you get her to give control back?" Kris asked as he paced.

"My Will."

Kris nodded. "I started using it more as she got older," he confirmed. "When I let Kezia escape, I knew there was the chance she'd be gone forever."

"*Kris!*"

He looked at me and shook his head. "A *chance*, Kezia, I said a chance. But as I told you that day, you are strong. So fucking strong, little sister, I knew you'd make a fight of it."

"Where is she now?" the shaman asked curiously.

"She isn't here," I confirmed. "I haven't felt her since I woke. We ran here as wolves, and I assumed the quietness was because my wolf was happy being out of bed and in the fresh air."

"And does she stay gone long?" the shaman asked me.

"A few days, sometimes more. Longer with Cannon some-times." Tilting my head back, I stared at the sky. "A passenger." *What the actual fuck?* "I thought she was my wolf." But as I said it, I thought about it, and I knew deep down that I had perhaps always known she was different. My beautiful white wolf never spoke to me. When we ran, we ran together, there was a shared awareness. Moonstar was very much a separate awareness.

"I'm sorry."

Lowering my chin, I looked at my brother. "You should be. It shouldn't be a male from another pack that tells me this." Glaring at Kris and the shaman, I felt my anger boiling over. "She wants to bodyjack me for fuck's sake! You couldn't warm me? Say to me that I was a complete freak show!"

"You are *not* a freak show," Cannon corrected me. "You're unique."

"Well, I don't want to be unique," I protested, frustration making my tone sharp. "How do we get her out of me?"

"First we need to know how she got in," the shaman said carefully.

Cannon stood, walking over to me. He took me by the elbow and led me back to the small circle we had formed. "Sit, we have much more to talk about," he told me quietly. Unresisting, I sat beside him, my hand taking a firm hold of his. "All these months, I've longed for you to stop talking, and now I wish I could hear you screeching," he joked lightly.

"Give me time," I muttered. "It'll come," I warned. The slight squeeze of my fingers took most of the heat out of me.

"I've been researching," Cannon told the shaman. "There is a shit ton of information out there, not a lot about spirits. Well, that's not true, not a lot about spirits who possess shifters. Because we aren't real to humans. Or we shouldn't be. But Norse, Celtic, Native American, and many other cultures all have their form of mythology. The nearest I can narrow it down to is either the Norse *vǫrðr*, a warden spirit, or Garmr, said to be a dog or maybe wolf guardian of the Goddess Hel's gate." He took a deep breath. "Even the Ireland myth of the *Faoladh*, which can allegedly shift into a wolf and is said to be a guardian or protector of sorts to others."

"Guardian," Kris murmured. "All three you've mentioned are guardians?"

"Yes." Cannon was nodding. "Their parents were murdered," he spoke to the shaman. "A traumatic event for anyone to witness, not to mention two gifted children. Alphas are powerful, we know this, but a child shifting so young? Gifted children are strongly tied to Luna. Their pain and fear would have been a strong beacon to any nearby spirit."

"We are always surrounded by spirits." The shaman was nodding thoughtfully.

"And when the ones that killed their parents were done, they'd have come hunting for their children." Cannon let my hand go when I tugged it free. "Two bullets in the back of the head would have done the job. Should have done the job," he corrected himself.

"And a wolf pup is more enticing than a young boy for a passing spirit," the shaman murmured.

"I think so," Cannon confirmed. "Whatever spirit is in Kezia, I believe it is, or was, a guardian. She protected her by ensuring she lived. When I shot Kezia with the silver bullet," Cannon spoke quickly, ignoring Kris's angry growl, "she told Kezia the silver binds. It slowed her down, it prevented her from shifting to heal, but she did not die, and more importantly, she did not shift."

"That's more important than the fact I didn't die?" I asked him incredulously.

"Don't be dramatic." Cannon waved my protestation away carelessly as he focused on the shaman. "Obviously, I can't shoot anyone else with silver to test it, but I think"—he paused—"no, I know, that any other shifter, they'd be dead. Because Kezia has the spirit inside her, it is her magic that makes her immune to the silver."

"Am I not another shifter?" Kris asked him. "I was also shot, you claim. Why am I alive?"

"Because you're Kezia's brother," the shaman spoke slowly as he thought about it. "If the alpha is correct, then when the spirit entered Kezia, she would have known only three bonds. The bond to each parent, and the bond to her brother. You. Two bonds were severed, meaning she only had you left."

Cannon was nodding quickly in agreement. "And when the spirit takes over Kezia's body, Kezia is weak afterward, or she takes a long time to recover. I had a conversation with the spirit that lasted no more than a few minutes, and Kezia took five days to regain consciousness." He looked at me. "You are strong, no one can deny that, but as a child? You would have been weak, plus you were dying."

"Which is why it took four years for us to recover?" Kris asked slowly, looking at me with wide eyes. "Whatever she did to Kezia to keep her alive, the familial bond in turn kept me alive as well?"

"I think so," Cannon told him.

"Is it why my hair is white?" When they both looked at me in varying degrees of confusion, I shrugged. "What? It's a valid question."

"It's a *vain* question," Kris scolded me. He pointed at his brown hair. "I don't have white hair."

"Your hair is silver, not white," Cannon mused before turning to Kris. "You confirmed you have the same scar as Kezia, which would suggest you were also shot with a silver bullet—"

"Or," the shaman interrupted, "he wasn't but was too young to shift to heal. With the exemption from Kezia, we don't usually shift so easily as children. Kris would have a scar because he wouldn't have been able to shift to heal until he was older."

I felt sick. It was all so much to take in, and confusing, and I had so many questions. I wanted my wolf to come forward. And then I remembered she wasn't my wolf.

She was a *passenger*.

I felt a little bit violated.

"Why would Kezia be the one to be shot with silver?" Kris asked them both.

"I used two bullets when I shot her," Cannon spoke candidly, ignoring my brother's anger. "If they shot your parents with silver too, then maybe it's as simple as there were only three bullets in the gun that were silver. The wolf pup was shot first and then the child. They may not have known she even *was* a shifter." He sighed. "But I don't know, it's all guessing, trying to figure out a puzzle, with pieces missing."

"Which leads us back to who shot us?" Kris sighed with frustration. Cannon grunted in agreement.

"Wait, all this, and you don't *know*?" I demanded, looking between them both.

"Well, I thought it was him, or his pack," Kris said defensively. "I mean, it still could be? Why *have* you got my father's buckle?"

"It was no one in my pack," Cannon growled. "The buckle? The wolf head?" When Kris nodded, Cannon turned to the shaman. "It was a gift I received with the invitation for the Luna Ball."

"A gift?" Kris demanded. "From who?"

"Me," the shaman answered simply.

CHAPTER 19
Cannon

I watched both siblings as they turned to look at their shaman.

"Why did you have dads buckle?" Kris demanded.

"Because I did," the shaman explained. "I found it a long time ago," he told them. "I woke one morning, Luna's presence all around me, and my wolf went for a run. We ran far from the packlands, something I don't do when I have no other to see for me. But Luna was my eyes that day, and when I stopped to rest, there was a buckle half buried in the dirt." His almost sightless gaze settled on the older of the siblings. "I knew I was to take it. I don't know why." The old male's head turned with eerie accuracy to look right at me. "When I heard Blackridge Peak had finally removed the curse of Rek from these mountains, I remembered the fierce wolf on a belt buckle I'd picked up years ago. I thought it meant nothing. I never knew it meant what it did."

"It was all for nothing?" Kezia asked, moving towards her brother. "I ran for no reason? I killed those men for nothing—"

"No!" I watched him grab her arm, giving her a firm shake.

"You will never feel guilt for that! They hurt you, they were going to do far worse to you than you ever did to them."

I wasn't so sure about that, but I agreed they needed to die. Especially after I knew it was so much more than she remembered.

"He's right." I watched her whirl around to face me in surprise. "They deserved to die."

"You have given me absolute hell over this. You do not get to change your mind without telling me why!"

"I gave you hell, as you put it, over the illegal fighting. You are not human, pup. Especially now we know how much more of you there is," I added. "When I spoke to her"—I wet my lips—"she implied the damage they did to you, the pain they caused, was more than you remember." Seeing her whiten and her eyes widen in horror, I rose quickly to my feet, crossing the distance to her. "They didn't," I assured her softly. "You're still—"

Her brother cleared his throat, and Kezia rolled her eyes. "A virgin," she said loudly. "Luna's grace, Kris, don't be such a prude. I've spoken with Cass. She told me all the kinky shit you've been doing. Don't be a hypocrite."

Turning my head, I tried to hide my laughter as Kezia just blurted out what everyone was thinking, as usual. Nothing fazed her.

My mate looked up at me, a small smile on her lips. "So, I'm still..." I nodded. "And you're my mate..." I nodded again, pulling her closer. "And you don't want us to..." I shook my head and was rewarded with a rush of heat to her cheeks. "Oh." She was trying to hide it, but her smile broke free.

"Later," I promised her. Dipping my head, I brushed my lips across her cheek. Turning back to the others, I pulled Kezia down with me as I sat back on the grass. "How do we get her out?"

The shaman was shaking his head. "I don't know, I've never heard of anything like this." He was frowning as he thought. "The Pack Council may help?"

"They will help put me in jail," Kezia muttered.

"We can explain it all," Kris assured her.

"The fighting is a breach of pack law," I reminded them. "She did that willingly. There will be repercussions, but we know we can explain away the savage murder."

"Savage?" Kezia's elbow dug into my ribs.

"You weren't really there," I reminded her. "Trust me, from what I found afterward, it was brutal."

"We also need to know who covered it up?" Kris spoke up. "If it was the Pack Council, then they would already be here for her."

"Agreed," the shaman said. "Who else would it have been?"

With a look at Kezia, I let out a breath. "Kezia had a *friend* in the human lands." Pushing down the jealousy, I still found myself reaching out and pulling my mate closer. "Although somewhere in between her meeting him and now, he became an enemy. When we took him, he had silver bullets in his gun."

"What do you mean, you took him?" Kris asked in alarm.

"He was a threat to your sister." I ignored her scoff beside me.

"Is he alive?" the shaman asked me.

Ignoring the attention of my mate, I nodded. "I have him at a secure location."

Kezia leaned forward. "You still have Vance at the pack?" she asked. "I want to see him!"

"Never."

"Cannon! It's only right that I get to ask him *why*?"

"I can tell you why, greed."

"But he kissed me!"

The small clearing went utterly silent, and I gave my mate a flat look. "I am very well aware of what you and *Vance* were doing the night I found you, Kezia."

Kezia kept her head averted, and I saw her flinch when her brother spoke. "A *human*?"

"Shut up," she mumbled, embarrassment flooding her scent.

"An interesting ploy," the shaman mused. "Gain her trust by protecting her, add in being attracted to her, to make her even more vulnerable to the betrayal."

"*Her* is still right here," Kezia grumbled.

"A human?" Kris asked again.

"I was curious," Kezia snapped. "I had a lot going on."

"Curious about what?"

Maybe I could learn to like her brother, after all. I sat back a little as he asked her the questions I was eager to know the answers to myself.

Kezia's eyes flicked to me once. "I'd learned Cannon was my mate, then Landon said *he* was my mate, and I've only ever been kissed by them. It was different with them. With one, I felt nothing, and with the other, I felt too much...I just wanted to know what *normal* felt like."

Her face was the color of a fire truck, and while it pleased me to know that she felt too much when I was with her, I felt a twinge of sympathy as she was forced to explain her experience to her brother, her mate, and the old male who had practically raised her.

"But a human?"

Kris wasn't moving on, and I wondered if the siblings realized they had more in common than they both accepted.

"I think we've exhausted this," I spoke in Kezia's defense, seeing the old shaman's lips twitch. "The point is, you won't be kissing anyone else, will you?" The gleam of defiance in her eyes as she looked at me made me want to strip her bare and claim her right here in the open. "Pup," I warned and fought back a laugh when she looked away from me with a small smile.

Her brother huffed and made himself comfortable once more on the ground. "This man is still alive?" I nodded and he looked at me shrewdly. "Can he still speak?"

I grinned. "His jaw is healing."

"Did he know of the coverup?" Kezia asked me eagerly. "What has he told you?"

"That you were the first shifter he met. He saw more of you than he should the night I found you." I reminded her of the night she shifted at the side of his house. "He knew you had killed his friends."

"They weren't his friends."

"Okay, you killed his *acquaintances*." I held her stare, relishing in her eagerness to know more but also defend her point. When I leaned back, she rolled her eyes, her hand waving me on to speak. "I can continue?"

"Fine."

"You sure?"

"Ugh, you're insufferable."

"So, there is a witness that Kezia shifted in front of someone who is not pack?" Kris asked me, his tone pensive.

"Yes." I looked around the small circle. "But he is unlikely to ever be heard by our Pack Council."

"Why is that?" the shaman asked me, and I didn't want to admit the truth to him. "You will kill him before then?"

"Yes." Then again, I'd never been one to shy from the truth.

"Good. Make him suffer a little," the shaman added. "Kezia is very dear to me. I dislike any duplicity when it comes to her."

Kezia got up on her knees and leaned forward, hugging the

older male tightly. "Thank you for always believing in me," she told him. "You never needed to know if I spoke the truth with a test." I saw her brother flush this time. "You always let me skip fish night in the canteen, you've listened to every tantrum I've ever had." She rocked back on her heels. "Which is why I cannot understand why you kept this from me."

"To protect you until you could protect yourself." He raised his head to look straight at me. "Or have someone at your side who cared more about you than I did." He sniffed delicately. "I knew he would be a rare find."

You did not call me for this, though, Alpha. Tell me what you seek.

You grant me a great honor, shaman.

I hadn't expected him to mindlink with me. I did not have a shaman in my pack. We had Doc, who could fix ailments that shifting may not. Shifters were resistant to most human illnesses but not immune. Viruses, we could not catch, but sicknesses that targeted our organs left us vulnerable.

The older packs expected dying wolves to leave the pack and die in peace.

What they meant was to die alone.

I would not let my pack, any of my pack, spend their last days in agony and alone. There were human medicines that Doc was adapting or trying to, to ensure my pack had better chances. He experimented a lot, but he had made progress.

But a shaman...a shaman was a direct link to the Goddess.

You wish to know if I have sought answers regarding the possession?

I don't want to know if, I want to know when you sought answers, what did you find?

"Luna has not answered me," he spoke out loud for the benefit of the others.

I sucked my teeth as I thought of the problem. "Ask again?"

The shaman laughed. "It is not like one of these electronic phones that are carried in pockets," he said with more bite than I expected. "I am Luna's vessel on earth. I do not have a hotline to her."

"Get one."

"Cannon," Kezia scolded. "Don't be so disrespectful."

"You have a rogue spirit who wishes to take over your body completely," I bit back. "She's getting stronger, pup. I think it's time to be disrespectful." I watched her as her eyes narrowed, ready to argue, and I caught her chin, my thumb stroking her jaw. "You haven't spoken to her like I have," I reminded her. She still looked like she wanted to argue, and then I saw her resigned acceptance.

"I understand you want to fight," she whispered. "But you can still be polite."

I wanted to kiss that smart mouth of hers, but instead, I let her go, sitting back once more, fighting the constant pull toward her.

"I will seek answers," the shaman spoke, pulling me out of my thoughts of Kezia. "Sacrifices will be needed."

"I'll kill whatever you need," Kris said fiercely.

Yeah, I could definitely grow to like him.

"We also need to stall the Pack Council," I said. "On the assumption you have called for them?"

"We did," Kris confirmed with an apologetic look at his sister. "Landon was quite vocal in his demands, and as pack leader, Bale had no reason not to." He looked as pissed off as I felt. "While

Landon keeps the claim you are his mate going, it's hard to deny him without outing you both."

"Or you." I saw his grimace. "Hard to tell a pack that's known you for so long that you are an alpha. Some will call you a liar. Some will feel betrayed. Some will remain loyal to their pack leader."

"I know," Kris told me evenly. "What's your point?"

"My point is that you need to make your move at some point if you want to *be* an alpha. A *true* alpha. If you want a pack of your own, for you, for your mate, for your children."

"For my sister."

"Your sister stays with me." I ignored her outraged gasp beside me. "As your mate will stay with you, or are you planning on letting her go?"

"Cass is everything."

"I'm sure she is." I held his stare until the shaman struggled to his feet. Kezia leapt to help him, and I slowly stood too. "I need all the help you can give me, shaman," I told the old man. "She needs to be free."

When the shaman held his hand out, I didn't hesitate. I didn't wince when he made the cut or when his tongue darted out and licked my blood. The shaman's head jerked back as he tasted me.

"Your rage rides you too much, Alpha." His tone was full of reproach. "You should be careful with that temper."

A warning? "I find a good fight works out most of my aggression."

"Pup." The shaman held his hand out to Kezia, who gave him her hand wordlessly. My wolf did not appreciate another's tongue on my mate's body, and I let the low growl out so *both* males could remember whose mate she was. "Your heat is complete," he told her with a smile. "Your wolf enjoyed stretching her legs today," he added gently. "I can taste the sense of freedom you felt."

Kezia stepped into the older male's space and wordlessly hugged him. Her voice was too low for even my hearing, but I heard the shaman's chuckle.

As she said goodbye to her brother, I stepped back, giving her the space for her farewells. I felt a thrill of satisfaction when she moved backward into me, seeking my presence and maybe my comfort.

Both Kris and the shaman chose to walk away. I wondered why they didn't shift but held my tongue. When she could no longer see them, Kezia turned into me, and automatically my arms encircled her.

"You did a lot when I was out of it," she muttered against my shirt.

"I've been doing *a lot* since I spoke to her the first time," I admitted. Looking down at her upturned face, I dipped my head and caught her lips with my own. The kiss was slow and leisurely, which was unlike us, and I found myself enjoying the slower pace.

When we parted, her cheeks were flushed, her eyes bright and her lips swollen. She looked stunning.

"And he said my heat was past," Kezia joked, hiding her vulnerability with humor.

"You feel too much with me?" I asked.

"I feel everything," she admitted freely. "It's scary."

Pushing her hair behind her ear, I searched her face, eager for the truth. "If we could break the mate bond, would you want it?"

Kezia frowned, moving back, putting distance between us. "The shaman said only death..."

"I have a doctor in the pack," I reminded her truthfully. "I don't want to lie to you. We think Doc can break it."

Kezia gulped loudly. "Oh." She wouldn't look at me. "I...I guess? I don't know. Do you?"

"There's a part of me that wonders if what attracts us to each other is a bond of blood and the Goddess Luna, which we have no control over. I wonder if we were free to choose, would we still choose each other?"

Kezia shrugged, looking down the mountain. "I don't think we would ever pick each other freely."

"Don't you?" Her quick look caused me to smile. Reaching out, I pulled her back to me. "Your heat has passed. You don't want to kill me right now. You are free of any other influence. We're almost as friendly towards each other as anyone can be." I'd moved us both so she was against the rock. My lips brushed hers as I spoke. "Tell me what you think."

Our kiss was sure, confident. Kezia kissed me back with equal passion. Her tongue stroked mine, her hands curled around my neck as I took the kiss deeper. My hands skimmed down her sides, round to her ass. Kissing along her jawline, I loved her small moan.

"Still not sure, Kezia?" I whispered, my nose skimming across her cheek as I kissed her mouth again. It was my turn to groan in pleasure when I felt her hands against my skin, lifting my shirt up, and then she was pushing me away. "Kezia?"

The woman in front of me undid me with her next words. "I want you. Now."

"What are you saying?"

"Fuck me. Right now. I need you."

CHAPTER 20

Kezia

CANNON TOOK A STEP BACK FROM ME, AND I STOPPED myself from reaching out to grab him. Pull him closer. Biting the inside of my cheek, I watched him warily as he took another step back.

"You're going the wrong way," I joked. "I think you need to be closer, right? To do this?"

"You want me to fuck you here and now?" Green eyes full of heat and passion watched me. The only emotion on his face was in his eyes as he watched me doubt myself. With a snort, Cannon looked away from me. "That's what I thought."

Turning, he walked away from me.

"Yes!" My heart was beating out of my chest. Dear Luna, what was happening right now? Rubbing my chest, hoping to ease my racing heart, I took a step towards him, and Cannon didn't move. "I do." Swallowing hard, I reached for him tentatively. "We've been skirting around it. You want me, I know you do." Pointing over my shoulder, I gestured to the rock face he'd just held me against. "You said you were sure..." Forcing myself to remain calm, I watched him watch me. "But you doubt me. You doubt that I'm sure, right?"

Cannon moved a few steps toward me. "Kezia..."

"Were you testing me?" I asked quietly. "Did you think I would run screaming?" I waved my hands by my face like a woman panicking as I rolled my eyes.

He snorted out a laugh at my teasing tone. "I didn't expect you to say...what you said," he admitted. He looked like he was struggling to find the right words. "Confirmation that you felt the attraction too, without your heat riding your senses, was what I was seeking. Not an invite to lie down and fuck you."

"Oh." My throat was so dry. He looked like a god standing there. His dark hair, chiseled features, and deep green eyes saw past every defense I had and saw everything that I tried to hide.

I didn't need a heat to know I was attracted to him. I didn't need a mate bond to *want* him. My nerves were strung too tight, but I knew what I desired. "Who said anything about lying down?"

The distance between us was closed quickly, and he was in front of me, his nostrils flared once, no doubt scenting my need. Cannon's hand rested lightly between my breasts, and with a gentle push, he walked me back a few paces to the rock face once more. He surrounded me. With the warmth radiating from him and just his sheer size, it was as if I was enclosed. Once more in a cage with him, but this confinement I didn't want free from.

"Cannon?"

The alpha moved even closer to me. There was no part of my body I couldn't feel him touching. My breath was coming in ragged gasps, my heart was thumping, and I knew I needed to calm down because the last thing I wanted was for him to think I was scared.

Cannon's head lowered, and his hand cupped my face, the other above me, his palm flat against the rock, holding his body slightly from mine. He tilted my head so he could speak in my ear.

"Do you want me to fuck you, Kezia?" he asked me, his tone low, the need in his voice evident. "Here? Now?" A sharp bite to my earlobe made me jump, and his dark chuckle did something wicked inside me. "You want it right now, don't you?" He drew back a little, his eyes searching mine for any doubts.

"I do."

His lips were just out of reach—if I stretched, I could reach him—but the way the alpha was looking at me held me in place, and I suddenly realized Cannon was holding onto his control as much as I was.

Maybe more.

The feeling empowered me. Any nerves I had left were gone. The alpha wanted me, and he was scared to let go. Reaching out, I caught his belt and pulled him impossibly closer so that he was pinning me in place. Keeping eye contact, I slipped my hand under his shirt and let my fingers stroke lightly over his abs. The ridged bumps made my fingers dip into the grooves of his body as I relished the feel of the smooth hard muscle beneath my touch.

Suddenly, his hand flattened over mine, stopping my upward journey, the shirt material the only thing that separated us.

His mouth moved to mine, almost touching, but not quite. He was so close to me that I could almost taste him. I yearned to taste him.

"We do this," he whispered, his lips against mine, "we could seal the bond."

We could?

"But I'm not in heat."

"But you *are* my mate."

We could seal the bond. We could be stuck with each other, for the rest of our lives. Wolves lived long fucking lives. I would be his and he would be mine.

Forever.

Shit.

Cannon held my stare, and all I could feel was our beating hearts, hammering in our chests, and I knew it didn't matter. He was as far gone as I was.

"This isn't a trick?" I asked him stupidly. "To bond me to you?"

"You're already mine, pup."

My tummy flipped over itself.

His tongue flicked out to wet his bottom lip, and I followed the movement before raising my eyes to meet his.

I don't know who moved first. Me or him. Cannon's hands were on me, pulling at my clothes as I tugged at his with equal desperation. He leaned back, his shirt pulled up and discarded to the side, and then he was pressing me back against the hard rock.

Hands cupped my ass, and he lifted me off the ground, my legs wrapping around his waist in a move that was becoming familiar to us both. How many times had we been in this position now? Him taking over and me hitched around his hips, urging him to take control. I felt his cock press against me, right where I needed to feel him, and his hips ground against me once, causing my nails to dig into his smooth taut back.

He drew back again, hooded eyes searching mine, checking I was okay. I was more than okay. Heat raced through my veins but not the heat I was used to. The uncontrollable desire that rode my sense of self wasn't there.

I was in control. Cannon's mouth moved over my neck.

Fuck. I was not in control.

Not at all.

But this wasn't the same heat as before. The mindless need to be consumed by him.

This was much worse.

This was desire.

Longing.

His mouth covered mine and I kissed him back as he took ownership of my mouth. My fingers curled into his thick dark hair, and I felt his hands at my waist, pulling at my leggings. Cannon stepped back to allow room for my legs to unhook from his waist, and he watched as I hastily pushed my leggings down, stepping out of them, kicking them out of the way.

His gaze flicked between my panties and my eyes once before the alpha gripped the material and tugged them free. The sting of pain as the material was ripped from me was gone the second he cupped me, his finger sliding over my wetness.

"Fuck," he hissed against my mouth.

Tilting my head back, I groaned when his large finger slipped inside as his thumb circled my clit once, causing me to whimper.

His jeans were rough against my skin, and I wanted them gone. Popping open his button, I popped the others free, my hand sliding in the opening, finding him bare and harder than the rock behind me.

Teeth bit my shoulder as I took hold of him and pulled him out. "Kezia," he mumbled as I began to slowly work his length. The longing in his voice caused me to squeeze him slightly, and he jerked his hips forward, making my hand move quicker.

"You want me to move faster?" I whispered against his shoulder. I didn't wait for an answer, picking up speed and then slowing down.

"Fuck!" Cannon grabbed my hips suddenly, breaking free

from my grasp and dropping to his knees. His mouth was on me. Licking and sucking, he worked two fingers inside me, hearing me gasp as I felt a stretch while he worked his tongue over me.

My hands were once more in his hair, holding his head to my body as he coaxed me towards an orgasm.

"Cannon..." My grip got tighter, and then I was screaming out his name as my body released waves of pleasure as I hit the peak.

Cannon moved up my body slowly, soft kisses peppered my skin, little teasing nips and bites of my flesh until his mouth was once more kissing me, letting me taste myself on his lips, while fingers stroked soothing circles between my legs.

"I need to fuck you," he spoke against my lips. "I need inside you. Tell me if you don't want it."

My eyes flew open as he pulled away slightly. I saw the raw hunger and I felt his desire in every cell of my body. "Don't stop now," I panted, pulling him closer by tightening my legs around him. "Not when it's getting good."

Cannon smiled against my mouth. "*Getting* good? It wasn't *already* good?"

"Meh," I teased, suddenly gasping when I felt the head of his cock at my entrance. "Cannon?" I heard the quiver of my voice.

"I'll take it slow," he assured me. "Yes?"

My body had tensed though. I'd never had sex, but I knew it could hurt, and Cannon was big and thick, and I had a sudden irrational thought that he wouldn't fit. Deft fingers dipped inside me, stroking, stretching, curling inwards at a spot that made me moan.

"Kezia?"

"I want you." My hips were rolling against his hand. "I want to feel you." I bit his neck, my tongue moving against his artery, feeling his pulse racing like my heart. "Please, don't stop."

The stretch wasn't the same as his fingers; it burned more than a little, but our simultaneous groans echoed around us as he slid inside me slowly. Inch by inch, he took me, his breathing shallow while my panting got louder.

"Fucking hell, Kezia." His head was buried in the crook of my neck. "*Fucking hell*," he repeated as he held still, his grip on my ass tightening. "You okay?"

I felt like I'd been impaled but in the best possible way as my body stretched around his cock. Cannon began to move slowly, and I was pretty sure my brain shut down as fireworks of pleasure set off all over my body. I couldn't focus on anything, pleasure was everywhere, even the stinging stretch as my body adjusted to the feel of all of him, paled into insignificance as I felt my whole being *come alive*.

"Luna," I groaned. "Holy Goddess, I never knew it could be this." I breathed him in as he moved slightly faster, my hands curling around his forearms, holding on and pulling him tighter towards me, feeling myself take more of him.

"Okay?" Cannon asked me, his voice deep and gruff, and somehow that made me want even more of him. Widening my legs more, I felt him reach deeper, and both of us moaned in appreciation.

"More than okay," I told him, my mouth taking his.

Everywhere was him. My sense of smell, touch, taste, everything. Cannon began to move faster, and I felt my body coil in anticipation. "Oh fuck."

My hips moved against his, and Cannon's hands gripped me tightly as he began to really drive into me.

"I can't hold on," I whimpered, and then my body spasmed as

I yelled out in the clearing when my orgasm exploded deep within me. My toes curled, my back arched, and my nails drew blood as I rode out my climax.

"*Fuck*!" Cannon thrust deep inside me, and with a groan and a curse, his body jerked inside me, reaching his own release.

With his forehead pressed against mine, we both panted, desperate to breathe.

"We need to do that again," I said breathlessly.

Cannon huffed out a laugh. "Yeah, we do. Soon."

Cannon moved back, pulling out of me, and I whimpered at the loss. He helped me stand on the ground, holding onto me when my shaking legs threatened to fold underneath me. Carefully he eased us both to the ground, curling around me as we regained our composure.

When we had recovered, he moved away from me, picked up his shirt off the ground, and handed it to me after helping me to my feet. "You can use this to clean up."

Taking it, I glanced down at his cock, about to ask him what he would use, but the words died on my tongue when I saw the trace of blood. A stark reminder I was no longer a virgin—as if I needed a reminder. My heart was still pounding within me from what we'd done.

Cannon looked down and then back up at me, moving towards me, reaching me, and folding me gently into his embrace. "It's natural," he soothed me. "Absolutely natural." He looked down at me. "You good?"

"Yeah." I shook my head to clear it. "I didn't expect to see it," I admitted and felt his lips as he pressed a kiss to my temple. I raised the T-shirt he gave me. "You want it first?" I asked, embarrassment flooding my cheeks.

"You go," he told me, moving away and picking up clothes. "We won't need these when we shift."

"We're heading back now?" Uncertainty hovering within me, as he got ready to leave.

He glanced at me. "You want to stay?" He looked around, then back at me, almost sheepishly. "We're quite exposed here." Cannon straightened as he watched me. "You sure you're okay?"

"Yup." I glanced at my naked body and the shirt in my hands. "Can you turn around?"

His grin was wicked, and my tummy flipped at the gleam in his eyes. "Don't tell me you're shy?" he teased. I liked this side of him. The playfulness.

"And if I was?" My smile widened as he caged me in once more.

"Then I'd need to rectify that," he told me, ducking down and kissing along my collarbone.

Smoothing my hands over his shoulders, I noticed the marks on his skin. "I think I marked you." Once more, embarrassment flushed my cheeks.

Cannon turned his head to look at the scratches on his skin. "They'll heal," he told me with a carefree shrug. His hand caught the nape of my neck, moving my head back to look up at him. "You want to stay here, or do you want to run and get back to the house?" His smile was wicked.

It wasn't even a question. "House."

"Me too." He kissed the tip of my nose. "Let's stretch our legs."

CHAPTER 21

Kezia

We had taken the long way back to the pack, or that's what it felt like. Cannon and I had run for hours, our wolves enjoying getting the time to spend time with each other. We hunted, played, and even relaxed.

Things were so much simpler when we were wolves.

It had been the perfect evening.

The two of us walked through the town, Cannon's huge black wolf imposing in size, but even in his wolf form, his pack called out greetings to him. Some even greeted me. It was nice.

It was the opposite of how I felt amongst the Anterrio Pack. The more time I spent away from them, the more I doubted that Anterrio was the pack I belonged to.

I wasn't sure how to tell my brother that I wanted to stay here.

The black wolf opened the back door to the alpha's home, and now I knew why his boot room was so big, because *he* was so big. Cannon shifted, uncoiling from a crouch, and my wolf sight appreciated the toned muscle as he stretched.

He half turned and I hurriedly shifted to human, alarmed he had just caught me checking him out. Again.

A white T-shirt was held out to me, and I slipped into it while he pulled on a pair of jeans.

"I keep clothes here," he explained as he buttoned his fly. "Not always sure who is going to be in the house, and although we're shifters, I don't flash too many of my pack too often."

"Makes sense." I tugged at the hem of the shirt, which reached mid-thigh. "In my pack, we must shift before we come back into town. Everyone has their own area where they keep spare clothes." I grinned. "Bit like a deposit box in a bank."

Cannon was frowning. "Your wolves aren't allowed in the town?"

"No." Shaking my head, I tried to untangle my hair from the mess I knew it would be. "Pack Leader Bale likes to keep our two natures separate. The town is for humans, the mountain is for the wolf."

Cannon didn't comment but I could see he didn't agree. I didn't either but there were many things that I didn't agree with in the Anterrio Pack. I'd been so grateful to be allowed to shift that I kept my opinion to myself about the when and the where.

"How do you feel about everything you learned today, now that you have had time to absorb it?" Cannon looked at me over his shoulder as he spoke. He was at the fridge, opening it. I heard him rummaging around, and I got sidetracked watching the muscles ripple on his back while he did the simple task of getting a plate of cold chicken legs from the fridge. "I hope you're speechless because you're checking me out and not because you want my dinner."

Startled, I met his amused smirk.

Reaching over, I took a leg from the plate and took a seat on a barstool. "It can't be both?"

The air suddenly grew heavy between us as the heat in his eyes grew. Placing the plate on the counter, he rounded the breakfast bar. Stepping between my legs, Cannon dropped his head and kissed me leisurely. It picked up in intensity quickly, and when his T-shirt was halfway off my body, the loud clearing of a throat made us spring apart.

"Alpha, Kezia," Royce greeted us, coming into the kitchen, pointedly ignoring me as Cannon pulled my shirt back down. "Productive trip?" he asked dryly. He saw the plate of chicken and helped himself.

"I'm older than you think." The information blurted out of me, and I watched as Royce hesitated mid-chew, his attention moving between Cannon and me.

"That'll be why it smells like sex in here." He took another bite of his food. "Was there anything useful uncovered?"

"Quite a bit," Cannon told him. He picked up a leg from the plate, nudging me to do the same with the one I'd discarded a few minutes before. "We'll discuss this in the study. I needed to eat first."

"I bet you did," Royce snarked, shaking his head, tossing the bones onto another plate.

"Beta." The soft tone of the alpha's voice held a warning, and after a deep exhale, Royce dipped his head slightly in acknowledgment. Cannon wiped his hands on a towel, passing it to me to do the same. When I had, he took my hand and helped me off the stool. "You should change before we discuss this with the others."

Looking down at my bare legs, I looked up at him. "Yeah, probably, I don't think this is somber-secret-meeting appropriate."

Cannon huffed out a laugh, exchanging an amused look with Royce. "It's not a secret meeting, it's just us, Nikan and probably Doc," he told me. "But no, that T-shirt isn't appropriate. Five minutes?"

"Make it ten, I want to shower." I was at the stairs, and they were going into the office when I hurried back to the kitchen and came back with a chicken leg for each hand. "Better."

"I have no idea where she puts all that food," Royce muttered as Cannon laughed at me while I ran up the stairs to my room.

I ate the legs quickly, wrapping the bones in tissue paper when I was done. In the bathroom, as I washed my hands, I studied myself. I didn't look different.

I'd had sex. Mind-blowing, toe-curling sex.

My shift to my wolf had eased the ache of my lower body, which I'd been a little disappointed with but also grateful for because Cannon's size was maybe a little ambitious for my first try.

Taking the shirt off, I snorted at my inner thoughts. First try? He was my mate, and he was my *only* try. Running the shower and waiting for it to heat, I quickly locked the bathroom door and then looked at myself all over. It was stupid and insecure, but as I studied myself in the mirror, I couldn't see why he'd be attracted to me. I wasn't ugly, I knew that, but I also wasn't curvy like Koda was.

My hips were narrow, and my breasts were small. Turning my leg inward, I noticed the curve of my thigh. Okay, I had nice legs. Maybe he was a leg man?

Thinking about our conversation before we'd had sex, he'd said it wasn't the mate bond that was pulling us together today, but what if it was? What if it was always the bond? Would he really want me if I was just another wolf in his pack?

The handle of the bathroom door turning and meeting resistance startled me.

A soft rap on the door, and then he spoke. "You okay? You didn't sneak down for more chicken, did you?" Wrapping myself in a towel, I opened the door, seeing his surprise that I wasn't showered. "What's wrong?"

"Nothing." My smile felt fake. "I'm daydreaming, sorry."

Cannon's eyes narrowed as he listened to me. "*Daydreaming*? And *sorry...*" Rubbing his jaw, he looked me over from top to bottom before he stepped inside the bathroom and closed the door behind him. "Two words I would never associate with you saying. Now tell me what's wrong."

"Do you feel different?"

He stared at me blankly. "No?"

"So, you think the bond isn't, you know, formed?"

"Do you think it is?"

"No?" Turning away from his scrutiny, I shrugged my shoulders. "I feel different," I admitted. "But I look the same."

Warm hands rubbed my shoulders. "It's natural to feel different," he assured me softly. "I don't feel different, but I feel good." Lips skimmed my neck. "*Really* good. Don't you?"

My insides were doing that nervous flipping sensation again. "Oh, well, yeah. I'm... Yes."

"Get showered." His hands left me, making me feel cold. "We've got people waiting downstairs, and if I stay in here much longer, they'll be waiting all night."

Turning, I caught his eyes as he made to leave, seeing that he was serious. He wanted me. Feeling sure of myself for perhaps the first time ever, I reached up and deliberately loosened the towel. Cannon watched it drop to the ground, and then slowly, so slowly, he moved his gaze over my body, and I felt it almost as if it were a caress.

"I'll be right out," I said as I watched him lick his lips.

The alpha flicked the lock on the door. "No. You won't."

~

LEO STOOD ACROSS FROM ME, and the longer I stood waiting, the quicker my patience was running out. We were in a large training room with several mats spread across the floor. On one side of the room hung four punching bags, and at the bottom of the space stood a bona fide fighting ring, but most of the room was open space with plenty of room to move and train lots of people at once. Another thing I liked about this room was the doors were open. There was no hiding the fact I was being trained.

I *genuinely* liked it here.

This room could be my favorite thing about this pack since coming here. Apart from the food hall. And the sex. It was maybe tied in place with the food hall. Sex was definitely on top for now. I felt a smug smirk and tried to ignore Leo's curious look when he saw it.

I'd had a late night. Neither Cannon nor I had made it back down to the study yesterday, and at some point—I *really* hoped it was quite early on—Royce and whoever was with him had left.

Sex was different in the shower, in the bed, and on the floor, and across the kitchen counter when we went down for a drink. I hadn't shifted to my wolf, and this morning, not only did I *definitely* feel different, but I also ached in places I never knew I could.

When Cannon woke me this morning, I'd been sleepy but

ready to participate in whatever he intended. He'd already woke me twice through the night. What he'd intended though was a six in the morning training session with Leo.

Thank the Goddess Luna for coffee, because that and the promise of a fully cooked breakfast was all that was keeping me upright right now.

"You've been staring for a very long time. It's beginning to feel uncomfortable."

Leo grinned. "I'm assessing your form, your dominant side, how long you can stay still...and also how long you can stay quiet." His grin got wider. "The last one was at the request of the alpha." His gaze shifted over my shoulder, and I spun to see Cannon leaning against the main door, watching me.

"Asshole!" I shouted, and with a laugh, he raised his cup. "Wait! Is that coffee?" Turning around to ask if I could get coffee, I barely missed Leo's punch. "What the hell?"

Leo circled me. "Cannon said not to pull my punches," he told me with excitement. "Let's see what you've got, Kezia."

"Now?" I asked, my shoulders relaxing as I prepared to defend myself. "No holds barred?"

"Give me all you've got."

Finally. A *real* fight.

I was right to go on the defense, as Leo rushed me, and his speed was almost frightening. I managed to block his punch to my jaw with his right fist, but my side took the full force of his left one. I tried to counter but he knocked my punch away like it was nothing.

Leo swung at me again, the initial surprise at his attack fading, while we jabbed and kicked at each other. His roundhouse kick landed firmly to the left of my ribcage, and we both heard the crack of bone, but he didn't let up. Dancing back out of his reach, I pressed my hand to my side.

Fuck, that hurt.

Leo charged at me again, and I dodged the high kick that was aimed at my head. Dropping to the ground, I bit out a curse as my ribs protested, but my leg sweep was worth it when I caught Leo's legs. He didn't lose his balance though, he merely stumbled and then literally threw himself on me, fists raining down on me, punching again and again into my ribs.

With a snarl, I grabbed the fucker's hair, and with all my strength, I brought his head down and bounced it off the floor. With a grunt, he rolled over, and I scrambled to my feet. In disbelief, I watched him flip up from the floor, and he was coming at me again.

We jabbed, punched, and kicked, and I knew my energy was fading fast. I wasn't going to last. I wasn't going to win.

Another sharp kick to my stomach, and I began to curse every martial art in the world. I didn't know what style he was using; it was nothing I'd been taught, but he was kicking my ass with it. I felt blood all over me, and my ribs were more than cracked now. I would need to shift to heal.

I'd never needed to shift after training. Not even when I beat Landon that one time.

I finally landed a right hook on Leo's jaw, and he countered with an uppercut that knocked me flying.

Flat out on the mat, I struggled to breathe.

"You done?" Leo asked me as he stood over me.

"Yup," I told him with a nod of my head, which hurt. "I'm done."

Smiling, he held his hand out and helped me to my feet. "You need to shift? You look like shit."

Glaring at him through my swollen eye, I snorted. "Hmm, I wonder why?"

"You were better than we thought," Royce spoke from behind me.

"Not as good as you think you are though." Nikan's voice made me turn to look at them both. My stomach dipped when I saw Cannon wasn't there.

"You've been watching?"

"How else can we assess you?" Royce asked casually. The two of them approached, and Nikan smiled at me in sympathy. "What d'ya think?" he asked Leo.

Pushing my hair out of my face, I winced at the pain in my ribs. "I think you broke them all," I grouched as I tentatively rubbed my side.

Leo was nonplussed. "It's what I was aiming to do." He looked me over. "I'd say advanced beginner." Nikan and Royce nodded.

"Advanced *beginner*?" I demanded. "You mean you don't even think I'm decent?"

"No stamina." Leo wasn't even being hurtful. He was just stating the facts as he saw them. "Your energy levels dipped early. You didn't even make the ten-minute mark." He shared a look with Royce, who nodded in agreement. "Your right side is dominant, and that makes your left side weak, so we need to work on that first. A balanced fighter is a better fighter." He scratched his ear, and I noticed he didn't even look *fatigued*. "The head move was good but desperate. If you'd executed it properly, you'd have snapped my neck." At my wide-eyed reaction, he smiled. "Don't worry, I can teach you how to do it properly. You didn't go for my junk," he added with what I think was disappointment. "You should have. It's a weakness to most men."

"Not you?" My words were muffled since my lip was split and swollen.

"Been punched in the nuts by Cannon more times than I can count. Think my poor balls are immune to the pain now."

Both Nikan and Royce laughed, and for a fleeting moment, I wondered what craziness I was in amongst, and then I realized I loved it.

"Where is Cannon? He didn't want to assess me?" I tried for casual, but I knew I failed.

Royce stepped closer while Nikan distracted Leo with a question about my ruthlessness to strike. I kind of wanted to know the answer, but Royce leaned down to talk to me quietly. "He left after a few minutes," he told me in a low whisper.

"Oh, right, that's okay." Was it? It didn't feel okay.

"Kezia..." Royce looked at me with disapproval. "He couldn't stay and watch you get beaten like that. It was either he left or Leo died. Which one would you prefer?"

I gulped hard. "Leaving's good."

Royce gave me a nod of approval. "That was our thinking too."

Leo wandered back to me. "All right, have you got your breath back?" When I nodded, he pulled off his shirt. "Excellent. Shift, and let's see what you've got as a wolf."

"You want me to fight you as my wolf?" I looked at Nikan and Royce with uncertainty.

Leo was already pulling down his gym shorts. "Of course, I need to see *all* your combat skills so I can train you to be better."

I looked between the three of them. "I've never done that," I confessed, my hand once more at my side, rubbing my ribs. Breathing was getting easier as my shifter ability healed me.

Leo hesitated briefly and then straightened, completely at ease with his nakedness. "Then we start fixing that today. Shift."

He was serious. They were all serious.

I felt for Moonstar, she wasn't present. Pulling off my tank top, I grinned, wincing as I re-split my lip. "This might be the best day ever."

CHAPTER 22

Kezia

THE BEST THING ABOUT THE DAY WAS THAT I WAS A much better fighter as my wolf when it came to fighting pack. My wolf had no mercy, and instinct overruled much, and when I shifted back, not only was I fully healed, but Leo was short of breath.

He did make me fight him one-on-one on the mat again, but this time, because my wolf had healed our sore bones and aching muscles and I had been watching and learning as we fought against the black and white wolf that was Leo, I didn't get my ass kicked quite as badly.

When Leo decided I could go get some food, I was practically skipping alongside Nikan as we walked to the food hall.

He laughed at me when I greeted a passing pack member with a "good morning" and a wide smile. "You look really happy." His hands were in his pockets as we walked, and I gave an eager nod as he watched me.

"I got to fight, *three* times, then get told the food hall is still open and I have to eat—and I quote—as much as I can. This is the best morning in the history of mornings." I took two big steps to put myself in front and spun around to face him as I walked backward. "*And* I also made Leo bleed that last time."

"Of course you'd be his mate," Nikan said in a low voice, but with a rueful smile. "You're as savage as he is."

My laugh was loud, and I winced when I realized I'd drawn attention to myself when I saw several people look my way as they went about their morning business, but whereas in the Anterrio Pack, I'd have received glares and mistrust, the pack here smiled openly and most waved at us as we passed.

At the entrance to the food hall, Nikan held the door open for me, and that simple gesture also stood out. Eager for food and coffee, I hurried to the counter to see what there was left, expecting it to be sparse. Instead, there was a full tray of cooked breakfast and two plates already made up.

"Morning," the women greeted. "Alpha said you'd be along around this time and asked us to make you up a plate. We can make more of anything you need."

There was a whole tray of bacon, pancakes, sausage, eggs, and French toast. Looking at it, then lifting my head between the woman and Nikan, I shook my head.

"I don't eat *that* much."

Nikan snorted while he took a plate from the counter, already laden with food. "Yeah, you do."

Taking the plate offered to me, I tried not to salivate over my breakfast. "I don't," I told her in a low whisper. But I still managed to reach out and take another piece of French toast. And then added a few more pieces of bacon. "They're exaggerating," I added while completely proving Nikan and Cannon right.

We sat near the counter, and I spent the next several minutes eating my breakfast, clearing my plate, and being rewarded with a second helping. When I finally looked up, Nikan was watching me over the rim of his coffee cup.

"What?" I picked up a napkin and dabbed my chin. "Do I have breakfast on my face?"

Placing his cup down, he shook his head. "No, I was just wondering if you're feeling okay. We established the..." He looked over his shoulder, but the woman who had served us was in the kitchen, and the only other shifter in the hall was an older male who was reading a paper, and I doubted he could hear us as the kitchen workers started to clear up. "We established before that your heat was near, or almost here, by your increase in appetite. Your *healthy* appetite," he clarified with a waggle of his eyebrows. "Know what I mean?"

"I just have a *healthy* appetite for good food." My cheeks warmed as I recalled what else I seemed to have a healthy appetite for when I thought of the last twenty-four hours and Cannon.

Nikan was frowning in thought, and I crossed my fingers in the hope he wasn't about to start making this awkward. "So, you feel normal?"

Finishing my coffee, I couldn't help but grin at him. "I've never felt normal..."

With a playful eye roll, he finished his own coffee. "Why am I not surprised?" Pointing at my plate, he made to stand. "You finished?"

"Yup." Jumping to my feet, I picked up my plate and cup and followed him through the double doors to the large industrial-sized kitchen. Several of the pack were either cleaning or prepping food for lunch or dinner.

Willy was one of the workers, and she gave me a hug in greeting. "Alpha added you to the chore list," she told me, wiping her hands on a paper towel. Nikan nudged me subtly and I followed her to a large whiteboard that I hadn't paid attention to that ran along a wall beside the fridges. Willy pointed at the far-left corner. "Alpha says you're a mean dishwasher." She glanced at my hands and then back up at the board. "You okay to start washing?"

"Now?" I admit it took me by surprise, but pack worked together; it's how we survived.

"No." She slapped my arm as she chuckled. "Alpha says Nikan is to show you how our pack works today, and then if it's all right with you, you're on lunch rotation tomorrow. Can you cook?"

It was a lot to take in, and *Alpha* sure said a *lot* it seemed about me, but not *to* me. Brushing it aside, I looked around the size of the kitchen. "I can cook, but I've never cooked for more than me and my brother," I admitted.

"Good, not too many bad habits to break." Willy looked pleased as she led me to the three huge sinks. "Rinse them, stack them." Opening one of the dishwashers, she showed me how the best way to stack a dishwasher was. I simply listened even though she was doing it all wrong. "If you're in for the slower mealtimes, we'll start you off slow by showing you how to cook for more than two, okay?"

"Of course."

Nikan spoke then. "Cannon thought kitchen to start with to ease you into the pack." He pointed to the other side of the whiteboard. "That's the schedule for combat and defense training. Tomorrow, you're on lunch duty here, from ten thirty to two. Then from three to four, you have training." I stepped closer as I read the shift pattern. "You still have Leo in the morning though, but tomorrow will be a shorter set." Nikan nodded at Willy, who had migrated back to her food prep. "See you later," he called out, waving to the pack and walking back into the main hall. "You may get a week, maybe two on the kitchen, then everyone rotates, and you get put somewhere else."

"Everyone rotates?" We were back outside, and Nikan was leading me away from the direction of the alpha's house.

"Any shifter that can cook, like really cook, they usually stay in the kitchen rotation, but they have the choice to move. Our rotations are simple." We were at a larger building, and as Nikan held the door open for me, I realized this was their general store. "Kitchens, serving, either in the hall or in here, teaching"—he glanced at me—"you won't be doing that, and hunting."

"Hunting?" I knew he could hear how excited I was at that.

"Yes, hunting, and we also do security too. Not sure you'll get put into that rotation."

"Security? The females are allowed to rotate?"

"Most packs operate this way." He picked up a bag of chips and two bottles of soda. "It's only the Anterrios who are so pigheaded about keeping the females away from roles that involve combat." He put the three things on the counter, and the young male was too busy staring at me to notice. "Do I need to kick your ass?" Nikan growled at him.

The male startled and flushed bright red. "No, Nikan! Sorry," he mumbled at me as his head dipped. He marked the three items on a computer screen against Nikan's name.

I waited for Nikan to pay but when he simply picked up the sodas and handed me one, he saw my frown. "We don't use money in the pack for food."

"It's free?" In the Anterrio Pack, in the canteen, if you ate with everyone else, you didn't pay for food, but in the bakery and store you did.

Nikan said goodbye to the store clerk, and I gave a small wave as we left. "So, in your pack, everyone has a specific role, and everyone gets paid for that role, right?" When I nodded, Nikan continued. "Here, there are very few of us who have one role. Cannon, obviously, is alpha, but he still works rotations, just limited, and he's more of a 'drop in when he can,' and to a certain extent, Royce and I do the same. Doc is, well, he's Doc. The teachers for the kids don't rotate, but that's obvious." When it was clear I was following, Nikan continued. "Cannon gives everyone, with those exceptions, the same amount of allowance. We hunt for our meat, and we grow our own vegetables—"

"You do?"

Nikan pointed ahead. "It's where we're going next," he explained, and I noticed we were heading out of the town. "If we hunt and grow our food, and everyone is involved, why would we pay for it?" Nikan shook the bag of chips. "Stuff like this, we buy in, and the store keeps a ledger, and it gets deducted from the allowance."

"Like a tab?" I'd learned of these when I worked in the bars.

"Exactly." Nikan opened his soda. "When our father was alpha, he made the pack pay for the store food, and he set the prices double or triple the retail price so that hardly anyone used it. He was such a dick."

"So where does the pack income come from?" I looked around at my surroundings. Every building was well-maintained, the sidewalks were clean, and as we neared the edge of town, I saw the land that was used for agriculture.

"We outsource our other skills." Nikan shrugged. "Most of the males my age and older, like Cannon, and some females served time with the military. Or there are some of the pack who were educated in human schools and colleges. Some went to trade schools. What we learn, we take back to the pack, and then we find jobs that require skills that we have."

"Like what? What skill do you have?"

"Graphic designer," Nikan told me proudly. "I design websites and do some coding, and the good thing about it is that I don't even need to leave the pack."

"You work with computers?"

We were at the side of a fence now, where several white poly-tunnels filled the field. Nikan slapped his forehead. "I forget how useless your old pack leader is. I hate his stupid ways. Everyone in this pack can use computers. Hell, most of us own one."

"Wow." I didn't have another word to describe it. "That's so... advanced."

Nikan laughed loudly. "No, it really isn't, Zia." He lost his mirth as he saw my look. "It's normal. Your pack is the anomaly, not ours."

"It makes me resent Bale even more," I said quietly, hating that my pack was so backward and restrictive in our leadership.

"He's a dick," Nikan agreed, tugging my arm to make me walk again. "But there are more than just Bale in that pack, and they know how it could be, and they *accept* it." Nikan scowled as he spoke. "They're the ones who make me angry." Turning to face me, he carried on. "Do you know your pack who have their own interest, like the she with the bakery? He takes a dividend from her for that. She pays rent, for fuck's sake, and he takes a cut of her profits too."

"For the pack, I assume?"

"For *himself*."

That was absurd. "I didn't know that."

"I bet he doesn't boast about it," Nikan grumbled. "Where is he?" He looked around, going as far as to climb up on the simple post and wire fence to use for a height advantage.

"Who are you looking for?"

"Cannon!"

I jumped when Nikan bellowed. "Dude, my eardrums!" Moving a few steps away, I rubbed my ear. "Mindlink him like a normal shifter."

"Can't." Nikan jumped down. "He's closed off today."

Trying to look casual, I asked, "Does he do that often?"

"Nah." Nikan rubbed his jaw. "Only when he's being secretive...*or*...doesn't want anyone to catch him *reliving* anything." Nikan's smirk was enough to make me blush. "I *knew* it," he said smugly. "It explains your appetite earlier, needed to refuel."

"Shut up."

He didn't say anything else, but with a quick check of the fields again, he jumped back down beside me. "He's not here, he's maybe with Doc." We were walking back when he stopped suddenly. "He treat you okay?"

My reaction of surprise that he would ask that, was enough to make him lose his casual smile, and I felt guilty. "Yes... Sorry?"

Nikan waved it off. "When I looked back on it all after we spoke, it was so obvious that you're his *you know*, I don't know why I never saw it." We walked in silence before he huffed out a laugh. "Way to ruin the day, Nikan."

Taking his arm like I would if he were Landon, and if Landon wasn't the giant asshole he was now, I linked my arm through Nikan's. "You've ruined nothing. I've loved my tour. Thank you for taking the time to show me your home."

He patted my arm in response. "We could go find my brother, or I can show you where the trades and maintenance are?"

I did want to see Cannon, but I also wanted to stay away from Cannon because I didn't know how to act around the man who kept me up all night having sex with me.

"Maintenance sounds good?"

"Avoiding him?" Nikan sighed. "Do you need an intervention?"

"Nope." I avoided eye contact. "He's alpha-ing, and I'm on a tour of your pack."

"You mean our pack," Nikan corrected.

"Why in Luna's name is it my pack?" I asked him, thinking he was teasing me.

We'd been walking back the way we came, and houses were around us, and I could hear pack ahead of us. Nikan looked ahead and then at me. "Because you're mates?" he said, keeping his voice low. "And this is now your pack."

I trailed to a stop as I thought about what he said. "No."

"No?" Nikan walked back the few steps he was ahead of me. "I don't understand?"

Neither did I. I wanted to tell him that this wasn't my pack, because we may be mates, but the intention was still to not form the bond. Well, until yesterday. Or maybe earlier than then. When did we change our minds? I was so confused. Chewing the inside of my cheek, I pulled my hair off my face as I thought about my answer. "It's... I'm... It's a lot okay."

"You're"—Nikan gave a furtive glance over his shoulder—"you know..."

"Yeah, I do. And until recently we were working on not being...you know."

He took a step back, confusion on his face. "But you had sex," he blurted too loudly for my comfort.

"Let's shout it a little bit louder, why don't you?" I hissed, grabbing his arm and jerking him forward. "Yes, we did, but what if that didn't *change* anything." He was gaping at me. All wide-eyed and mouth open. He looked like a caricature of himself. "Stop overreacting," I warned him.

"You think it didn't change anything, or Ca—" At my warning look, he took a deep breath. "Or *he* doesn't think it did?"

"What kind of question is that?" I wailed. "I don't know, ask him."

"Why would I ask him?" Nikan looked bewildered. "Unless you want me to? Are you asking me to ask him?"

"No! What is *wrong* with you? Why would *you* ask?"

"That's what I said, but you said *ask him*." His arms were flailing like a windmill. "So did you say that because you *want* me to ask him, because I don't even know how to start that conversation, or if I even want to! And—"

"Oh for fuck's sake, Nikan, I didn't mean actually ask him," I scolded. "Are you crazy? You can't just walk up to him and say hey, bro, so I was wondering, anything changed on the whole you-know thing?"

Nikan looked thoughtful even though my tone was mocking. "I could..."

"No!" I whisper-yelled. "That is insane. I'm not asking, and you aren't asking, and neither of us is even *thinking* of this anymore."

"But don't you want to know?"

Throwing my hands in the air, I glared at him as he came to stand beside me. "Oh my Goddess, will you shut up?"

"Fine." He hesitated as we started walking again. "But you know—"

"Shut *up*."

"Fine."

"Or...you stop having this conversation in the street, and both can ask me at the house?"

Turning slowly, I faced Cannon, who was standing behind us, with his arms crossed and an eyebrow raised. I knew I was the same color of red as a cherry tomato. "Hey?" I avoided making eye contact while blushing furiously and wishing I was anywhere but here.

"Hey, yourself," he greeted me, and I saw him checking me over out of the corner of my eye. "Got something on your mind, pup?"

Ah damn it all to hell.

CHAPTER 23

Kezia

"WE WERE JUST TALKING," NIKAN SAID BESIDE ME, AND I felt him shift his feet nervously. "Nothing important."

Had I been able to glare at him without Cannon seeing me, I would have. Instead, I nudged him in the ribs to shut up, but I heard Cannon's low chuckle.

"Kezia, would you like me to walk you back to the house?" He walked forward until it was so obvious I was avoiding looking at him, I had no choice but to lift my head.

"No?"

Cannon laughed loudly and I jumped in surprise. "Come on," he said jovially, walking past us both to lead. "This isn't a conversation for the street. You two aren't as subtle as you think you are," he added dryly.

Nikan huffed when I jabbed him in the side, but like dutiful chastised children, we followed the alpha through his town, and as we walked, I looked even more closely at the buildings and the pack we met along the way. This pack was *happy*. It was so obvious, when I watched them interact with each other, that they were content.

The Anterrio Pack weren't unhappy, but we were much more reserved with each other. It wasn't even just with me, although they were a lot more standoffish; they were simply a quiet pack that kept to themselves. But as I observed the Blackridge Peak Pack, I couldn't help but wonder if this was how pack life would be and if this pack was different because they had a better alpha.

Better alpha?

Was Cannon better than Bale? I knew that he was. If we didn't have the whole awkward mate thing happening, this would be a pack I could easily stay with. But was I only here because of the Goddess's sick, twisted sense of humor, and was I only being shown around because Cannon probably thought I was in his pack too?

I wondered, if we managed to break or resist the bond, if I could still stay. Like the universe itself was toying with me, I saw Koda up ahead, looking like one of the fashion models on TV. She was wearing simple black pants and a loose shirt. But with her hair down and luxurious looking and her perfect-looking face, I knew I didn't measure up to her. Looking down at my simple borrowed shorts and T-shirt that had a couple of food stains, I looked grubby.

There was no other word to describe it. I dressed in whatever was comfortable because I didn't care what I looked like.

Koda obviously cared and made the effort.

Is that what he liked? Girls whose hair bounced when they walked?

Self-consciously I patted my ponytail. I had no idea what my hair looked like, probably like a female who had spent the morning fighting and barely showered.

"Why are you frowning?" Nikan asked quietly. He followed my gaze. "You've nothing to worry about there," he assured me.

Cannon looked over his shoulder. "Worry about where?" Coming to a stop, he waited until we were beside him. "Who's worrying? You?" His look was searching. "What are you worried about?"

I was going to punch Nikan by the end of the day, I just knew it.

"I'm not worried about anything." Pulling at the hem of my shirt, I pointed to the stain. "Coffee stains." I looked closer. "Could be bacon stain?"

Nikan snorted. "It's not food, not the way you eat," he teased, just as Koda was almost beside us. "You're like a mechanical digg —" I punched him. "Ow!"

Cannon looked at me and I shrugged. "Knew it was going to happen today."

"Alpha?"

Oh great, now *Seductive Koda* was looking at me in horror, having obviously witnessed me punching Nikan. Looking between her and Cannon, with her hand *on* his arm like he was a possession and him not shaking it off, I stepped back.

"I'm going back for a shower," I told all of them. "I'll catch up with you later," I added to Nikan.

"Zia?" Nikan called after me, but I ignored them. All of them. I was overreacting, I knew I was. I just felt confused, and I needed time. I needed time to just get my bearings and feel within myself how I felt about everything that had happened to me over the last few days.

"Do you want to talk about it?"

I jumped ten feet in the air.

"Luna!" I fixed him with a glare. "Why the fuck are you always creeping up on me?"

"I don't creep." I could see him trying not to smile though. "Are you all right?"

"Yes." *No.*

"You know you are really bad at hiding your emotions," Cannon commented quietly.

"Then be a gentleman and don't look." We were almost at his house, and I picked up the pace.

"You running from me?"

"No," I scoffed. "What's the point? You always find me," I added bitterly. Circling my hand in the air, taking in the town, I added, "Plus this is your pack, where could I possibly run?"

"So just avoiding me then?"

I leveled him with a look. Standing at the top of the steps to get into his house, I looked down at him, standing on the path. "I just want a shower."

Cannon put his hands in the back pockets of his jeans and rocked back slightly. The move showed off the definition of the tone of his arms, his dark gray T-shirt pulled across his upper body. His jeans were the same dark ones I liked, the ones that sat a little bit low and hugged his ass just right.

The jeans I liked? He had jeans I liked? Dear Luna, what was happening to me?

"Something wrong?" His tone had dropped slightly, his voice huskier.

My tummy fluttered and my lower body wakened. "No." Forcing myself to look at him, I reached for the door handle. "I just need a shower. You"—licking my lips, I remembered the last time I was in the shower with him—"you don't need to come in."

Cannon didn't move, his expression didn't change, he simply nodded. "Okay. You sure?"

"I'm fine." I was almost inside, and Cannon hadn't moved from the path. "You can go do your alpha things."

He smiled widely. "I'm due in the fields. We're planting for spring harvest," he told me. "I was late, and then hearing you and Nikan, I got distracted." He looked over his shoulder briefly. "We can talk if you have things you want to discuss?"

"Nope. No questions or anything to discuss. Just need a shower. I feel grubby."

His smile turned wicked. "I like you grubby," he said so softly that only I could hear, and that part of my body that knew only him wanted to get to know him some more.

We held each other's stare for a moment until a *nauseating* floral scent overloaded my senses.

"Alpha, Doc's looking for you."

Koda looked perfectly innocent, but I knew I would never trust her. Realizing I was jealous, I stepped inside the house. "I'll see you later," I told Cannon. I never heard his reply. I was already halfway up the stairs to the bedroom.

A quick shower later, I searched the bathroom and then the bedroom for a hair dryer. Coming up empty, I decided to check Cannon's bathroom.

Pushing the door open, I checked over my shoulder, making sure he wasn't behind me in one of his creeping-up-on-me tricks. Seeing no sign of him, I stepped into the alpha's bedroom and was at once surrounded by his scent, which hit me so hard that I stumbled. My nostrils flared as I breathed his scent in, filling my lungs with the familiar, welcoming presence of my mate.

"*Luna,*" I breathed shakily. Cannon's room was devoid of anything personal, but it was so overwhelmingly *him* that I drank it all in, from the plain white linens on his bed to the two pillows straightened with military precision, the closet door slightly open, and the simple wooden bookshelf crammed with books of all genres, which sat beside a large desk with papers on it and a simple desk lamp. I frowned at the hole in the wall, wondering what happened there.

A high-backed gray chair sat in the corner beside the window, and I wondered why he would need a chair here when he had a window seat, until common sense reminded me that Cannon was just too large of a frame to sit there comfortably.

My feet took me across the room, and soon I was sinking into the sturdy chair, surprised at how comfy it was. Dark blue drapes hung on either side of his window, and I hoped they shielded me as I sat on the alpha's chair and looked out over his town. The simple act made me feel closer to him, causing me to shake my head at my romanticism. He wasn't even here, and I felt him all around me. I could feel how being able to sit here and watch his pack go about their lives would please him.

I could practically feel how content he would be sitting here.

A sense of peace spread through me, and I let myself feel it before I gently pushed it away. I didn't need to be here, experiencing this. This was his space, and I was an intruder. Ignoring the sense of disappointment, I stood and walked to the adjoining bathroom. Papers on his desk made me pause.

Without thinking about it, I moved the top papers aside, picking up the one that had caught my eye.

"Vance Forbes," I read. "Twenty-eight, weighs one-hundred-eighty-nine pounds, height five eleven. Blood type B positive. Criminal record, arson, grievous bodily harm, possession of drugs, illegal fighting." I swallowed, my hand shaking as I read the next note. "Targeted Kezia when she returned to the human world, sought her out. Employed a large network of eyes and ears for a white-haired girl. Unknown why he wanted her, but three guns were retrieved, all carrying—"

"Silver bullets."

Dropping the paper, I turned to the doorway where Cannon stood leaning against the frame. "Three guns?"

Cannon nodded, entering the room and closing the door behind him, and I felt the room seal with the same magic as the study.

"You need soundproofing in here?"

"Not everyone needs to hear their alpha snore." He was in front of me, reaching for me, and I went unresisting, eager for his kiss. "Among other things," he teased, kissing me lightly. Anticipating my outrage, he kissed me more firmly. Our mouths softened against each other, and then he was kissing me the way I hadn't realized I desperately needed him to.

When we pulled apart, Cannon kept me close to him. Reaching behind me, he picked up the paper and scanned it. "I told you all this." He frowned. "Did you not believe me?"

"I saw his name, and"—I took a deep breath—"I'm ashamed to say I forgot he was even here." Pushing against Cannon's chest slightly, he loosened his grip, and I stepped back. "I've been so disoriented lately I can't keep track of all the shit in my life," I sneered at how easily I had lost sight of everything.

Cannon's large thumb brushed over my lips as if to wipe the sneer away. "I don't like that look on you," he murmured. "You've dealt with everything you've had thrown at you. Let me deal with this."

"I want to see him."

"Absolutely not."

"I think I have the right—"

"You thought wrong."

I gaped at the alpha in front of me. "I'm sorry, did you just tell me what I can think?"

"Yes." He saw my outrage. "No," he said with a sigh, rubbing his head. "You can think whatever you want, you can be whoever you want here."

"But I can't see Vance?"

"No."

"Even though it was me he was going to shoot with silver bullets?" I demanded.

"*Exactly* why you can't see him."

"That's *exactly* why I *should* be the one who sees him. Why I should be one of the *only* people to see him!"

Cannon crossed his arms over his chest. "I said no."

With wide eyes, I pointed at him. "I don't give a damn what you say."

"Too bad." Cannon turned his back on me, heading back to the bedroom door. "Why were you in here?"

"I wanted a hair dryer." Hurrying after him, I pushed the door closed when he opened it, feeling the spell reengage. "Do not walk out on me. I want to discuss this."

"There's nothing to discuss, Kezia. You asked, I said no. End of discussion." Cannon jerked the handle, and the door opened so sharply I needed to step out of the way. "I think there's a hair dryer on the bottom shelf of the vanity."

He left me. I watched him as he walked down the stairs without looking back, and I heard the front door close.

"Asshole."

Pulling my damp hair off my face, I quickly braided it, ducking back into my bedroom for a hair tie. Checking my clothes and deciding I was stupid to be put off by Koda's appearance, I hurried down the stairs in my leggings and a T-shirt. I had bigger things to worry about other than how I was dressed for an alpha who didn't even listen to me.

On his front porch, I scanned the streets for him. Seeing him nowhere, I jogged down the steps, and then I was making a beeline for the bunker.

He could *tell* me whatever he wanted. Didn't mean I had to listen.

The bunker was unguarded, which took me by surprise, but then it dawned on me that the pack would have no reason to be here. Carefully I entered and took the stairs slowly, waiting for a pissed-off alpha to appear at any time. The corridor was empty, and slowly I made my way to the door that was damaged, stepped inside, and saw the room with my cell.

"It looks bigger," I spoke out loud, walking closer and seeing the bars pulled apart, a stark reminder of her strength and the fact I wasn't alone inside myself. I'd let too much be put aside while I enjoyed the benefits of being with the alpha. I had so much to work out and get through that I shouldn't be letting physical plea-sure be the reason I got sidetracked. "I'm not thinking with the head on my shoulders," I scolded myself.

Before I left the room, I hesitated at the approximate spot where the alpha had shot me with silver bullets. "Asshole."

In the corridor once more, I picked a direction and listened for movement as I walked along. The bunker was far bigger than I thought, and I was in danger of getting lost when I saw a door ajar and a light coming from it. Praying to Luna, I pushed the door open, vaguely seeing Hannah, but my entire focus was on the back of the room and the man who sat on a cot, watching me as I approached him.

"Vance."

He held my stare as I looked him over. He was thinner and had a few bruises, but he looked okay.

He looked *fine*.

Irrational anger surged through me. How *dare* he look fine! He was going to shoot me with silver fucking bullets. As I moved forward, the cool hand wrapping around my upper arm surprised me.

"Hannah?"

"He can't hear you," she told me gently.

"Why?"

"He's sealed in. It's a pod."

"A pod?" I looked more closely, seeing the enclosure for what it was. It was a cell with no bars and no obvious exit. "Magic?"

Hannah nodded. "Mixed with science." She tugged my arm, turning me away from Vance. "Let's not give him the chance to lip-read," she murmured.

"I need to talk to him."

"Nuh-uh." Hannah glanced at Vance and then me, and I suddenly knew how her children felt being chastised, because she was definitely wearing a "mom" expression. "And does your mate know you're here?"

I could lie. I could avoid the question. Instead, I shrugged. "If he knows me as well as he seems to think he does, then yes, he does."

Hannah groaned loudly. "For Luna's sake, Kezia. Are you just trying to make him lose his temper?"

"He's a pigheaded asshole."

"Who has done everything to keep you safe," she scolded. Her look was speculative. "I thought you had sex?"

My eyes widened in shock and embarrassment. "Did he put it on a bulletin board?" I demanded incredulously.

Hannah chuckled, taking her seat at a computer desk. "No, silly. Royce was in the house when he concluded that neither of you were coming back down."

"Oh."

We both jumped when the door was open, but my spike of apprehension settled quickly when I saw it was only Doc.

"Kezia?" He looked surprised but it was gone quickly. "What are you doing here?"

"I want to talk to him."

Doc looked over my shoulder at Vance and then me and nodded. "Sounds reasonable."

"Doc?" Hannah stood. "Is this a good idea?"

"He can't get out, and maybe he'll answer her, because he's said shit to me. I need a pad and a pen."

Turning, I faced Vance and saw him leaning forward, his elbows on his knees, his eyes missing nothing of the exchange, even if he couldn't hear us. He looked at me with expectation, sitting back, entirely comfortable despite being in a pod.

I smiled widely as I took him in. He wasn't fooling me. Not again. "Oh, he'll talk to me. I guarantee it."

CHAPTER 24

Cannon

HEADING BACK TO THE FIELDS, I KNEW THAT I WAS barely holding onto my temper. Why was she so infuriating? It had been a pleasant and *welcome* surprise to find her in my bedroom. Even though she had been snooping, she looked *right* as she stood at my desk.

She looked like she *belonged* there. With her hair damp and her eyes narrowed in concentration, my mate looked right at home in *my* room, amongst my things.

"And then she spoke and ruined everything," I muttered with a grunt. I saw Royce ahead, laughing and joking with one of the other pack members. A male who had hunted Kezia down with me. Who had seen her in the ring the night I toyed with her and brought her home.

With a frustrated breath, I looked past both of them. I didn't want to be cheerful. I wanted to hit something. Preferably Vance fucking Forbes or, if I thought she could fight me and hold her own, Kezia.

I frowned at myself. She could hold her own, she just had shit training. But when she was trained and I knew I wouldn't hold the advantage over her with my training and strength, I relished the opportunity to kick my mate's backside.

Maybe knock some sense into her.

"Why do you look like you're about to go to war?" Royce asked me only half-serious. At the look I gave him, he nodded with a sigh. "Right. Of course. Zia."

"Her name is *Kezia*," I stressed.

Royce didn't give a fuck I was pissed off. He pointed to the wagon with the grain. "You know what to do. Go do some manual labor, work her out of your system."

Ignoring them both as they grinned at me, like they knew what it was like to have their mate get on their very last nerve, I shouldered past them. The trouble was they didn't know.

No one I knew, *knew* what it was like. When I was younger and beginning to understand that I was the next alpha of our pack, I had sought out shamans. I had no one to teach me. Luna knew my father, Rek, was never going to embrace his successor with welcome arms. He thought I was merely a shifter. I hid my alpha scent from him, and I hid it well.

That didn't help me with the way of an alpha though. I had sought out shamans in other packs, their duty to Luna overriding their duty to the pack when an alpha came seeking answers in secret.

A shaman in a pack that preferred the very far north of Canada had explained the mating bond to me. Luna needed strength and loyalty, and there was nothing more loyal or unbreakable than a mate bond.

A pack that had a strong alpha and his mate was a good pack. A pack that would do anything for each other. I had that already. My pack and I were loyal to each other. I had done everything I could for them, and they deserved a strong alpha female.

Did they deserve Kezia?

I wasn't sure I deserved her. She was a riddle I may never work out.

Picking up the first bag of grain, I carried it to the harvester machine, emptying it and shaking it loose. That was unfair, I reproached myself sourly. Kezia was wild and untamed, a fact I liked about her. Of course, my pack deserved someone who would fight for them.

I snorted. Luna knew Kezia loved to fight. About everything. She may be a puzzle, but I wanted to be the one to figure her out, I knew.

I emptied the next grain bag. Was it my fault she was irrational?

No.

It was her brother's.

Stooping to pick up the next sack, I realized I *did* know another alpha who was mated.

Kris.

He'd had more years than anyone to deal with the spitfire that was my mate. He would know how best to control her. Again, I winced at the terminology.

I didn't want to *control* her. I just wanted her to listen. To understand the risks that she ran at full-on, they affected others and not just her.

"It's only been four sacks," Royce spoke quietly beside me. "You lost that fire quick."

Straightening, I looked at him. "I'm an ass. She makes me act like an ass."

He half shrugged. "She's female. It's in their genetics, I think." He beamed at me. "It's what makes them so fun."

I shared his smile. "Yeah, I don't know if I'll ever get to the fun, but she makes it interesting." Reaching to my back pocket for my phone, I remembered I left it on the kitchen counter. I'd gone home earlier for it and been distracted by Kezia in my bedroom. Looking around, I looked back at Royce and saw his knowing look. "I—"

"Need to go, yeah, I know." Patting me on the back, he pushed me away. "Get whatever it is out of your system, come past the house later. We need to plan the next move. Right?"

"Absolutely." I was already backing away. "I just need to make a call."

"Sure." His eye roll made me realize he thought I was going to find Kezia. "Just make sure you close the door," he added quietly.

I nodded but I was already planning on it. Not to disguise the sound of sex from my pack, but to hide the conversation I was about to have with my mate's brother. Thinking about Kezia and sex reminded me how good it had been.

Thank the Goddess, I'd had the sense to close her bathroom door last night, and then the other times, I'd reminded her to be quiet, but Luna, I needed to hear her scream like she had in the open yesterday. But the last thing my pack needed to suspect was me having sex with someone else's mate. As far as they were concerned, she was still Landon's mate.

The very thought of that made me want to punch the imbecile's face.

When she told me all those months ago that the prick had his hands on her ass, *my* ass, and he'd kissed her, I'd almost gone looking for him that night to rip out his innards. Thank Luna for Royce and his voice of reason.

Then I saw her kiss that vile bastard Vance, and no will in the world would have stopped me from slapping her ass that night in the ring.

She needed a good spanking. The thought of her screeching if I spanked her made me laugh. She would never allow that, and the idea of her fighting it was what made me like the idea even more.

I loved her fight. Her spirit. I hated her inability to keep herself safe.

Blowing out a breath, I jogged up the steps to my house. "Kezia?" I called out, heading to the kitchen and seeing my phone on charge where I left it. Taking the stairs two at a time, I poked my head into her bedroom, saw it was empty, and didn't find her in mine either. "Where are you now?"

She'd told Nikan she would see him later, I remembered. He'd told me he had yet to take her to the trades warehouses, where the skilled pack worked. She was still on her tour, and checking the time, seeing it was lunchtime, I guessed she was either still on her tour of our pack or in the food hall.

Closing the bedroom door, I sent a text to Kris.

> Cannon: Can you talk?

> Kris: What's happened?

Realizing he would immediately think the worst because his sister was such a magnet for danger, I quickly typed out a reply.

> Cannon: All is good.

> Kris: Why are you texting me then?

Luna, he was as difficult as his sister. No wonder they clashed so much.

> Cannon: Can you talk or not?

Kris: Give me 5

Pacing my bedroom, I felt awkward as I waited for the phone to ring. When it did, I almost dropped the fucking thing.

"Hello."

"Is she okay? What's happened?"

"I told you she was fine," I barked. "Calm down."

"Don't tell me to calm down. You text for no reason, when you know I'm being watched—what is it?"

"You're being watched?" I asked, my focus sharpening.

"Of course I'm being fucking watched," Kris seethed. "I'm an undeclared alpha mated to the pack leader's only daughter, whose twin is declaring that *my* sister is his mate."

Shit. He was right, his situation was dangerous. "I'm...sorry." I exhaled slowly. "I shouldn't be adding to that risk. Go."

"You said sorry." Kris sounded curious. "What's she done?" he asked warily.

I couldn't help the smile at his correct assumption I was phoning because of his sister. "Has she always been so infuriating?"

"Every day of her life."

Rubbing the back of my neck, I closed my eyes as my awkwardness returned. "How do you not strangle Cass?"

I heard his snort of laughter. "Because she has me wrapped around her finger," he told me, and I heard the fondness in his tone. "Wait...have you had...is it formed?"

"We have, and no it isn't, not properly, she wasn't in heat."

"She slept with you anyway?"

"Should I be insulted you sound so surprised?" I asked him dryly. Looking out my bedroom window, I ran my hand over the chair. I could scent her here. Had she sat here earlier and looked out as I was now? Something inside me settled at the thought of her being so comfortable in my home.

"I'm surprised," he admitted. "Kez is...determined and can't usually be dissuaded. She was determined not to like you."

"I don't think she's dissuaded," I told him with a grunt.

"So...you called to tell me this?" he asked dubiously.

"No. I..." I didn't know how to say it. "I want to either kill her or fuck her. When does it pass? The urge." I grimaced when I grasped what I'd just said to her *brother*. Clearing my throat, I added, "No offense."

"I don't know," he told me simply. "Cass frustrated me too." I was grateful for him brushing past my implied violence to his sister. "It eased with her heat. I'd waited so long..." I'd forgotten his mate was still a teenager. Unlike mine, who had four years robbed from her. "Once her heat passed, we were more at ease."

"And the fact that she isn't as irrational as your sister helps."

Kris laughed. "Cass is just as unpredictable. She may look innocent, but she's responsible for more trouble than Kez ever was, I'm realizing." He was quiet for a moment. "You need to be together during her heat. It helps." Once more, he cleared his throat, clearly as uncomfortable as I was with the conversation topic. "The shaman told me it settles us. The bond intensifies all the small things that we find irritating and all the things we find... attractive. A completed bond creates balance."

Despite the topic, and who I was discussing it with, I was glad I swallowed my pride and phoned her brother. He had the advice of a shaman. Advice I lacked.

"Right." Glancing at the phone, I put it back to my ear. "I was thinking..." I took the plunge. "I was thinking extreme thoughts that aren't me and I knew were severe. I told her she wasn't allowed to think for herself earlier," I admitted, my gut clenching with embarrassment.

"Went down well?" I heard his huff of laughter.

"Like a lead balloon."

"We had a few moments like that on the days running up to Cass's heat." I heard him moving. "To be fair, there are still days like that, but our reactions aren't as exaggerated."

"I get it."

"I need to go," he told me, his voice lowering.

"You okay?" Concern for his safety surfaced once more.

"Yeah, I just need to be careful." There was a pause. "You good?"

"Yup. I appreciate the...this."

"Don't make it a habit."

"If you need to," I told him, becoming serious, "grab Cass and come here. We'll deal with it."

"That's what family's for, right?" Kris quipped. "I have it under control, but thanks."

We said goodbye, and with a grin, I dropped the phone on the chair. "Well, that's one thing, I suppose," I told the empty room. "The need to throttle her is the bond not complete."

Glancing out the window, I erased that rational thought when I saw my brother walking up the street, alone. "Where the hell is she?"

And I knew. Of *course*, I knew.

"*Damn* it, Kezia!"

Rushing out of the house, I grabbed my brother as I passed him, spinning him in place as I half dragged him behind me.

"Whoa!" Nikan protested. "I'd like to keep my arm!"

"Where is she?" I asked him, shoving him away from me as I headed to the bunker.

"Who?" Dragging Nikan in front of me, my nose touched his, and I saw him flinch as he looked at me. "Zia? I don't know. She went for a shower, didn't she?" He looked at me in panic. "She run?" he whispered urgently.

"No." I let him go. "She did something much worse." We were at the bunker. "She's in here."

"Ah, fuck, Zia." Nikan and I shared a look. "I'll get Royce?"

"I don't need my beta to babysit me," I growled at him as we went inside.

"I'm already here," Royce spoke from behind us. "Hannah texted me," he explained as he joined us. "Doc's letting her talk to him."

I felt my jaw drop, and thank fuck for Nikan, who said what I was thinking.

"Is he fucking crazy?"

Royce shook his head slightly, but his eyes never left mine. "Alpha?"

"We go in. We remove her. Someone stand in front of Doc." My voice was quiet and firm. "My wolf is *not* happy. I don't know if I'll control myself enough not to react."

"A quick, simple extraction," Royce confirmed.

As we approached the door, I held my hand up, seeing it wasn't closed firmly.

"Hannah," Royce whispered in explanation. "So I can get in."

The three of us listened.

"Why isn't he speaking?" Kezia's voice floated out to us.

"Cannon wasn't exactly gentle in his interrogation," Doc sounded sympathetic.

"*Can* he speak?" Kezia demanded. "He's useless if he can't tell me anything. He may as well be dead."

I heard her disgust, and my wolf felt less panicked. She wasn't here to save him.

"I've been working on fixing his throat," Doc told her. "Tricky, but I think it's working."

Exchanging a look with Royce, who looked as surprised by this as I felt, I made a mental note to ask the Doc a *lot* more questions.

"I don't have time for him to regrow shit or whatever," Kezia snapped. "Can you write?"

We heard movement and then Hannah's clear voice. "Don't go near him, Kezia. He can write. He won't, but he can."

My wolf urged me forward, and I took in two guilty faces and one of relief when they spun to face me as I walked into the room.

"You better not start talking," I warned Kezia. "You." I pointed at Doc. "I'll deal with later." Looking past all three of them, I locked eyes with Vance. "And you, I should have killed already."

"I need answers." Kezia stepped in front of me. Her hands came flying up to stop me. "I'm not protecting him," she told me softly, her eyes pleading with me to understand. "I need to know who knows. How did he know? He never knew before, I swear." She swallowed. "I need to know if he hurt anyone I care about when he came to find me."

"Care about?"

Kezia nodded. "The town Bullet found me in that time, I had friends there. Two women who cared for me. Lottie." She licked her lips. "Lottie was older. She was on TV, asking whoever had taken me to return me." Her eyes narrowed in anger. "I need to know if he hurt them." She stepped towards me. "Please?"

"Pup—"

"Pup?" The hoarseness of Vance's voice had all six of us turn our attention to him. He was leaning back, his shoulders shaking with laughter. "You call it pup." His voice was scratchy and raspy. It made my throat itch to hear it, but it had a different effect on Kezia.

"You!" Her body went unnaturally still.

I reached for her, but catching me off guard, she moved so fast that my hand clutched nothing but air as she launched her attack on Vance.

"Kezia!"

She was already on him. He'd gone from sitting on his cot to kneeling in front of her, with her arm locked around his throat from behind. Kezia's lips were at his ear, but her eyes were on me.

"He was in the truck."

My mind was racing, not connecting him and the truck at first until I saw her arm flex.

"You were in the truck," she hissed in his ear. "Why didn't I see you?" she demanded. "Were you the driver? How did you disguise your voice so I wouldn't recognize you then?"

The look on his face was vile, and malice was in his stare as he looked at me. "She tastes good, doesn't she?"

Kezia growled but I moved forward cautiously. "Loosen your hold," I told her. "He's doing it to antagonize you. Let him go," I instructed more firmly. "You won't get answers if you strangle him."

"Maybe I don't need answers."

"What was her name? Lottie?" I asked, and Kezia visibly flinched.

"*Kezia.*"

She leveled me with a glare, but she stepped back, letting Vance drop forward. "Come here. Beside me." I reached for her, and when she took my hand, I yanked her closer, pushing her behind me as I faced Vance.

"All the information you gave me, you never mentioned tasting her." I stepped closer. "Because you haven't. You may have kissed her, but just now, you played with her fear that you and your *friends* did a lot more to her in that truck."

"You'll never know." His voice was so ravaged it hurt to listen to it, but it didn't matter because I knew it hurt him a lot more to speak.

"But I do know," I told him, seeing his confusion that he couldn't hide. "The women? Are they harmed?"

He sniffed and spat to the side. "One fought, one didn't."

I heard Kezia let out a sob, and I forced myself not to turn to her. "You told me you learned of what we were the night Kezia changed form at your cabin." I saw his sneer. "A lie?" He smirked. "When did you know?"

"When she kept coming back for more." The disgusting vermin winked at me.

My wolf growled but I pushed it down. Anger wouldn't serve me now. He was talking because she was here. Because Kezia was hurting hearing this. For all the walls that she built to protect herself from the way the Anterrio Pack treated her, she had trusted Vance.

"I don't believe you." It was Royce who spoke. My beta stood beside me, both of us blocking the others from seeing Vance, or him them. "I know humans. No one assumes someone's a shifter. No one."

He was right. We'd served. We'd done some humanly impossible stuff in tight situations for our regiment, for our brothers and sisters in arms.

Humans didn't accept the possibility of the supernatural; they put the impossible down to adrenaline.

"Who recruited you?" I asked Vance.

He smiled and I watched him as he got to his feet, taking a seat on his cot like it was a throne.

"We will speak with him, Alpha."

My insides froze as I recognized the tone of *Moonstar* in Kezia's voice. I almost didn't move aside, but firm hands slipped between Royce and myself as the slight frame of my mate moved between us.

Her step was smooth as she approached Vance. She took a step to the side, and he followed her movement, his eyes narrowing when Moonstar tilted her head to the side, assessing him. Even in his ignorant state, he recognized the *she* in front of him was not Kezia.

"What the fuck is this?" he asked, looking between me and the being who occupied my mate.

"Nikan, take Hannah and Doc," I murmured. "Now."

"I—"

"*Now*, Nikan," Royce growled.

We heard the door close, and despite the high tension of the situation, I felt Royce's relief that his wife was no longer in the room.

I didn't feel any relief, because my mate was in more danger than ever.

Kezia

THE CHILD WAS HURTING. WE DIDN'T LIKE IT WHEN the child hurt. This human caused her pain, and this human would pay for that.

"You killed the old human?" we asked him. We remembered him; he had his hands on us. We had not liked that.

"Was he in the truck?"

We turned to look at the alpha, our eyes narrowing. He had put us into a deep sleep.

We did not like that either.

"Alpha, we will deal with you next."

The alpha did not look as afraid as he should. He would know fear.

"The night they took her," he said to us clearly. "Was he in the truck?"

We shook our head. "No. There were only three humans that took us." We looked back at the human. "But there was another voice." Looking at the alpha, we thought back. "Three humans but four voices."

"Bluetooth," the alpha murmured to the beta. He returned his *gaze to ours. "We need to know everything he knows," he told us, the meaning clear. "Do whatever you need, but…" We watched him as he took a deep breath. "Keep it from her."*

We raised our head and faced the alpha straight on. As we assessed him and considered who and what he was, we recognized this was the alpha we respected.

"She slumbers," we told him.

"I'll be waiting when she wakes," he told us firmly. "Do not doubt that."

We'd see.

We moved in front of the human, bending to look him in the eye. The white wolf moved within us, and we felt our eyes change color to the amber of the wolf. His eyes widened in fear and horror as our nails extended into claws and our fangs grew.

The human scrambled backward, his back hitting the wall, and he tried to dodge to the side.

Silly, silly human.

We smiled at him.

"What secrets are you hiding?" we murmured, moving forward. We didn't care that the wolves were here. Wolves were predators, and they knew how to hunt.

We did not mind them seeing how we hunted.

"I remember your friend prayed to his God and wept." We ran a claw down the side of his face, smelling the blood as it ran from the cut we made. "Will you weep?"

"What the fuck is she?" the human shouted past us to the alpha behind us.

"Justice."

That pleased us.

"Get us answers," the alpha spoke to us.

That did not *please us, that he would order us, but we would play his game.*

For now.

"You killed the old one?" He nodded rapidly. We tried to remember, that there had been the old one with huts in the woods and the other one who worked in the place with all the chemicals. We did not like the chemical smell. "The one in the bar?"

"They're dead."

The child would cry. She had liked them. They had helped her. For that, we took his kneecap.

His screams were amusing, but when we looked at the alpha, he rolled his hand as if to say hurry up. The alpha was beginning to annoy us.

"What do you want to ask?"

"When we caught him," the alpha spoke, "he had three guns filled with silver bullets. I want to know where the knowledge of silver bullets came from and who gave them to him."

"Silver burns," we hissed as we turned back to the whimpering human. "You will tell us everything."

When we finished with the human, we turned to the alpha and his beta. The beta had lost color and looked wild about the eyes, but the alpha...oh, the alpha stood strong.

The alpha walked up to us and picked the half-dead human from the floor. With a quick snap, the human's neck broke. The alpha faced us, and we got ready to fight him.

His Will surrounded us, and we fought against his power. But his power was so strong. His Will too strong.

Sleep, Moonstar.

⌒

I WOKE up in the guest bedroom of Cannon's house. Completely disoriented, I didn't know what day it was or how I got here. Struggling to sit up, I saw the glass of water and the protein bar. Drinking my water, I got out of bed, not liking how weak my legs felt. What had happened?

I was in sleep shorts and a tank, with my hair braided over my shoulder, and I patted it self-consciously. It was a far neater braid than I ever managed.

After I'd been to the bathroom and brushed my teeth because my mouth felt as dry and musty as a desert, I came out of the bathroom, ready to go in search of answers when I found Cannon already in the room.

"What happened? Is he dead? How long was I out for?"

Cannon held his hand up to stop my questions and pointed to the bed. "In."

"There's nothing wrong with me," I insisted but somehow still managed to find myself climbing back onto the bed.

"Just humor me," Cannon grumbled, taking a seat at the side of the bed. "How do you feel?"

I thought about it, checking how I felt. My wolf was sleeping. Running my hands over my legs, I shrugged. "Good."

Cannon nodded. "Eat your protein bar."

"Why is there no food?" I asked him with a grin. "I thought I was predictable. I thought my appetite was a source of your amusement?"

Cannon's eyebrows raised briefly as he looked away. "I've got a lot to tell you." His voice was subdued. "You'd be better off lying down."

I sat cross-legged on the bed, and I saw his flat look. "Best I can do when you look and sound like that." I heard the defensive tone in my voice and was relieved when I saw his small smile.

"You've been gone a long time," he told me.

I'd been about to take a bite of the snack, but my hand lowered when I saw that he wouldn't meet my eye. "How long?"

"Two weeks."

The protein bar bounced off my lap and onto the floor. "What the fuck?"

"Moonstar took over when you learned of Lottie's passing," Cannon began. "Do you remember?"

I remembered the pain of grief and then...nothing. "Sorry."

Reaching out, he patted my knee. "I'm sorry for your loss. I think she meant a lot to you."

Wiping the tears away, I nodded. "Maggie and her, they took me in. Maggie gave me a job, and Lottie gave me somewhere to sleep." Rubbing my nose, I stared at his hand on my knee. "They cared. I was, I was..."

"Happy."

Looking up at him, I nodded. My shoulders lifted and dropped. "I was happy with them."

"They were your friends." Cannon took his hand off my knee, and I mourned the loss. "It's not your fault what happened to them." He glanced at me briefly. "If it's any consolation, and I know it won't be, their deaths were quick."

He let me cry. He didn't move to console me. He kept himself on the edge of the bed, rigid. It was for that reason that my tears dried up quickly while I pushed my pain down, realizing there was worse to come.

"What else did he tell you?"

"Your ability to come back so often to his fighting ring made him suspicious. Bullet?" I nodded. "Bullet had heard a rumor, a folktale of werewolves that some friend of his had said was more than a fable, he'd seen one. We know the humans have their tales, but years ago, this friend had smelted silver and formed bullets. And went hunting."

"Oh my Luna." My hands were pressed into my stomach.

Cannon nodded. "Killed mostly wolves, I think, but he caught and maimed a shifter. Silver slows down the shift. Your *guardian* calls it binding. It binds us to the form we are in when we're shot, but it's not permanent. It does slow us down, and that's what can be fatal."

"It slows us down enough to bleed to death?"

Cannon nodded grimly. "It would be an excruciating way to die, because, well, as you know, it burns."

"What happened to the shifter that was caught?"

Cannon rolled his head on his shoulders. "He was let go."

I gaped in surprise, but again the alpha's look was grim. "Why don't I think that's a good thing?"

"Because it isn't." Inhaling deeply, Cannon sucked his teeth. "According to Vance, a deal was made."

"A deal? What kind of monster makes a deal with a human who has silver bullets?"

Cannon met my question head-on. "Bale's father."

My gasp reverberated around the room. "Fuck off."

Cannon huffed out a laugh. "Let me tell the story first," he teased with the first real smile I had seen from him since I woke. "Stefan was a man of limited thinking. I remember that's how my father described him when I was younger, and trust me, given that Rek was as small-minded as they come, that's quite the insult." Cannon's hand was back on my knee, and I wasn't sure he was aware he had reached out to me. "Stefan struck a bargain: he would provide shifters for them to hunt, and they would use their silver bullets if he ever needed them."

My hand clutched Cannon's. "Tell me this is a lie."

Cannon was shaking his head. "No, it all adds up." Pulling his hand away, he rubbed his face. "Did you know your mother was Anterrio Pack?"

My heart felt as if it stopped. "Wh-what?"

"I spoke to your shaman while you slept," Cannon spoke softly. "He has told your brother what we've uncovered. Your mom was Anterrio Pack, and it's possible she was to be wed to Bale."

"Bale murdered my parents?" I was aware I was shouting.

"I can't prove that, Kezia."

"Can you prove he didn't?"

He blew out a breath. "No."

I was out of the bed, heading to the bedroom door, when Cannon lifted me off my feet and put me back down on the bed.

"Cannon!"

"Think!" he scolded me as I struggled. "If not about yourself, for your brother."

That stopped me cold. "Kris? Is he okay?"

Cannon eased off me and sat back, allowing me to sit up once more. "Yes, but he must be careful, Kezia. We don't know if Bale was involved, but your brother is in the best place to find out." He saw I was about to speak when he raised a finger to my lips. "And your brother is *mated* to Bale's daughter. Kris will not put Cass at risk, and honestly"—Cannon shook his head—"I don't envy him that conversation."

"You have to get him."

Cannon grimaced. "Trust me, I was halfway there to do exactly that."

"But?" He looked at me, and I rolled my eyes. "I know there's a but coming."

"Kris talked me out of it."

I waited, my eyes bugging out of my head. "Oh, my Luna! Is that *it*? You didn't go and get him because my stupid, knuckle-headed brother told you not to?" Tugging at the end of the braid, I gawked at him. "Please tell me that isn't why you *left* him there!"

"I cannot kidnap the head of security of the Anterrio Pack."

"Why?"

Cannon gave me a dry look. "I just told you why, and your brother asked me to hold back."

"Okay, I get it." I didn't, but I wasn't telling him that. "I'll go back." I got out of the bed again, heading to the closet.

Firm hands gripped my upper arms and turned me back to the bed. "You will not be going back."

"My brother needs me."

"He needs you *safe*," Cannon chastised me. "Here, I have the proof."

He handed me a phone, open to a message screen.

Kris: I need to think

Cannon: I'm coming to get you and your mate out

Kris: No. She won't understand, I need time.

Cannon: And if you don't have time?

Kris: Keep Kezia away from here, while I figure it out.

Cannon: I don't think I can do that…she's your family.

Kris: Keep my sister safe, Alpha, or I'll hunt
you down and take you out

Cannon: If I keep her here she'll do it for you!

Kris: Kezia is smart, smarter than we give her
credit for. She'll understand, she'll also bust
your balls but keep my sister away from here,
Cannon. That's all I ask.

Kris: and also a place to stay when I grab my
mate and run...

Cannon: Call for me, I'll be there

Kris: counting on it brother

I read the messages again.

"He called you brother." My tears dripped onto the screen.
Looking up, I saw his pain. "I'm scared for him."

Cannon nodded, drawing me close. "I know, I am too."

"We should go anyway."

"Remember he said you were smart?"

I pushed the alpha away. "I *am* smart. I'm smart enough to
know that he's being stupid."

Cannon sighed and tilted his head back. "It's not just that,
pup."

"Tell me."

"I send her back, but each time, you're taking too long to
resurface." Cannon looked worried. I'd never seen that before
today, and I knew I didn't like it. "You must learn to fight her,
Kezia. I can't..." He stood, shaking his head as he moved away. "I
don't think I can keep doing this, the worry, the not knowing if

you'll come back to me, I just—" Cannon ran his hand through his hair, watching me helplessly.

Come back to me.

It hit me like a ton of bricks. Cannon cared for me. *Actually* cared. He cared for my brother. For my family. That was huge, and I was struggling to breathe easily.

Shit. I cared for him too.

Whoa. I really did.

I hadn't expected that, but the realization filled me with warmth, and I needed to show him. To touch him. Kiss him.

Love him.

Getting off the bed, I crossed the short distance to him and wordlessly slipped my arms around his waist. He pulled me tight into his embrace and hugged me back. I felt his cheek rest against my head as he held me, and I felt weirdly emotional.

"She's getting stronger?" I whispered, berating myself for this being what I addressed first.

"So much power," he said in the quiet of the room. "I have to use my Will on you," he said, his hold getting tighter. "I don't like it. And...I think she could resist it. At any time. I don't think I have enough power to hold her."

Looking up at him, seeing the anguish and worry in his eyes, I raised myself a little and brushed my lips across his. "You can't get rid of me," I teased lightly. I lifted his shirt and ran my hand up his back, over his smooth skin. "I keep coming back."

Cannon's eyes closed at my touch. "Fuck, Kezia, you just woke up," he scolded lightly, but when I pushed my other hand against the front of his jeans, his look turned hungry.

"You said I needed to be in bed," I reminded him, popping open the top button of his jeans. "Are we alone?"

Cannon's eyes darkened as I gripped his hard length and

began to move my hand. "Yes, we're alone," he growled, "but this isn't what I meant when I said you needed to be in bed."

"It's what I meant," I told him, continuing to stroke him, kissing his neck. "And...and I need to forget for a little while."

Cannon groaned, his hand slipping down my back to squeeze my ass. "Kezia...I need you to be checked by Doc."

"You mean a physical?" I smirked up at him, giving him a light squeeze, enjoying the way his teeth grazed his bottom lip as he watched me with hooded eyes. "You can give me a physical. Right?"

He resisted for maybe five seconds, and then he kissed me, and after that, my clothes came off, and then his came off, and he allowed me to forget everything I'd woken up to as his hands worked their magic on my body, and finally he slid inside me.

Completing me.

When I was with him, he made me feel that I could handle anything, that *we* could handle anything.

Him and me. *Us*.

I realized I was no longer hating the sound of that.

CHAPTER 26

Kezia

Cannon made me stay in bed all day because Cannon was a controlling worrier, who didn't believe people when they told him they were fine.

The bonus was he stayed in the room with me, not always in bed. I think he had gone down to the study at times when I was asleep. For all my protests that I was fine, I was still very tired.

Having sex with Cannon helped ease the pain in my heart, but he did tire me out. I was blaming him, even though I knew I only had to look inside to know who the real culprit was.

He'd woken me up earlier with a glass of fresh orange juice and a promise that he wouldn't be long, I remember I mumbled something, but his low chuckle that tickled my ear probably meant that my response hadn't been understandable. I remember the kiss to my temple, the squeeze of my hip, and then I slept some more.

I'd gotten up a while later—I wasn't sure how long after he left—and had a shower and was relieved to feel like me again. A careful search and I knew my wolf was asleep and sated for now.

I didn't feel Moonstar. I hadn't for a long time, and I knew at one point I would need to deal with the fact that Moonstar was not the name of my wolf; she was something else entirely.

I didn't know how to deal with that, so I did what I did best: I ignored it until it wasn't the first thing I was thinking of.

When I looked in the closet, I saw that I had clean clothes. New clothes. Jeans, leggings, shirts and T-shirts, there was even a pack of underwear.

Cannon bought me clothes.

Blowing out a breath, I looked at them as they hung there. The first thing I noticed was that none of the clothes were like Koda wore. Reaching out, my fingers trailed over a simple three-quarter-sleeve, fitted blouse. It was pretty, but it was also *me*. So me. It had no decoration, nothing fancy, just a simple-cut white blouse that I would pick to wear for something like a date...

Picking a sports bra and plain boy shorts, I got ready for the day in jeans, and a black T-shirt. The jeans were a little loose, but I wouldn't complain. I spotted the white tennis shoes just as I prepared to come out of the closet and saw that they were also new, as I slipped them on.

My hair was half-dry, and after realizing Cannon had moved the hair dryer to the other bathroom, I took the time to dry my hair properly. I didn't mind he'd moved it. He had left his bedroom door open, his room lay as I remembered, and he hadn't moved the hair dryer because he didn't want me in the room, but because he was making it easier for me.

Studying my reflection, I wished for maybe the first time in my life, that I had mascara and some lipstick. My blue eyes had lost their sparkle, my pale skin was whiter than snow, and I lacked any color at all in my cheeks. Even my lips were such a pale pink I took a step back when I suddenly recognized that I looked like a corpse.

This absolutely wouldn't do.

Nikan's tour the other day...week? My brain shut that door firmly. Nikan's tour had failed to show me a clothing store. There hadn't been clothes in the grocery store, but these new clothes had to have come from somewhere, so with a plan in mind, I left the house and went searching.

"Hello, Kezia," Willy greeted me as she approached me. Stepping forward, she hugged me closely. "It's so good to see you on your feet."

"I'm sorry." I remembered I was supposed to be on kitchen rotation. "I'll ask Cannon to put me back onto chores."

Willy laughed. She easily looped her arm through mine, and a gentle tug encouraged me to walk. "I'm pleased to see you recovered from your spell."

"Spell?" Did she know? Had Cannon told his pack I had an unknown spirit inside me?

"It's hard when you are far from your mate," she told me with a gleam in her eye. "The pull can be unbearable."

She meant Landon. They all still thought I was supposed to be with Landon.

"Resisting it only makes it harder," she scolded. "Where are you heading this morning?"

"A clothes store? Do you have one?"

"We do," Willy told me, coming to a stop. "I'm headed in that direction." She pointed across the street. "You want to head in that direction."

I followed her movement and nodded. "Cool, so maybe I'll see you later?" I liked Willy, she was nice to me, and I had a vague recollection of her being there the night my heat came.

"You can count on it, and, Kezia?" She moved closer, her

voice a whisper. "Stop stalling with our alpha and seal the deal." The gleam was back in her eye.

"Landon," I blurted. "You mean Landon."

Willy laughed. "Sure, I mean *Landon*." With a shake of her head, she patted me on the shoulder as she said goodbye and then headed in the opposite direction of where I was heading.

Chewing the inside of my cheek, I watched her leave with narrowed eyes. "Huh."

Turning, I followed the road and only had to ask two more of the pack where the store was. I was claiming it as a success when I pushed open the store door. Only to be filled with dread when I saw Koda. Of *course* she would be the one to work in the clothing store.

It was too late to duck back out; she and the other female had seen me.

"Hey." I raised my hand in an awkward wave. "How are you?" Walking to one of the clothing racks, I hid behind it like the coward I was. Pack clothing stores were a huge mixture of different kinds of clothing stores that humans had. When I had lived amongst the humans, they had stores called thrift stores, where anything and everything was sold, but the items were mostly used. Or there was one huge store that Maggie had taken me to that sold everything. From food to books, electronics, and clothing.

A pack store was like that. Some things were other packs' cast-offs, and some things were brand new. In the Anterrio Pack, the females used to do shopping sprees as they called it and would go every two months to the city to shop for the pack. It's how Cass always had a new dress for events. They also had several catalogues that they ordered from, with a drop-off point near the base of the mountain. I'd never really cared to go with them, and I think the only reason I was ever asked was because of Cass.

Looking around the store, I realized Blackridge Peak Pack must have worked a similar system.

"The alpha bought you clothes." Koda's voice wasn't as sweet when the alpha wasn't around, I noticed. "What do you want?"

What I wanted was some better, prettier underwear. Cass had always been talking about sexy lingerie, and while I was comfortable in a plain sports bra and boy shorts, I wanted something a little...frillier...for that white blouse.

I couldn't tell Koda that though. The shifter in front of me would probably wear that blouse to clean in. I also didn't want to discuss lingerie with the female who probably wore frilly things as her normal attire.

"Well?"

"Um, I..." Yup, I had nothing. The other female walked closer and smiled at me in greeting. "Hi."

"Hello." She had the softest voice. "It's so nice to meet you finally," she told me, and I saw that she was sincere.

We both ignored Koda's snort.

"I'm Kezia."

"Barbara." She was staring at me, and what had been nice was now kind of becoming intrusive.

"Okay, well, I just wanted to know where here was," I said, looking around, avoiding eye contact with both. Which is when I saw it. The white lacy bra with soft cups, and I wondered how I could get it past them, knowing I couldn't. "See ya."

I said goodbye to the bra more than to the two shifters.

I walked quickly with my hands shoved in my pockets when I heard the footsteps running behind me. Turning, I got ready for the attack and almost fell over when Barbara skidded to a halt, fear on her face.

"I'm not going to hurt you!" I shouted as she backed away. "Sorry, I'm..." I squared my shoulders. "I get nervous," I told her, feeling stupid. "I'm sorry."

Cautiously, she took a step forward. "I know better than to run up behind Andrea's daughter." Barbara dipped her head briefly. "You look so much like your mother, Kezia."

My world was spinning, sound rushed into my ears, and I hadn't appreciated I'd stepped forward and grabbed her arm until I felt the cool touch of her other hand gently fold over mine.

"Oh Luna." I hastily let go. "I'm sorry, I didn't mean to grab you, I'm—" Shaking my head, I looked at her. "You knew my mom? Really?"

Barbara's smile was gentle. "She was my best friend growing up."

Holy Luna.

"I need to know everything."

Barbara nodded, watching me as closely as I was watching her. "I have freshly baked scones at home. Would you like one?" At my nod, she seemed to lose some of her shyness. "It's not far," she told me, and I followed her eagerly.

My back pocket buzzed, and I pulled out the phone I forgot Cannon had told me I had to carry everywhere with me. Glancing at it, I saw his text.

Cannon: You're not where I left you pup...

Kezia: Met Barbara, she knew my mom! Going for a scone

When I looked up, I saw we were outside a wooden-clad, single-story house. Barbara looked between the phone and me.

"Overprotective alphas," I told her, jamming the phone back into my jeans. "Is this you?" I pointed at the house.

"If the alpha needs you…"

I waved away her concern. "Most definitely does not. Come on, I'm hungry, a scone sounds wonderful," I told her as I hurried past.

As I waited impatiently at her door, I saw her try to hide her smile. "It seems like you inherited your mother's impulsiveness." She pushed her door open. No one locked their door in this pack.

"What else do you think I inherited?" I asked her eagerly, following her inside. "Did you know my dad?"

Barbara gestured to a stool beside the kitchen counter. "Sit, I'll make some tea, and you can ask me every question you have."

I looked at Barbara in wide-eyed wonder. "Every question?" I took the seat, blindly reaching out for it, and almost fell off because I wasn't paying attention. "You don't know me—I can ask a *lot* of questions," I warned her.

Her laughter was light, and I watched her get cups after filling a kettle and placing it on the stove. "Another thing you inherited from your mom," she teased.

I sat on my hands while I waited for Barbara to make tea, biting my tongue as question after question went unasked, and when the loud banging on the door made me jump with surprise, I rolled my eyes as I knew exactly *what* was trying to knock down her door.

Or *who*.

"Luna, don't let me stab him," I muttered after Barbara rushed to the door and returned with one very pissed off alpha.

"Hi." I waved at him. The look he gave me made me grin. "What brings you here?"

The look got darker.

"Alpha Cannon, we were just having some tea. Can I pour you a cup?" Barbara was shaking and looked ready to collapse. Recalling the way she reacted when I spun on her earlier, I reached out and pulled Cannon to my side, and then I stepped in front of him and approached Barbara.

"Hey, are you okay? Cannon won't hurt you."

"Hurt her?" Cannon sounded confused but also *loud*.

"Shut up," I hissed over my shoulder. I was surprised when he gently moved me out of the way. In fascination, I watched as the alpha bent his knees slightly to meet Barbara's eyes.

I heard the *thrum*, looking around for the source of the noise, and then realized he had mindlinked with her. Cocking my head, I listened to the gentle pulse around me. I'd never spent much time around alphas, and now that I knew Bale was *not* an alpha, it made sense that he wouldn't want his pack to see it either.

Cannon stepped back, turning to me. Barbara was staring at him in wide-eyed wonder, and I had the ugly thought that he didn't need any more females hero-worshipping him. His ego was already big. By the smirk on his face, he knew exactly what I was thinking.

"Barbara is new to the pack," Cannon explained to me. "She hasn't been here long."

The shifter moved out of the shadow of her alpha. "My husband died," she told me quickly. "The pack we were in, well, they'd never felt like home. I chose to move on."

"The Anterrio Pack was your original pack?" I guessed, and Barbara nodded. "Where you knew my mom?"

"Yes." Her eyes were full of uncertainty. "Alpha Cannon says you are from there?"

I could see why she would be confused. My mom left the Anterrio Pack to live the life of a nomad with my dad. Barbara probably didn't know Kris and I had gone back there.

"Bale took us in when we were young," I told her, retaking my seat on the stool.

"Us?"

"My brother, Kris."

Barbara's hands flew to her mouth, and tears filled her eyes. "He survived?"

Cannon's look sharpened. "Why would he not?"

Barbara hurriedly wiped her eyes and looked around her kitchen. "I think we need to move to the couches." Her voice was shaky. "We have a lot to tell each other, I think."

"You can go," I told Cannon reluctantly as the other shifter started piling things on a tray, even though the couch and coffee table were within walking distance. "I know you have stuff to do."

Cannon shook his head at me, exasperation clear on his face. "Stuff?" he grumbled. "The only thing I need to do right now is be here."

Reaching out, I caught his fingers, my own curling through his. "Thank you," I whispered. "I really would have been pissed if you left."

The alpha gave me a very un-alpha-like roll of his eyes before he turned and offered to carry the tray.

When we were all settled on the couch, I looked at Barbara expectantly.

"Well? Start talking."

CHAPTER 27

Cannon

I looked at Kezia in disbelief before turning to the older shifter. "Kezia lacks social skills," I apologized for her. "A *lot* of social skills."

The wolf beside me tutted as she leaned forward. "I say it like it is. You told me you had a lot to talk about, well...let's talk. I want to know everything you know about my mom and dad, Bale, and who killed my parents." She glanced at me. "And who tried to kill my brother and me, and why you thought they succeeded and that he was dead."

Barbara looked between the two of us, and as she reached forward for her cup of tea, I saw the tremor in her hand.

"You don't need to be scared of either me or Kezia," I spoke gently. "This is a safe space for you," I assured her. "Neither Kezia nor I will speak of what we learn here to any other."

Kezia straightened up and dug her elbow into my ribs as she did. "Well, I can't promise that," she told Barbara honestly. "I will tell my brother. The alpha will probably tell his beta, Royce, who the alpha will think isn't the same as telling someone, but Royce will tell his wife, Hannah, and I believe it will go no further.

However, my brother Kris will tell Cass, his mate, and…" Kezia cleared her throat. "Cass is Bale's daughter."

Barbara looked between the two of us, wetting her lips when she looked away. "Anterrio Pack is a pack set in the past. It's a reason both Andrea and I were eager to leave. We both hoped for matches outside of the pack." The older shifter patted her hair. "My Lee was from a pack out west. We met at the Luna Ball, and while he is no alpha, I knew he was mine and me his." She turned her attention back to Kezia. "I am glad that Kris is an alpha," she spoke honestly. "I worry who the Goddess selected for him, but Luna is as mysterious as the moon." Barbara sipped her tea. "How did Bale take it when Kris took over the pack?"

"He hasn't."

Barbara paled. "Does he know?"

"Yes," I confirmed. "It seems the Anterrio Pack likes to fudge the truth about mates, and no one has questioned what it means that Kris and Cass are true mates."

Barbara was nodding. "It was always that way. It wasn't until I met Lee that I realized we'd been fed untruths. Pack leaders don't have the same authority or power as an alpha. The mindlink is so weak. The first time Lee spoke to me in my mind, I thought he was shouting."

Kezia was getting more restless beside me, and I knew she was barely holding on to her manners. Not that her manners were good at the best of times, and I knew she'd snap soon.

"You were happy with your husband?" I asked. Barbara nodded enthusiastically. "And your marriage was a good one?"

"The best," she told me with a weak smile.

"The point?" Kezia asked under her breath.

"The point is that I am wondering why a female who was in a loving marriage left her pack when her husband passed and jumps at the slightest thing." Sitting back, I looked the shifter over. She was slight in stature, almost frail. Mousy brown hair and light brown eyes made her overwhelmingly average. "Who hurt you?"

Barbara swallowed. "Alpha, I don't know wh—"

"I told you that you are in a safe space," I told her with more bite in my voice than I intended.

Or do you prefer to talk without Kezia knowing your tale? The she's eyes widened as her gaze darted to Kezia.

My husband loved me very much, Alpha, but his pack is hard. They fight amongst themselves and are...restless.

I took her in one more time. Her skin was almost as pale as Kezia's. Her nervousness was ingrained in her. If I had to guess, I would say that her husband had beat her, but I heard her truth when she spoke about her love for him. But it was more than that, and I took a guess.

You said you were west? You were with the rogues to the north of Seattle?

Barbara lowered her eyes from mine and gave a simple nod.

Did they harm you? When Lee passed? A simple shake of her head, but I noticed she was shaking again, and I didn't believe her. *You are safe here. You are at no threat. My pack is no longer the same as the pack that my father ran.*

"I know that, Alpha." She extended her hand towards Kezia. "I am not ashamed of the fact I took flight from that pack." Her shoulders straightened. "My Lee never let any of the others near me. We were a hard pack, strong, but too many males together and..." Once more, her eyes darted to Kezia.

"And strong males prey on the weaker females," Kezia said with understanding. "Your husband was one of the pack leaders?" Barbara nodded in confirmation.

"This is a good pack," Kezia told her, reaching over and

taking her hand. "I've been raised in the Anterrio Pack, and you won't be surprised to know that they still keep to themselves. The whole time I've been here, everyone has been friendly. They are happy. They greet him like he's a god," she told Barbara with a jerk of her head towards me. "And I will deny this was ever said outside these walls, but I think he may deserve their respect."

My wolf rumbled happily at the praise from my mate, and I hid my smirk of satisfaction behind my hand.

"I have been here a few months." Barbara squeezed Kezia's hand. "I have seen the lightness in this pack." She shifted her gaze to mine. "A big difference from the last time I was here when your father still lived."

"An alpha should never abuse his position," I murmured.

Barbara nodded in agreement. "Stefan, Bale's father, was like Rek, although not as cruel. Not as openly." With precise movements, she cut open three scones, buttering them as she spoke. "Andrea and I were born weeks apart. We had no siblings, and much to both our parents' disappointment, we were female. Stefan's rule was that only one child could be born to each couple. Unless they birthed a male first." Barbara added jam to each scone half. She handed me a plate first and then placed the scone on the plate. "Needless to say, Andrea and I were friends from the cradle onwards." A fond smile played around her lips. "Andrea was so fierce. She rebelled against everything Stefan and his pack stood for. And I, as her willing accomplice, got punished as much as she did."

"What kind of things did you fight?" Kezia asked, taking a huge bite of the scone. "Oh Luna, this is amazing," she said, chewing and peering at the scone.

"Thank you." Barbara blushed. "Hunting. We were only

allowed to go with the males. Andrea and I hunted when we were supposed to be learning how to run a house."

Taking my bite of the scone, I echoed Kezia's approval. "Run a house," I scoffed. "So archaic." I pointed at Kezia's empty plate and my own. "You seem to have picked up some skills though."

"I agree, it is barbaric," Barbara said with a nod of approval. "I learned to bake when I married. Lee taught me how to cook better, but baking filled in the nights when he was hunting."

"Raiding, you mean," I corrected sharply. The female's cheeks flushed but she let it slide.

"This isn't telling me about my mom," Kezia added with impatience.

Barbara placed her plate with her half-eaten scone on the table. "Andrea and I were in trouble a lot. But we were also part of the pack, and we both knew that neither of us wanted to remain in a pack that repressed us. I was lucky. Lee attended the Luna Ball just after I turned seventeen. We courted and I was wed within three months. We convinced her parents to let Andrea come with me to Lee's pack. While I settled in, it would be helpful for me to have a friend."

"Stefan fell for that?" I asked in surprise.

Barbara smirked. "You have no idea, Alpha, of how much trouble Andrea could get into."

With a glance at Kezia, I pursed my lips. "You've forgotten I've met her daughter." I was rewarded with another dig in my ribs. "See?"

"Nate was a loner," Barbara continued with a smile at us both. "He was an alpha," she confirmed, and I saw Kezia nod. "But he didn't want the responsibility of the pack." She caught me frowning and gave a half shrug. "Not all are suited to rule."

I agreed with that, but having met both Kris and Kezia, I was surprised that their father wouldn't also be a strong independent wolf.

"What pack was my dad from?"

Barbara looked sympathetic. "I don't know. He never told us, and my Lee, well, he always suspected he was born of a rogue." Looking between us, she carried on with her story. "Andrea was his mate. It was so much stronger than my bond with Lee. I worried I wasn't loving my new husband enough, but Nate explained the alpha bond to us." She averted her gaze when she spoke next. "Honestly, that craving that the bond creates, the connection and hold it has over the ones bonded? I wouldn't want it."

Out of the corner of my eye, I saw Kezia shift in her seat. "The bond creates balance for the alpha," I spoke quietly. "Have you noticed that the packs with no bonded alphas are the ones that are unhappy?"

"I don't think it's as simple as that," Kezia muttered.

"Isn't it?" She saw the challenge in my eyes and looked away.

"Nate and Andrea were bonded under the full moon by a shaman on his way to join a new pack."

Kezia sat up excitedly. "My shaman?"

Barbara looked at me with uncertainty. "I...I don't know. You have a shaman?"

"The Anterrio Pack has a shaman," I explained. "Is it possible it was him?"

Barbara looked unsure. "There was no shaman in the Anterrio Pack when we left."

"Where did my mom and dad go when they were married? Back to Anterrio?"

"No. Married, to an alpha especially, a female is not required to return to her pack. She belongs to her alpha."

I grinned at the look of horror on Kezia's face. "*Belongs*?" she screeched.

"Balance," I reminded her.

I was rewarded with the full force of her fury as she snapped her head around to meet my gaze. "*Belongs* to her alpha?" she asked scathingly. "Fuck that."

I heard Barbara's gasp. "Kezia, your language," I scolded softly, holding back my laughter as I watched her eyebrows disappear into her hairline. The look on her face told me in no uncertain terms that we would be discussing this later.

"Keep talking," Kezia ordered Barbara, giving the older woman her attention once more.

Luna, her manners would need work. I couldn't have Kezia present during pack negotiations if she had no restraint. Her wild and free nature was alluring, but I also needed someone with discipline and control. I didn't envy my future self *that* conversation.

"Nate was visiting all the packs in the area. I don't think he had any intention of joining any of them," Barbara carried on with her story. "Andrea was tasting freedom for the first time. She loved that Nate allowed her to do whatever she wanted." She sighed. "It came as no surprise the next time I saw her that they were choosing to live as nomads. She was pregnant and glowing." She smiled with fondness. "Everything about them both was so..." Barbara paused as she searched for the right word. "Content."

Kezia sat back, her face stricken but her eyes full of longing. "I knew they would be happy," she whispered to no one. "Kris always said he remembers their laughter."

Reaching out, I pulled Kezia into my side, offering her comfort, which she took as she pressed into my side. I saw the other female's look of surprise and hoped I looked like an alpha offering a pack member comfort and not an alpha needing his mate at his side.

"How does Bale fit into this?" I asked, hoping to take the female's attention off my mate, who had rested her head on my shoulder.

"Andrea was like her daughter," Barbara told me simply. "She was beautiful."

I felt Kezia stiffen at the compliment.

"Bale liked pretty things, but he hated her wildness. He told the pack that he intended to marry Andrea, another reason why she was so eager to escape with me and Lee." Barbara looked down at her hands. "I never thought he would go after her."

"He definitely followed her?" Kezia demanded, leaning forward.

Barbara nodded. "Yes, he came to my wedding. He made a fool of himself, as usual." She scoffed. "Luna, I hated that male. Always watching us, trying to get Andrea to go places with him alone. Claiming her as his no matter how much she objected. He would know when we sneaked out, and he would tell his father, and then we would be punished on our return."

"Punished how?" I asked.

"Holding cells. To give us time to reflect on our actions."

"Under the hall?" Kezia asked knowingly. When Barbara confirmed it, Kezia once more looked at me. "Another thing my mother and I have in common... Being locked up by someone thinking they know better."

"Now, now," I murmured. "Let's not confuse an obsessed stalker and an alpha protecting his pack." At Kezia's unimpressed snort, I grinned. "Your brother put you in the cells, too, remember." Kezia opened her mouth to argue, but Barbara's next words caused both of us to stare at her in shock.

"Other times, they would flog us." Barbara rubbed the back of her neck. "I believe that stopped when Stefan died."

"He whipped you?" Kezia's jaw was slack. Turning to me, she ran her eyes over me. "Don't get any ideas," she warned me, and I bit back my grin.

"So, when Andrea rejected Bale, he did...what?" I asked Barbara.

"He left." She thought about it. "When I saw Andrea when she was pregnant, she told me he had confronted her one more time, as she and Nate had visited Anterrio Pack one final time."

"She went back?" Kezia's surprise was like my own.

"Andrea wanted her parents to know she was happy and about the child."

"Bale wouldn't have liked that," I mused.

"She told me he flew into a rage, and Nate challenged Bale." Barbara looked uncomfortable as she spoke. "The hunters attacked them that night and ran them from the pack. They barely made it out alive."

"But they didn't kill them," I spoke out loud, absentmindedly reaching for Kezia and taking her hand. "Did you see them again?"

Barbara shook her head. "No, we moved west. I heard about her death years later. They told me she was attacked by rogues killing her mate and her child."

"Rogues like your pack?" Kezia challenged, her voice tight with anger.

"Yes." Barbara met the challenge head-on. "It's why Lee and I went there. I wouldn't settle until I knew the truth, and he was unhappy with the current pack."

I watched as she spoke, my senses alert for any hint of a lie. "And what did you find?"

"A pack that was rough and undisciplined but that wouldn't kill a child." She took a deep breath. "But one that would be easy to blame." Sitting up straighter, she looked like she was struggling with what to say next. "What I say next, you may not believe me, but I have no reason to lie to you."

"Tell us," I encouraged.

"Stefan was deranged." Barbara adjusted herself in the seat one more time. "He didn't shy from torture, and although we were flogged and locked up, or withheld food, it wasn't the worst he could do to us. In that way, we were lucky." Barbara ignored Kezia's scoff. "But we heard rumors." Nervously she licked her lips. "It was said amongst his team that he had a far worse form of punishment."

Once more, I watched the shifter in front of me pat her hair nervously. "Which was?" I asked.

"Silver," Kezia whispered.

Barbara looked at Kezia, her eyes wide. "How did you... Did they use it on you?" Her timidness was gone as she lurched forward in anger. "Did they torture you?"

"No." Kezia reached for her to comfort her. "I was shot with it." Pulling her hand away, she pointed to her upper arm. "And I have the scar to prove it."

Barbara's eyes were glued to the spot where *I* had shot my mate, and it was my turn to move with discomfort in the seat. I saw Kezia's lip curl upwards, and I pressed my knee into hers and was rewarded with a little nudge back.

"How did the pack use it?" I asked Barbara.

"The rumor was they melted it and poured it on open wounds."

Both Kezia and I winced. The agony would be... I shivered at the thought and once more pulled Kezia into me. Her shiver was more pronounced than my own. She'd been shot; she knew the pain like no other in the room.

"My parents were murdered," Kezia said softly. "Kris remembers that males came for them. He remembers our mother screaming for us to run." Tears slipped down her cheeks. "He thinks we ran."

Barbara was also crying. "I'm so sorry, Kezia."

"You thought Kris was dead," Kezia spoke to her. "But you recognized me as my mom's daughter. How?"

I hadn't known that bit and watched the older female with interest.

"You look so much like her," Barbara explained easily. "I knew who you were the moment I saw you." She looked between us. "The resemblance is uncanny."

"If that's true, then that means Bale has always known exactly who you and Kris are," I realized.

"And that means he's always known Kris is an alpha!" Kezia looked at me with alarm. "And that we are older than we thought, because he would know when my mom was pregnant!" Kezia gripped my arm. "Cannon, we need to get Kris out of there!"

"We still can't say with certainty that Bale is responsible," I reminded her, watching her eyes narrow in fury. "Think before you speak, pup," I warned.

Kezia pulled back, her jaw clenched tightly, but I knew that she was merely retreating due to Barbara and that the fight was merely on hold for now.

After some more time with Barbara, we made our leave, Kezia hugging her close when she left.

Walking back to the house, Kezia walked with her head down, her eyes on her feet. "I have so many questions," she broke the silence. "I went there for answers and now I just have more questions."

"We can't make assumptions," I reminded her.

"I can," she muttered darkly. "Especially when everything points to a certain pack leader."

I had to agree with her, but I knew not to encourage her too much. My mate was unpredictable. "It may be a good thing the Pack Council is coming," I muttered as we walked up the path to my house, and I moved in front to open the door for her.

"Landon."

That made me stop and look back at her. "Forgot my name already, pup?" I tried to tease, but it pissed me off she just spoke his name.

But Kezia was staring across my yard, to the side of the house and the pathway that led from the bunker. "It's Landon."

Stepping away from the door, I saw the son of the pack leader who could have killed Kezia's parents walk into my town like he belonged here. Just like the cocky, arrogant little shit he was.

"What the heck does he want?" Kezia whispered beside me.

The growl I let out caused my mate to look at me with apprehension. "Let's find out."

CHAPTER 28

Kezia

I felt myself move closer to Cannon as I watched Landon approach us. His hands were in the pockets of his jeans, his posture relaxed, and for the first time in my life, I wondered where he got his confidence from. I knew he could have had it easier in the pack. He was the pack leader's son after all, but Landon did his chores like the rest of us.

Sometimes, Kris would scold him for slacking off, but considering Cass did nothing, pulling Landon up for relaxing instead of working wasn't as effective. Of course, now I knew why my brother wasn't scolding his mate. I resented all the times I was berated for taking advantage of the friendship of the twins.

With a narrowed gaze, Cannon watched Landon approach, and I wanted to link our fingers together to let him know I was here, but we were in the open, and for the few pack members who saw Landon approach, they all thought *he* was my mate. The thought made my stomach turn.

"This isn't going to end well," I murmured so only Cannon could hear me, "if you don't keep your temper," I warned, my voice barely a whisper, and felt the whisper of a caress across my mind from the alpha beside me.

Landon hesitated at the gate, his eyes full of mirth as he grinned insolently at Cannon. "And here was me thinking I'd have to search this town, and I find you as soon as I come over the hill."

"What do you want?"

So much for holding onto his temper.

"What do I want? My mate, of course." Landon pointed at me as if there was any doubt to anyone watching he meant me.

Cannon moved forward, and I grabbed his arm. "Let's go into the study?" I spoke loudly. "Landon, inside. Now."

Instead, Landon leaned on the gate and grinned at Cannon. "Bossy, isn't she? Is she like this when you fuck her?"

I grabbed at Cannon, but I missed him as he jumped the steps and barreled towards the male I once thought of as a friend. Landon jumped backward not to run, but into a defensive stance.

I couldn't take in the craziness, but I was already running after Cannon, but it was the bundle of muscle that threw himself between the alpha and Landon that got there first. Royce pushed Cannon back, just as Nikan raced between them also, and he pushed Landon away.

"Let's all calm down," Royce spoke firmly but pleasantly, his eyes hard as he looked at Cannon. "Alpha," he warned.

"We were going into the study," I told him, feeling anxious.

"Excellent idea," Nikan agreed. I noticed he had a hard grip on Landon and practically dragged him towards the house. Cannon hesitated and I was sure that the alpha wasn't going to move, but he did. As he turned on his heel, his gaze clashed with mine, and I saw his barely restrained fury. Then we were all following him inside the house.

The study had several chairs and couches, plenty of seats for everyone. I sat perched on the edge of a seat while Cannon chose to remain standing. Royce took a seat on the couch, as did Nikan, leaving Landon with a chair or a smaller couch. The couch was nearer me, and when he moved to sit beside me, Cannon sat down, his legs kicked out in front of him, his hands on his stomach as he watched the fair-haired male with an almost violent insolence.

Landon chuckled as he took the seat. "I prefer not to bullshit either," he told Cannon when he sat down. His cool gaze turned to me. "Kez, you look great."

I ignored *his* bullshit. "Why are you here?"

Landon let out a dramatic sigh. "Would you believe I missed you?"

"No."

"We've been friends for years, Kez. You wound me."

"I wouldn't mind wounding you," Cannon drawled with a smirk. "Permanently."

Landon threw his head back and laughed. "I bet you wouldn't," he said, his grin wide. "But I think you've had enough time to break her in. I want her back. It's my turn now."

The silence was deafening and then chaos erupted. The whole couch was tipped backward when Cannon launched himself off it and landed on top of Landon, the sound of fist meeting flesh echoing in the room. Landon was ready for him, but he was no match for a pissed-off alpha whose mate had just been insulted.

Royce and Nikan struggled to pull Cannon off as he and Landon punched the shit out of each other, and when I tried to dodge the male limbs in the area, I got an unintentional smack across my face, causing me to curse in pain as I jumped back.

My cry penetrated Cannon's temper, and suddenly he was beside me, his hands cradling my face.

"Fuck, baby, who hit you? Was it me?" Cannon frantically searched my face, only calming when I placed my hands over his.

"Baby?" I tried to tease him. "That's new." I moved closer to him, seeing him calm down as he watched me. "It wasn't you, and I'm not hurt," I assured him. Cannon dipped his head, his lips brushing over mine gently, and I reached up for another kiss.

"I'm right here, Kez."

Cannon stiffened and I squeezed his hands.

Don't let him get to you.

Cannon's eyes widened in surprise and then delight as he heard me through the mindlink, and he was kissing me again. Not softly, not tentatively. Full-out kissing, and I dimly heard another smack on flesh and figured Nikan or Royce had punched Landon for whatever he had just said.

The alpha stepped back, letting me go with reluctance. He turned and straightened the couch, pulling me onto his lap when he retook his seat.

Overkill, no?

Fuck him. Figuratively not physically.

My snort was loud in the quiet of the room. With effort, I turned my attention back to Landon. "Why are you such a dick?" I cut him off before he could speak. "I'm not your mate. You know it, I know it. And"—I played my trump card—"your father knows it."

Landon watched me, his eyes flicking now and then to Cannon's large hand, which rested with familiarity on my hip. "Says who?"

I blinked. "What?"

"Who says I'm not?" Landon eased himself back in his seat, appearing completely relaxed. "You've never denied it."

"I never accepted it either!"

He leaned forward with the speed of a striking viper. "And you've never *denied* it." Easing back, he inspected his knuckles. "So, I ask again. Says who?" He glanced at Cannon. "Many mates fuck around first, and honestly," he said with a sigh, "I wasn't looking forward to fucking a virgin, the whimpering and the inexperience, gah. So, thanks for that." He gave Cannon a nod, and I felt the alpha's fingers bite into my hip, but he said nothing. "But it's getting embarrassing now, Kez, so pack your shit and let's go."

There was a low rumbling growl, and I almost, *almost* wanted to let Cannon punch him again, but something wasn't adding up. I'd known this male for most of my life. This wasn't the carefree Landon I knew.

Not taking my eyes off him, I spoke quietly. "I need the room." Silence once again surrounded me, and when I turned to them, Nikan and Royce were both looking at me in varying degrees of shock. Turning on his lap, I locked eyes with my alpha. "I need a moment alone with Landon."

"No."

I knew that was coming, so I gave him an eye roll and was pleased to see his top lip curl upwards. "Search him," I told him quietly, knowing the others would still hear. "But then leave me with him." Swallowing, I leaned forward, kissing him lightly. "Please."

Cannon was no longer smiling as he watched me, but after a long moment, he nodded, and I heard his brother and his beta's reaction.

"Make it quick, Royce," Cannon told his beta, standing with me still in his arms. The noise of the three others in the room allowed Cannon to move me until I was fully facing him with my legs around his hips. "Whatever you think you're doing, it isn't happening," he whispered in my ear.

Moving into him, I moved my mouth to his ear. "Trust me, Alpha," I whispered back, my teeth catching his lower lobe.

"Pup..."

Pulling my head back, I looked into his eyes, and I felt a thousand emotions race through me as we held each other's stare. Cannon kissed me with urgency and passion, and I kissed him back, even as he unwrapped my legs from around him and lowered me to the ground.

"You have five minutes." He let me go. His look was hard when he spoke to Landon. "Touch her and you die. I don't give a fuck whose son you are."

"I'll wait 'til she's no longer full of your saliva," Landon grunted as he took his seat.

Trust me.

I am, pup. Don't make me regret it.

He was at the door to the study when I sent the next message. *I'll make it up to you tonight.*

He looked at me over his shoulder, and I saw the gleam in his eye. Hiding my smile, I turned my attention back to Landon, who was watching me openly. The door closed and I felt the seal of magic enclose us, as did Landon, whose eyebrows rose in surprise, and when he got off the seat to come towards me, my punch landed him on his ass.

"That's for the way you spoke about me." I shook my fist. "Don't get up. I will quite happily punch you a hundred more times. What the fuck, Landon?"

Rubbing his jaw, Landon slowly got to his feet, his other hand out to hold me off as he retook his seat. "We even?" he asked me. "You hurt me with your fist, I hurt you with my words."

"No! We're not *even*, you dipshit." Sitting on the couch Cannon had just left, I tried to calm down. "Why are you here?"

"I told you, I want you to come home."

I waited, but when he said nothing further, I knew I was gawking. "Home? Anterrio Pack has never been my home!"

"Bullshit, Kez." Landon stood abruptly but it wasn't to come towards me, it was to pace. "How can you say that? Cass and I are your family! We've known each other almost our whole lives. And Kris? Is your brother no longer home?"

He was right, but he was also wrong. "You three will always be my family," I agreed, then gave him a pointed look. "You may be the family outcast after the shit you've said today, but three people don't make a pack—"

"Don't they?" Landon watched me closely. "It was enough for your parents."

My heart lurched. "What do you know?" I asked, my voice barely a whisper.

Landon looked away from me. "I know enough."

"Tell me."

He turned back to me, and I saw his gaze harden. "No."

"Landon!"

"No." Pushing his hands in his pockets, he shrugged. "I told everyone you were my mate. You didn't deny it. Cass has started planning a wedding, for fuck's sake."

"*What*? Why?"

"Because she believes you're my mate!" he roared in anger.

"I'm not your mate, you asshole. I'm *his* mate!" I pointed to the doors and then realized what I'd said, snapping my mouth closed, although I knew it was too late.

Landon looked so shocked I almost laughed, and then he was shaking his head. "How?"

"Luna?" I said tiredly, dropping back onto the couch. "Just tell me what you know about my family, Landon."

"I don't believe you."

"I don't fucking care!" Curling over my knees, I dropped my head in my hands, trying desperately to hold onto my temper. "I am not your mate." I lowered my voice. "It doesn't work like that." Straightening, I watched him as he took his seat, avoiding my stare. "But you know that already, don't you?"

He didn't meet my glare. Instead, he made a show of reading the titles of the books on the shelves. "You need to come back with me."

"So you don't lose face?" I guessed and saw his slight wince. "Is that what this is? You saving face?"

"The Pack Council can break any bond. Fathers already checked with them."

I felt my mouth go dry. "You knew Cannon was my mate. How long?"

Landon glanced at me and then returned to looking at the bookshelf. "Your heat. The time you were in the cells, Kris was with you. *Him* I could have gotten past, but that fucker? He guarded your door the whole time. His eyes changed to his wolf, and he almost took Grant's head off when he tried to take water down to you."

"I don't think Cannon even knew then." My voice was quiet as I watched my childhood friend.

Landon snorted. "He knew. He was fucking furious when Kris came back without you."

"Then if you know this, why are you trying to make me go back to a pack that never wanted me?" I leaned forward. "Your face is decent enough; you don't need to save it." I tried to be lighthearted even though I was in knots on the inside. "And I think the pack may be relieved if you are free to pick another."

Landon's flat stare held more animosity from him than I had ever seen. "Alphas have mates," he bit out. "You will be my mate."

Rising to my feet, I backed away from him. "No. I won't. You are *not* an alpha, and my mate, *my* alpha, is out there."

Landon crossed the room with surprising quickness. His hand wrapped around my throat, tightening as he pulled me closer. "I know everything that happened with your parents, Kez. *Everything.* Agree to this, and I'll help you kill the ones who killed them."

My hands were clawing at him as I struggled to breathe.

Landon pulled me closer, his lips almost touching mine. "Do this, and Kris lives." He saw the panic in my eyes, and he nodded. "You think you're the only one who will suffer if you continue to be a selfish bitch?"

"Landon!"

"Think about it." Releasing me and pushing me away, he straightened his T-shirt. "I'll be waiting at the alcove you fucked him at."

My brain was scrambled, and my breathing was coming in pants, but I watched him like a hawk. "You were there?"

Landon snorted with contempt. "Fuck no. I could smell you both when I went to see where our pack beta and the shaman had sneaked off to."

"Why are you doing this? We were friends, I was never this for you. Why is this happening?" I struggled to understand. "If you need help, we can help you."

Landon tipped his head back and laughed. When he stopped, he cocked his head as he watched me. "You're as naïve as always, Kez. I'll wait one night."

"Or what?"

"Or you better say goodbye to Kris before it's too late."

I lashed out at him, but he caught me, turning me so my back was to his chest. "You tell that fucking animal outside, or any of his pack, and Kris dies."

"You wouldn't do that to Cass," I countered desperately, struggling to get free. "Kris is her mate, her *true* mate."

"Just like I wouldn't threaten your brother," he taunted in my ear. "Right?" His hand cupped my breast and squeezed, freezing me in place. "At the alcove, you come tonight, you come back to *our* pack, *our* home, and you will mate with me. Reject Cannon, and if you do all that..." His tongue licked up the side of my face. "You do that, and I will tell you everything you need to know about the day your parents died. I'll hunt those left down with you, and you and your brother will have your vengeance. Plus, both you and Kris will live."

Landon stepped back, and I watched him carefully, fear in my belly when he smiled at me like he always had done. "You'll adapt to this, Kez," he told me casually. "You're a fighter. Do what you need to survive."

The doors opened and Cannon walked in, his eyes on me. "Kezia? Are you okay?"

I couldn't look away from Landon, the male I grew up with. The stranger in front of me, who looked just like the male I knew.

"Kezia?"

The sharpness in his voice startled me. "Yeah?" I tried to smile when I saw his concern. "I'm fine. Landon understands now," I told him. My lips felt swollen as I lied to him. "Everything is sorted."

"Kezia is right," Landon said as he looked at the others. "I should head back. My ego is bruised, but as I was reminded, we're survivors." I felt Landon's eyes on me, and I looked away from

Cannon, who was ignoring Landon, to meet the blue-eyed look of a former ally. "No hard feelings, right, Kez?"

"None." I willed my heart to slow down before Cannon demanded answers that I couldn't give him. Answers that put my brother at risk. "Have a safe journey back to the pack." I swallowed. "Say hi to Cass and Kris for me."

He gave a sharp nod of his head, understanding my compliance, and I felt sick. I didn't pay attention as Landon was escorted out of the alpha's house. I was caught in the hard stare of an alpha.

"What the fuck did he say to you?"

CHAPTER 29

Kezia

"WE TALKED IT OUT."

"It was five minutes," Cannon said flatly, moving closer.

Was it? It had felt so much longer. "What can I say, I'm a fast talker."

"You're also shit at bullshitting," he told me as he stood in front of me. "Talk to me."

Looking away from his penetrating stare, I made a pretense of looking for Nikan and Royce. "Are they walking Landon out of town," I joked. "Or is he going via the cells?"

"You have marks on your neck," Cannon growled, tipping my head back gently. "He's going via his grave." Cannon made to walk past me, and I jumped in front of him.

"I punched him!" I blurted, holding my fist up. "For the way he spoke about me, I punched him. He hit back." I clung onto his arms, trying to drag him back. "We're shifters, Cannon, we fight." I took a wild gamble. "Isn't this what Leo is teaching me? Training me for? To hold my own against opponents?"

Cannon looked even angrier. "To fight fairly! Not to be

assaulted verbally and physically by a jumped-up little prick who needs a good beatdown!"

Despite his anger and the shit Landon had just hit me with, I smiled. "You're overreacting because I'm your mate." Cannon opened his mouth to deny it, but it snapped shut again, and he looked away from me guiltily. "It's okay," I soothed him, rubbing my hands over his biceps. "He's gone."

"I need to get your brother out of there," he said. "I don't give a fuck if his mate comes with him, he needs out. Now."

I was nodding. "Yes, you should text him," I told him eagerly, hope rising within me. If Kris left, then I wouldn't have to go back. We could get answers to my parents' death another way.

"I did. He hasn't replied."

"How long does it usually take?" I asked, trying not to show my dismay.

"Sometimes he's instant, other times it can take a day or two."

Two days? I didn't have two days. I had *today*. I heard Landon's threats settle around me like a noose upon my neck. What if they had Kris already? What if they had already hurt him?

I fought to remain calm, but when Royce came back through the door, banging the door off the wall accidentally, I jumped in fear.

"Whoa, sorry, Kezia," he apologized as he came into the study. "He's gone. Nikan is keeping an eye out to make sure he doesn't return." Royce looked at me. "Well, he's a piece of work, isn't he? Guess the apple doesn't fall far from the tree."

"He's never been like that before," I told him sadly.

Royce looked between us both. "Well, love makes us stupid."

I snorted. "He doesn't love me," I told him, anger beginning to rise. "He told everyone I'm his mate, and the longer I stay away, the worse he looks."

"Ego?" Cannon said with disgust. "This is about his *ego*?"

When I nodded, he shook his head, contempt clear on his face. Pulling me close, he pressed a kiss to my temple. "You're better away from that pack," he soothed.

"I am." And I was. I could be happy here. This pack. Him. I suddenly realized how much it all had come to mean to me in such a short time. Now I had to leave it all behind. "It's been a day," I said to neither of them. Rubbing my forehead, I let out a light laugh, thinking about this morning. "All I wanted was a pretty bra."

"I bought you underwear." Cannon was looking at me with confusion.

My cheeks flamed as Royce pretended he had forgotten he had somewhere else to be. We said goodbye and I felt a pang in my chest at the thought I wouldn't see him again for a long time.

"Kezia?"

Turning my head, I regarded the alpha. "I wanted something pretty." He frowned and I hated that I had to explain this. "You bought me a white blouse," I told him, and he nodded. "And it's prettier than I usually wear, and I wanted pretty underwear for... you know."

His slow smile and the heat in his eyes made my pulse spike. "You wanted lingerie...for me?"

I could tell him it was for me. I could deny it. I could do so many things, but why play pointless games? Instead of denying it, I gave a simple dip of my head. "I've seen Koda, remember?" I told him, my cheeks burning with embarrassment. "And I'm just me, and I thought—"

"You thought what?" His smile had faded, and a frown marred his forehead.

"I thought you were used to...more."

Strong hands circled my waist, and with a gentle tug, the alpha brought me into his chest. A finger hooked under my chin and slowly tilted my head until I was looking into his deep green eyes. "Have I ever made you feel less?" Wordlessly, I shook my head. "I don't want *more*." Cannon brushed my hair back. His thumb traced over my cheekbone. "I just want you."

"The mate bond—"

"Can suck my dick."

Blinking rapidly, I stared at him in surprise. "Cannon..."

"You drive me insane." I watched the soft smile on his full lips as he spoke. "You also challenge me, intrigue me, and give me more shit than one shifter should be able to dole out." He held me tighter when I tried to move back. "But...I wouldn't want anything else. Whether Luna picked you for me or not, I think it would always be you, Kezia." He gave a soft laugh. "Want more? What more could I want?" he asked me fondly.

Oh shit, I was going to cry.

"It could still be the bond talking," I protested weakly. I heard his long-suffering sigh, and moving closer, I rested my head against his chest. "But I think...you're probably right."

"I'm always right." The grunt he let out when I kicked his shin made me smile.

"Don't get cocky," I murmured, feeling safe and content within his arms.

"You love when I'm cocky," he whispered in my ear, and once more my pulse spiked. Cannon moved back and looked down at me. "You've had a lot to deal with today. Do you want to rest?"

I understood what he was saying. "You need to see to the pack. Reassure them because Landon was here." Pushing my hair off my face, I sighed, knowing I needed time to myself. "I think, if you don't mind, a nap would be good."

"I'm not sending you to your room," he told me suddenly, flushing. "I do think you need time to process."

"I don't think there's ever going to be enough time for that."

"I could stay…"

Wrapping my arms around myself, I shook my head, taking a step back. "No, your pack needs to see you. Especially after you and Landon almost coming to blows outside. You have stuff to do, not babysit me." I saw his reaction to the term *babysit*, and I waved his protest away. "You know what I mean, poor word choice, that's all."

Cannon kissed me quickly as he passed. "I'll be home in a couple of hours," he assured me. "Try to sleep, you'll need it later," he added with a wink.

As I swatted him away with a laugh, he was smiling as he left the study. "Horndog!" I called after him, forgetting the doors were open and any passing shifter could hear me.

Alone again, I wandered up to my room where I looked around it and then went to Cannon's. He still hadn't fixed the hole in his wall, I noticed. Sitting in his chair, I watched the pack go about their afternoon. I watched two females talking in the street as their children wrestled at their feet. Neither mother paid much mind as the youngsters played rough. The shifter with the one arm paused to scold them when they rolled onto the street, and I found myself smiling when the youngest boy jumped up onto his back, and then the three of them were play fighting.

Movement caught my eye, and I slowly turned my head, my skin prickling. The shifter Cannon had words with the night I was let out of the cells was standing in a shaded corner, leaning against a wall, his stare on the house. I couldn't recall his name, but the more I looked, the more I believed he was watching me.

"Tev." It was nothing more than a whisper, but I watched him straighten, and then he quite deliberately tapped his wrist, the message loud and clear. I was wasting time.

Standing up, I moved deeper into Cannon's room, tears threatening as I considered all my options.

I could tell Cannon.

I could.

I wanted to.

To tell him put my brother at risk. Fear clutched at my heart. He was the most overbearing brother that ever breathed, he had tested my very last nerve more times than I could count, and me his, I had no doubt. But he was my brother.

We had each other, and we had already lost too much.

And Cass? How did she fit into this? Was she complacent to her father and brother's treachery? Or was she as much a victim as we were? Then I remembered that Bale had asked the Pack Council if a bond could be broken.

It wasn't for me and Cannon, I realized with horror. It was for Cass. I *had* to go back. My brother needed to be warned.

If I left Cannon without telling him, would he forgive me? Would he understand? I felt the tears spill over. Whichever choice I made, I lost. But only one decision meant lost lives. The other one, the one to go to Landon, that choice kept us all alive. Once I was back in the Anterrio Pack, Kris and I could fix this, and we'd figure out a way to get us *all* out. If Cass resisted, I wouldn't feel any guilt knocking her on her ass. Or my brother if she truly wanted their mate bond broken.

Remembering what Landon said made me pause once more in my pacing. He said the Pack Council knew how to break the bond. Gnawing my lip, I thought back to all those months ago, when Cannon, Royce, Kris, and I sat in the shaman's house, and after Cannon and Royce left, we spoke about breaking the bond.

The shaman never mentioned the Pack Council. Neither did Kris. Why would the shaman, Luna's vessel on earth, why would he not know how to break a bond?

Sitting on the edge of Cannon's bed, I moved back until I was comfortable, my legs crossed beneath me. We thought it was perhaps the Pack Council who covered up my part in Bullet's death. What if it wasn't?

What if it had always been Bale?

They knew about shifters, and the Anterrio Pack knew where to get silver bullets. I wondered how close the pack still was to the humans who liked to hunt shifters for sport.

Lying back, I stared at the ceiling, my head on Cannon's pillow, breathing him in as if he were here with me. Tears slid out from the corners of my eyes, sliding down into my hair as I soaked in the scent of my alpha.

My mate. My alpha. Mine.

I allowed myself a few more minutes of self-pity, and then with a final deep inhale, I sat up, pushing myself off the bed. In the bathroom, I took a shower. I wanted Cannon's scent off my skin before meeting Landon. Working quickly, I washed and pulled my hair back into a tight braid to save drying it. With my mind made up, I needed to move fast. The alpha could come home any minute, and I knew I may weaken if I was in front of him.

Wearing my usual wardrobe of black leggings and a T-shirt, I pushed my feet into tennis shoes, then grabbing a hoodie, I headed out. At the door, I looked back into the bedroom and took one last glance around. Hardening my heart, I closed the door and ran down the stairs, careful of anyone being in the study or the rest of the house.

Luna was with me though as I slipped out the back door and

onto a silent street. I scowled as I glanced at the darkening sky. The moon was barely visible. Luna wasn't *with* me, if she'd been with me, I wouldn't be in this mess.

On the outskirts of town, I glanced back once. A shadow detached itself from a building, and I watched as Tev waved at me, a sneer on his face.

"Fuck you, asshole." Giving him my back, I hurried away from the town. I was halfway up the mountain when I suddenly thought I should have left Cannon a note.

An explanation.

Would he think I had betrayed him? *Had* I betrayed him? I had lied to him. Kept a truth from him. As I climbed the slope, I hoped he would understand why.

My only consolation was that we had never truly formed the mate bond. In time, if I had to remain with Landon, Cannon would be able to move on. Nausea swept over me as I thought of him with another, and as I raced to the meeting point, I vowed that I would never let Landon touch me. Kris and I would find a way to be free of that hateful pack, and if Cannon truly rejected me, well, I would adapt just like I expected him to.

I ignored my inner voice screaming at me it didn't work like that.

My feet slowed the nearer I got to the alcove. My throat was dry, and it was taking every ounce of willpower to keep walking. I hated myself for the speed at which I got here. I hadn't shifted; I didn't want to arrive here and be naked. Shifters spent most of their lives naked, but the idea of being vulnerable right now kept me in my human form.

Rounding the wall face, I saw Landon sitting on a rock, chewing his nails, a trait he only did when he was nervous. He was looking up as I approached, and I was taken aback when he looked at me with such relief. As he rushed forward toward me, I jumped back, my hands held up in warning.

"Stay away from me, asshole."

Landon slowed, his own hands up as he took a step back. "I can't believe you came." His voice was a whisper. "I'm so sorry, Kezia."

"Sorry?" I saw his eyes dart over my shoulder, and I turned, seeing nothing there. When I turned back, he was in front of me. "What the—"

Landon clamped his hand over my nose and mouth, the cloth he held pressed tightly to my skin, the chemicals overwhelming my senses as his fingers dug into the back of my skull to keep me in place.

"I'm sorry, Kez," he whispered as I struggled against the numbness that was spreading through my limbs. "He has my mom," he told me as he followed me down as blackness threatened. "He'll kill them all if I don't bring you back." I felt something wet hit my cheek and realized Landon was crying.

My hands struck his futilely, but the chemical smell had robbed me of my strength.

"Forgive me."

It was the last thing I heard.

Epilogue

JOGGING UP THE STAIRS TO THE HOUSE, I WAS whistling. It had been a long day, but I was home now, and I wanted to wake Kezia up, nice and slowly. I didn't sense her downstairs, and I ran up the stairs, hoping she was well-rested but ready to be awake. What could I say, my mate made me crave her.

Her bedroom door was closed, but I already knew she wasn't in it. Pushing the handle down gently, I crept into my room, looking around in confusion when I found it empty. Checking the bathroom, I scratched my head. I could smell her, she'd definitely been here.

Heading back downstairs, I wondered if she was with Hannah. It was unlikely, but I started to walk that way, and then I thought of Barbara. A connection to her mother would be irresistible to my curious mate, and with a smile, I turned in that direction.

Seeing Tev walk toward me, I tried to keep my pleasant outward countenance, but internally I longed to punch the fucker. Berating myself for being a piss poor alpha towards a male who had served his penance for the part he played in my father's pack, I dipped my head in greeting as I passed. The surly old bastard ignored me, which I was used to.

"Hey, boy."

Grinding my teeth, I turned back to look at the bitter old male.

White hot pain erupted in my side as Tev drove the knife deeper into my body. I felt the knife tear at my insides as he twisted it. Burning pain exploded, bringing me to my knees, and he followed me down, the knife held tight in his grip.

My head jerked up in confusion as I tried to shift and nothing happened. He grinned at me, his breath foul on my face.

"I'll kill you for this."

Tev laughed. "You'll be dead soon." Leaning into me, he gave another short stab into the small of my back. "Silver will bind you," he told me, hate swimming in his eyes. "I hope you feel every drop of spilled blood as it leaves you," he sneered. "You deserve this."

Standing, Tev looked down at me and spat on the ground. Wiping his mouth, he looked me over. "Kezia says fuck you."

Kezia? What did Kezia have to do with this?

With a laugh, Tev stepped over me, walking away whistling. Reaching behind me, I tried to reach the knife, but the more I moved, the deeper it seemed to lodge.

Pain, so much pain.

How had she survived this?

Was this her revenge? To make me feel what she had.

Falling to the side, I called for Royce, but the mindlink was faint, the power out of my reach. Fire burned through my veins as the silver took root, and I had no strength to rise.

I had no strength.

As I struggled to breathe, fighting to survive this, I had only one thought.

Kezia, what have you done?

About the Author

Eve L. Mitchell is a USA Today Bestselling author who writes Contemporary Romance, and New Adult Romance but also dabbles in Paranormal Romance.

If you like a morally grey alpha-hole, then chances are Eve's got a male character for you to claim as your next book boyfriend.

As an avid reader from a young age, Eve still considers herself a reader first. She believes there is nothing better than getting that new book either on your e-reader or in your hands, and the fact she may bring that excitement to a fellow reader fills her with wonder. She writes under a pen name; otherwise, her Secret Agent status will be revoked.

Eve lives in the North East of Scotland, with her three coffee machines and her significant other, Mr. M. She enjoys NFL Football, music (played loudly), and having long conversations with the voices in her head, which sometimes turn into the stories she writes.

How to Connect with Eve:

Join my newsletter and keep up to date with the latest news and updates on my books and releases: http://bit.ly/Eves newsletter

Connect with me on Facebook: http://bit.ly/evesfacebook page

Also by Eve L. Mitchell

<u>CONTEMPORARY ROMANCE</u>

The Boulder Series

Unbroken Devotion (Boulder Series Book 1)

Dark Heart (Boulder Series Book 2)

Unbroken Bonds (Boulder Series Book 3)

Dark Soul (Boulder Series Book 4)

A Very Boulder Christmas (A Holiday Novella)

The Denver Series

Her Greatest Mistake (Book 1)

Beautifully Broken (Book 2)

Keeping Harmony (Book 3)

The Ruthless Devils Series

Ruthless Heart (Book 1)

Ruthless Desire (Book 2)

Ruthless Charm (Book 3)

Ruthless Devil (standalone)

Torn & Broken Duet

Torn by Grace

Broken by Faith

A Collection of Short Romances: Volume 1

<u>FANTASY</u>

The Akrhyn Series

Into Darkness (The Akrhyn Series Book 1)

Lost in Darkness (The Akrhyn Series Book 2)

From the Darkness (The Akrhyn Series Book 3)

<u>PARANORMAL ROMANCE</u>

The Watcher Series

A Glow of Stars & Dusk (The Watcher Series Book 1)

A Flame of Stars & Midnight (The Watcher Series Book 2)

A Blaze of Stars & Dawn (The Watcher Series Book 3)

The Blackridge Peak Series

Wolf's Gambit (The Blackridge Peak Series Book 1)

Wolf's Betrayal (The Blackridge Peak Series Book 2)

Wolf's End Game (The Blackridge Peak Series Book 3)

<u>WRITING AS AVA SPEIRS</u>

Order of the Ravens Series

Knight of Sword & Shadow (Book 1)

Knight of Sacrifice & Shade (Book 2)

Knight of Dagger & Darkness (Book 3)

Knight of Trials & Twilight (Book 4)

Title TBC - New Series - Coming Autumn 2024

THE DENVER SERIES

The Denver Series is a three-book mafia romance shared world series. Each book is a standalone, featuring cameos from the other books. Although it is recommended that the books be read in order, it is not necessary to do so.

The series covers tropes of opposites attract, enemies-to-lovers, and forbidden romance (stepcousins).

The Denver Series is a steamy contemporary romance series that dabbles in the mafia romance genre, with book one hinting at it and the other two exploring the darker side of this much-loved genre.

A complete three-book series where sassy heroines meet and fall for their dark alphahole heroes.

The series includes **Her Greatest Mistake**, **Beautifully Broken** and **Keeping Harmony**.

GET THE SERIES

WWW.EVELMITCHELL.COM

THE RUTHLESS DEVILS SERIES

A college sports romance series following twin brothers and their cousin. Three football stars who have it all: looks, money, talent and the world at their feet. No one messes with the Devils. Each book deals with a different Devil and their love interest who will either make them or break them.

The series covers tropes of enemies-to-lovers, second-chance romance and forced proximity.

This is interconnected three-book series with an underlying story arc that carries through from book one to book three, and therefore the series must be read in order. The series deals with some elements that sensitive readers may find triggering.

This series includes **Ruthless Heart**, **Ruthless Desire** and **Ruthless Charm**.

GET THE SERIES

TORN & BROKEN DUET

The Torn & Broken duet is a duet with a twist. You can read either book as a standalone. *Torn by Grace* was written first and one of the female side characters in that book is the main character in *Broken by Faith*, however, you don't need to know what happened in *Torn by Grace* to enjoy *Broken by Faith*. There is a little bit of crossover, but no spoilers.

Torn by Grace is a second chance, enemies-to-lovers, brothers-best-friend romance.
Broken by Faith is an enemies-to-lovers, forced proximity, fake relationship romance.
The series includes **Torn by Grace and Broken by Faith.**

THE WATCHER SERIES

The Watcher Series is a paranormal romance trilogy that will take you on a journey where you will get lost in a world that will hold you in its depths. With a blend of steam, humour and angst, be ready to buckle up for the ride.

With demons, devils and one sassy, clueless witch, what more could you ask for? Join Star as she gets a crash course in what not to do when you get involved with the Watchers.

An enemies-to-lovers story that has all the emotions packed between the pages as the heroine deals with love, betrayal, loss and so much more.

This series is a trilogy and must be read in order. If you love cliffhangers, this series is for you. If you hate cliffhangers, don't worry, the next book's already written.

The series includes **A Glow of Stars & Dust**, **A Flame of Stars & Midnight** and **A Blaze of Stars & Dawn**.

GET THE SERIES

THE BLACKRIDGE PEAK SERIES

The Blackridge Peak Series is a wolf shifter series about rival packs, hidden secrets, a little bit of magic, and a girl who's trying to find her way amongst a pack that doesn't want her.

Kezia is an outsider, and when given the chance she leaves the pack that never truly accepted her. But trouble follows Kezia and she soon learns that only an alpha can protect her.

An alpha who may be her mate.

The series includes **Wolf's Gambit, Wolf's Betrayal, and Wolf's Endgame.**

THE AKRHYN SERIES

Creatures of evil roam the shadows - the Drakhyn. They may look like humans, but their taloned hands and razor-sharp teeth serve one purpose only; killing.

A Sentinel's purpose is to patrol and protect. They are highly trained soldiers with superior skills and abilities. Whether they be Vampyres, Lycan, Castors or gifted Akrhyn, their purpose is the same; hunt the Drakhyn and rid the world of their evil presence.

This fantasy trilogy covers tropes of chosen one, fated mates, good vs evil.

The series includes **Into Darkness**, **Lost in Darkness** and **From the Darkness**.